'I loved this book! *The Intern*'s Josie is smart, funny, compassionate and absolutely impossible not to love. Gabrielle, too, is one of those special types of authors that you feel compelled to want to hang out and eat pizza with — you just know she'd make you giggle and be an amazing best friend.'

Dannielle Miller, author of *The Girl With The Butterfly Tattoo* and *Loveability*, CEO of Enlighten Education

GABRIELLE TOZER

📚 Angus&Robertson
An imprint of HarperCollins*Publishers*
harpercollins.com.au

Angus&Robertson

An imprint of HarperCollins*Publishers*

First published in Australia in 2014
by HarperCollins*Publishers* Australia Pty Limited
ABN 36 009 913 517
harpercollins.com.au

HarperCollins*Publishers*

Level 13, 201 Elizabeth Street, Sydney NSW 2000, Australia
Unit D1, 63 Apollo Drive, Rosedale, Auckland 0632, New Zealand
A 53, Sector 57, Noida, UP, India
77–85 Fulham Palace Road, London W6 8JB, United Kingdom
2 Bloor Street East, 20th floor, Toronto, Ontario M4W 1A8, Canada
10 East 53rd Street, New York NY 10022, USA

National Library of Australia Cataloguing-in-Publication data:

Tozer, Gabrielle, author.
  The intern / Gabrielle Tozer.
  978 0 7322 9705 3 (pbk.)
  978 1 7430 9948 3 (ebook)
  For secondary school age.
  Journalism—Juvenile fiction
  Interns—Juvenile fiction.
A823.4

Cover design by Hazel Lam, HarperCollins Design Studio
Cover images by shutterstock.com
Author photograph by Simona Janek, gm photographics
Typeset in 10.5/17pt Sabon by Kirby Jones
Printed and bound in Australia by Griffin Press
The papers used by HarperCollins in the manufacture of this book are a
natural, recyclable product made from wood grown in sustainable plantation
forests. The fibre source and manufacturing processes meet recognised
international environmental standards, and carry certification.

5 4 3 2 1   14 15 16 17

For JT, my first reader and fellow sweet tooth

1.

Melons. The girls. Gazongas. I could rattle off every nickname in the world for my boobs — oops, nearly forgot jubblies — but it didn't change the fact they were small. Embarrassingly small. Think grapes over melons, fun-size bags over fun bags, shot glasses over jugs.

Which was why I shouldn't have been surprised when my boobs were the catalyst for squeals of laughter from my younger sister, Kat, on the eve of an important day. A Very Important Day.

'Geez, put those puppies away,' Kat smirked from my bedroom doorway. 'Some of us haven't had lunch yet and I'd hate to lose my appetite.'

I paused from rifling through piles of crumpled clothes on my bed. 'What? I don't know what you —'

'Just look down,' said Kat, tossing her jet-black ponytail. I hated when she did that.

Following her instructions, I looked down and saw my left nipple peeking out of my bra. 'Argh!' I yelped, yanking at the faded material. 'Kat, get out! Get out!'

Kat cackled, then plonked onto my bed, squashing the heaving mass of clothes. Too tired to argue, I sat down next to her and double-checked that my boob hadn't made another escape.

Kat fussed with her thick fringe. 'So, found something to wear tomorrow, Jose?'

Broken shoes, stained shirts and fraying dresses burst from the wardrobe, spilling into an unwearable mess. A personal stylist would've come in handy to tell me why I shouldn't tape my sneakers together instead of buying a new pair, and how to dress like a normal seventeen-almost-eighteen-year-old.

'Yep. Well, maybe. Probably. No. I'm screwed. My sister just saw my boob and I'm screwed.'

Cursing, I lay back on the bed. Kat reapplied her lip gloss. It smelled of cherries, reminiscent of summery desserts.

'Hey Jose?' she said.

'Yeah?'

'I won't tell anyone I saw your boob.'

'Thanks.'

'Well, except Tye,' Kat added. 'I tell him everything. You know, boyfriend rules and all that.'

I sighed. One of those melodramatic I-hate-my-life sighs, where the air rushed up from the depths of my stomach and exploded with a raging 'whoosh'. But if Kat noticed, she didn't show it.

'Hey Jose?' she said again.

'Yeah?'

'You're going to have to look amazing tomorrow, you know?'

'I know.' I know. I know. I know.

'*Amaaaazing.* Seriously, tomorrow's important. Mum's been yabbering to everyone about it.'

'Heard you the first time.'

During the past few weeks, Kat had been firing off tips about the Very Important Day (I swear she was sixteen going on thirty sometimes). Wear this, don't wear that, do this, don't do that, say this, don't say that. I knew she was trying to help me reduce the risk of embarrassing myself, but it only made me more panicked. You see, life loved handing me something amazing, only to backhand me almost straight after. It had always been that way. In Year Eight, moments after my first kiss, the delectable Pete Jordan vomited from food poisoning and hadn't spoken to me since. At Year Ten presentation night, I was named 'Most Likely To Succeed', only to faceplant the ground as I walked back to my seat. Some moron recorded my historic fall, making me an overnight YouTube sensation. I won't even go in to what happened at my Year Twelve formal, although it involved a spiked punch bowl, ninety rolls of toilet paper and a paddock of mud. I don't know why I thought the next day — the Very Important Day —

would be any different, but I was counting on a fairy-godmother-shaped miracle.

Most girls I knew, like Kat, spent their allowances or pay on make-up, jewellery, fashion, music, phone credit and *magazines*.

For me, magazines were a sparkly fantasy filled with smiling, shiny people who looked too happy all the time. That didn't stop me from leafing through Kat's magazines when she was out, but instead of checking out the fashion I was reading the feature stories, scoping out who wrote them and looking for spelling mistakes.

I'd studied hard at high school for six years because I was destined to be a news journalist at a newspaper or radio station. So it had come as a huge shock to everyone, including me, to discover I would be interning at a magazine as part of my uni degree's second semester. And not just any magazine. I'd been signed up to (translation: pushed into) a one-day-a-week internship at one of the hottest women's magazines in the country, *Sash*.

When I told Kat my news, she was thirteen per cent excited for me and eighty-seven per cent envious. In her world, my inability to use a curling iron meant I didn't deserve the intern position. Her warning of 'Don't say anything stupid to the *Sash* girls and ruin my chances of working there one day' hadn't filled me with confidence. Unless I underwent the world's first personality transplant

4

between here and the city, I knew I'd find a way to put my foot in it.

Kat picked up a ratty floral dress from the top of the pile and threw it into the rubbish bin near my desk.

'Hey! What are you doing?' I said. 'I've had that for ages.'

'Exactly,' she shot back, rolling her blue eyes in a flurry of mascara, eyeliner and eye shadow. 'Tomorrow you need to look hot *and* cool. You can't wear your crappy old clothes at a place like *that*. Now, here's what I'm thinking ...'

I sighed and tuned out. I couldn't handle another one of Kat's pep talks where she criticised my worn-out sandals, mismatched socks, lack of bold lipstick, split ends and under-plucked brows.

'... so come on, it's makeover time. We're getting our shop on,' barked Kat, unaware that I'd been ignoring her rant.

'I'll sort it. Trust me.'

Grunting in disbelief, Kat held up a daggy blue skirt and waved it around. 'This opportunity is wasted on you — and your small boobs!'

She threw the skirt back onto the bed and stormed out, her ponytail whipping behind her. I heard her bedroom door slam — twice, just in case I missed the first. I held the skirt up against my lower body and took in the reflection grimacing back at me. Mousy brown hair, scruffy but fine. Eyes, green and wide, easily my favourite feature. Eyebrows, semi-unruly but manageable. Lips, pouty and pink, no major complaints, but occasionally clownish. Nose, free from any wart-like protrusions, so doing okay. Boobs, small in size — *obviously* — but apparently confident enough to jump free of brassiere on a whim. Everything from the waist down blurred together: hips, thighs and legs were all … just there.

I gazed at the skirt. Sure, I'd owned it for five years, and it was a hand-me-down from my weird cousin Tracey, but it was all I had. I needed another opinion.

'Mum, can you come here for a sec?'

Moments later, Mum appeared in the doorway, balancing an overflowing washing basket on one hip. Her shaggy brown hair was pulled into a loose bun at the nape of her neck and held with a rusty peg. A yellow daisy played peekaboo from behind her right ear. Mum loved plucking flowers from the garden and wearing them until they wilted. Her dress — another bargain from the op shop — had faded to a musky pink and clung to her body in all the wrong places. But none of these things detracted from her pretty features, which glowed without even a hint of foundation, blush or mascara.

'Yes, love?' she asked, readjusting the basket on her hip.

I held up the skirt. 'How hideous is this? Would you say it's send-me-home-to-change hideous or let-me-stay-but-bitch-about-me-behind-my-back hideous?'

Mum shrugged, then patted me on the shoulder. 'Josephine Browning, you always look gorgeous.'

'You have to say that.'

'Not true. When you were a child you were chubby with enormous ears — reminded me of a baby elephant — and I was the first person to point that out.'

'Mum!'

'But I do like that skirt.'

'Kat thinks I need a new outfit — new dress, heels, the works. You know, for tomorrow.'

'Wait, is that my skirt? I thought I'd passed it on to your cousin Tracey. I should've hung onto it if it's back in fashion, love.'

I forced a smile. Kat's outburst about my lack of options suddenly didn't seem so hysterical. It was time to admit defeat to the self-proclaimed fashion queen of the house, which ranked number two on my Things I Hate To Do List. (Number one: cross-country running.)

I knocked on Kat's bedroom door with its 'Stay Out' sign sticky-taped above the doorknob. Rock music pounded from within and I imagined her writing in her diary about her ugly, frumpy, older sister. Either that, or sneaking out the window to meet up with Tye. I doubted she was dabbling in the rare option of cleaning her room, although when it came to Kat I could never be sure.

The door cracked open. 'Whaddya want?'

'Um, what were you saying about the shops?'

'Not another word, I hear your unfashionable cries for help loud and clear,' said Kat, scooping up a handbag from the floor and swinging it over her shoulder. 'Get your wallet, Jose, because when we're done you're *definitely* going to need it.'

I looked like a tarted-up pageant queen. As I stared into the full-length mirror, all I could see were big green eyes, big pink mouth, big bold jewellery, big bright patterns and big high-heeled shoes. Everything was big, even the price tags. I smelled like a perfumery and my face itched from the foundation and bronzer caking my skin. Kat beamed, admiring her work. She'd taken me on a whirlwind tour of the department store, trialling make-up products at every counter. Before I could stop her, she called out to a saleswoman who was hovering nearby.

'She looks amazing, right? Like, *amazing*,' Kat said.

'Oh yeah, *amazing*,' gushed the woman, fuelled by the anticipation of a sale. 'Hon, you should seriously get that whole outfit.'

I blushed, reminded of when Mum took me to buy my first bra in Year Six and invited the shop owner into the change room to admire my 'growing buds'. Like Mum, Kat had the intuition of a dead caterpillar when it came to sensing my discomfort. I squeezed my wallet a little tighter as the saleswoman circled me, eyeing me up and down. She'd detected my fear the moment we'd walked into the store and I'd cried out, 'Is that a belt or a skirt?' Mentally, I double-locked my piggy bank and buried it in a safe three hundred metres below ground level, complete with security guards and CCTV cameras.

I snuck another peek in the mirror and cringed at the loud colours competing for my attention. The dress felt tight, but Kat was convinced it fitted perfectly. I had to admit, it was creating curves in places usually hidden by baggy T-shirts or baby-doll dresses.

To my right, a mannequin wearing the same outfit, down to the bright yellow peep-toes, was looking rather fashionable. 'How do you do it?' I muttered to her.

'Okay, I'll say it: this is the best you've ever looked,' said Kat. 'Wear this tomorrow and you'll kill it. That dress is hot.'

'Weren't we aiming for hot *and* cool?'

Kat rolled her eyes. 'Let's not go crazy, Jose. It is you we're talking about.'

The saleswoman cleared her throat. 'So do you want to pay with cash or credit, hon?'

I ran through my wardrobe options at home one final time. A montage of outdated playsuits, daggy dresses and worn shoes danced in my mind, the blue skirt at the forefront. I had no choice: I was getting the outfit.

'Cash, thanks.'

I handed over the crumpled notes. There was no turning back now.

2.

Magazine-shaped butterflies fluttering in my stomach woke me up on the big day. I filled an overnight bag with a change of clothes, Kat's make-up case and a packed lunch. The plan was I'd stay at my cousin Tim's place in the city the night before and after my internship day. This first time, however, I was going straight into the *Sash* office.

Mum came with me to the train station, and kept dragging me into hugs smelling of flowery cleaning products with a dash of cigarette smoke. She'd started smoking after Dad left and I was trying not to give her a hard time about it.

She squeezed me again. 'Give it your best, love.'

I bit my lip to stop myself crying. Kat had done my hair, nails and make-up that morning and the last thing I wanted was mascara streaking down my face.

'You'll call me when you get there?'

'Yes, Mum.'

I hated leaving her, even just for the night. She didn't

admit it, but I knew she was missing Dad. He'd walked out last November, so suddenly we'd almost missed it.

I'd come home early due to a free period to see him storming down the driveway, sunglasses on, wheeling two suitcases. His cricket bag was already in the back of the car, next to an esky. I'd shouted out 'Hello' but he didn't turn around. To this day, I didn't know whether he'd heard me or not. I'd convinced myself he hadn't; that he was so caught up in his own thoughts they'd drowned me out.

When Mum got home from work I told her how Dad had driven off. She'd nodded, walked into her bedroom and closed the door behind her. She didn't come out all night. I sat outside with my back against the door and my knees up to my chin listening to her sob for hours. Kat cried too, lying on the couch with her earphones in, tears streaming down her face.

The next day, Mum discovered Dad had taken a chunk of cash out of their joint account. In my mind, he'd become a raging gambler who'd disappeared to Vegas to spend our family money. But I didn't know the truth and probably never would.

We hadn't heard a peep from him since, except for a scrawled letter for Kat's birthday.

Guilt nipped at my ankles for hopping on the train and heading off to the city, but Mum was the one who'd encouraged me to go for the internship. She wanted more for Kat and me. She always did.

'Julie said Tim's excited about your visit,' she told me.

I smirked. Why did relatives always exaggerate the truth? Aunt Julie was Mum's older sister, and her son, Tim, was twenty-two. I hadn't seen him for four years and he probably couldn't remember who I was. Last time we met I had braces and he was bragging about his bike and ducking classes to make out with his girlfriend. All I knew about him now was that he'd changed his uni degree four times and was letting me crash on his couch.

I nodded. 'Great.'

'You've got his number in your phone, haven't you? Or just call me if you need anything. The city's a big place, love, lots of weirdos.'

'Mum!'

'Actually, I'll call you tonight. Or you call me. Or we'll call each other. Let's just call each other.'

'Yes, Mum. Love you.'

Mum cuddled me close, then let go to blow her nose. 'Go on now, you can do this,' she said, half to me, half to herself.

She shooed me onto the train. I found a double seat, dumped my bag next to me and glanced through the window. It was impossible not to spot Mum on the platform with her wild, curly hair and even wilder outfit: a bright green muu-muu spattered with orange lilies.

Moments later, the train purred to life and I strained my neck waving as we chugged away.

I settled back in my seat and watched the scenery whizz by, my mind racing just as fast with thoughts of the city. I was nervous and it wasn't only because I was wearing my expensive new outfit. I could tell this was the beginning of something exciting.

I'd applied to intern at the best newspapers in the country, but those positions had gone to older students. My journalism lecturer, Professor John 'Filly' Fillsmore, had told me there were only two positions left: at *Sash* or *Cats Quarterly*. Even he couldn't hide a grin while telling me about the *Quarterly*'s tea-sipping cuckoo readership. Apparently *Sash* had had a last-minute dropout, creating a spot for me. Filly used words like 'exclusive' and 'highly sought after' to describe the placement. I didn't know the first thing about fashion or beauty, but I was determined to score a high distinction for the internship, even if I had to fake my way through twelve weeks at a magazine. I'd read about high-powered magazine editors climbing the ranks to successful careers in newspapers and television so I wasn't completely put out. And I was happy to escape the kitty litter at *Cats Quarterly*.

But ever since I'd accepted the internship, my imagination had immersed me in graphic daydreams of what *Sash* magazine would be like. There'd be six-foot supermodels sipping cocktails, chiselled handymen fixing photocopiers, glamorous fashion writers giggling and flashing their company credit cards. Models, musicians and celebrities would hang out in hammocks in the office, while the staff tossed around creative ideas and took early marks to go shopping. Unlike me, everyone would have Proactiv-perfect skin, whitened teeth and a boyfriend who sent roses to the office. Above all these, my biggest worry was surviving a day in heels; I could barely stand up straight in ballet flats.

Shiny-haired glamazons swinging designer handbags and wearing killer heels dotted the city's main street. The air was thick with the smell of coffee, bacon, perfume, bus exhaust fumes and cigarette smoke. City slickers lined up at fruit stalls, or mindlessly played with mobiles while walking along the footpath.

The crowd swallowed me up. I allowed myself to be swept past sushi shops and high-rise buildings, bumping people with my overnight bag and apologising when they glared at me. I also had a handbag bouncing off my right hip and a smaller tote holding my resumé and certificates.

Despite taking six wrong turns, I arrived at the *Sash* office early, so I took a seat inside a cafe across the road. I'd heard internships involved lots of coffee-fetching, and wondered if they expected me to remember their orders off by heart. I had visions of screaming girls clawing at me because I'd bought them a skim soy latte with no sugar instead of a rice milk tea with three sugars. A cute waiter wearing skinny jeans and a black tie interrupted my panicked thoughts.

'Tea? Coffee? Hug?'

I looked up. 'Pardon?'

'Just kidding. What can I get you, doll face?'

I blushed redder than the lipstick Kat had ordered me to wear.

'A water would be great, thanks.'

'No worries,' he replied. 'You know, I haven't seen you in here before.'

'I guess I'm new.'

'Oh yeah? What brings you here?'

Damn, I clearly wasn't channelling my inner glamour enough yet. Maybe I needed more eye shadow.

'A magazine internship.'

He nodded. 'Nice. Funny, though, I thought magazines and newspapers were dying off? Isn't new technology taking them down and all that?'

Stunned, I didn't know how to reply. 'Oh. I, ah, I ...'

'What would I know? I'm sure it'll be great. I'll go grab that water,' the waiter said. 'Have a great internship, Magazine.'

He walked off, humming, and I smiled at his little nickname. City people aren't so bad, I thought. But then I saw the girls stalking into the building across the road. They looked scarily like the people in my daydreams: glamorous, slim, tall and modelesque. I imagined them chattering about their weekend spent on the family yacht or at a hot-people-only dinner party on Saturday night. 'I only drink water fetched from a spring in Finland and blessed by a nun,' one perfect-complexioned diner would titter to the other. 'Did you happen to catch up with Brad, Angelina and the kids over the summer?' her companion would reply. 'We tried to, but you know what they're like, all work, no play. Luckily George was free so he showed us the sights instead.' I was so deep into my daydream that I almost didn't notice when my water arrived (sadly, not from a fancy spring in Finland).

A quick glance at the clock on the cafe wall showed it was time to leave. I stood up and checked my reflection in the window. On a normal day, I had the bad habit of hunching over like Quasimodo reaching for a dropped coin. But today wasn't a normal day. For a start, I was in heels. Expensive, probably-going-to-snap-my-ankle heels that made me taller than usual. I rolled my shoulders back, straightened my spine and tilted my chin upwards. You can do this, I told myself. You're the most likely to succeed, remember? You blitzed school, you're wearing a new dress and you're destined to be a brilliant journalist. You. Can. Do. This.

I hoisted my bags over my shoulder, picked up my overnight bag and headed for the door. Milliseconds later, my heels slipped in a puddle of juice, sending me crashing to the floor. Everyone glanced around — my screech probably had something to do with that — but no one came to help, not even the cute waiter. I scrambled to my feet and out the door, cursing Kat and her insistence on heels for my first day in the office.

It was only at the traffic lights that I realised my dress was now stained with juice.

'No, no, no, this isn't happening,' I muttered.

Rubbing at the wet patch with a saliva-soaked tissue didn't help. I realised I'd have to walk around all day with my hand placed over the stain. It's not ideal, but you'll be okay, promised my surprisingly supportive internal voice. (Surprising, because usually it would've suggested I give up right then. I appreciated the shift to a more positive outlook, even if it was just a one-off.)

I took a minute to soak up the immensity of the building I was about to enter. According to the company website, it held almost sixty magazine offices and more than a thousand employees. And one new intern, I reminded myself.

I teetered across the sleek marble floor of the foyer. Framed magazine covers lined the walls. Despite my heels, I felt two centimetres tall alongside the statuesque women striding through the doors, swiping their security cards with one hand, balancing a takeaway coffee cup in the other, all the while chatting on their phones. A sturdy guard handed me a security pass and told me to wait to be collected, so I sat down on an uncomfortable black couch. I double-checked my hand-on-stain positioning. So far, so good.

A thirty-something woman with straight blonde hair came over to greet me. She wore a loose, flowing top, jeans and ballet flats. Yes, *flat shoes*. I was going to kill Kat for forcing me into a pair of torture devices. The woman beamed at me and extended her hand, and that's when my plan to hide the mark on my dress fell apart. I reached out to shake her hand, exposing the darkened stain.

If she noticed it, she pretended not to. 'Hello, you must be Josephine. I'm Liani, *Sash*'s deputy editor.'

'Ah, hi. Yes, Josie. Browning. I mean, hi, I'm Browning, Josie Browning.'

'Hi there.' Liani chuckled, a joyous sound that almost stopped me from feeling like the biggest moron to grace the foyer. Almost.

'Um, just to be clear, I didn't mean to sound like James Bond then,' I said.

'Got it.'

'Can I start over? I'm Josie. Thanks so much for having me.'

'Pleasure, Josie.'

Liani signed me in to the building and took me into a huge mirror-filled lift, chatting about her husband, the weather and her baby boy, Dylan. She reminded me of Mum and I instantly wanted to crawl onto her lap and weep about the juice incident. Luckily, I restrained the urge.

Liani led me out of the lift and down the hall toward the *Sash* office. I didn't know what to expect behind those big glass doors, but I was about to find out.

3.

'Nice stain.'

'What happened to your dress?'

My hand-over-stain mission failed again within one minute of being inside *Sash* headquarters. Liani had stepped into her office to drop off my overnight bag and grab some paperwork, leaving me with two immaculately dressed girls on the couch in reception. As they leaned closer to eyeball the mark, I speculated whether or not the couch had an invisibility button or teleportation capabilities. I'd even have welcomed an alien abduction at that moment. Instead, I unleashed my inner journalist-in-the-making in an attempt to distract them.

'So what are you guys here for? A photo shoot?'

'Internship,' smirked the taller, slimmer and older-looking of the two. 'Although I do model occasionally, when I'm not singing or acting. I'm Ava.'

Ava had long, curled red hair and shaped brows over dark and piercing eyes. Judging by her appearance she was early to mid-twenties, although I couldn't be sure.

She sat up straight, her lithe legs crossed neatly at the ankles. Unlike me, everything about her was groomed. A diamond — and no doubt expensive — engagement ring sparkled on her finger.

The other girl had short, shaggy blonde hair and green eyes. I spotted a tattoo on her wrist, but her arm was so laden with chunky jewellery it was hard to make out.

'Hey, I'm Steph,' she said. 'Internship for me, too.'

Unlike Ava, who was dolled up in heels and a dress, Steph had her own style, somewhere between grunge and glam. She looked like she'd stepped straight from the pages of a fashion magazine. When Ava asked about her career in the past year, Steph shrugged and said she'd been travelling through Asia, and was keen to buy an around-the-world ticket and head off again. I admired Steph's confidence. She gave bare-minimum answers to Ava's nosy questions; nothing more, nothing less. I, on the other hand, blabbered like a fool when Ava fired questions at me.

'What have you been doing for the past year, Josephine?'

'Uh, you can call me Josie. Well, what have I been doing? Er, high school mainly. Final year and all that. I'm in uni now.'

Ava leaned forward. 'God, how old *are* you?'

'Seventeen. Almost eighteen. I was young for my year.'

'You can't even legally drink! I feel ancient.'

Steph glanced at me. 'So how'd you go, Josie? Pass alright?'

'Yep, got through it,' I said.

Luckily, Ava butted in before I spouted off my results. 'So you want to be a writer then, a journalist?'

'More than anything.'

Steph smiled. 'Seventeen and you already know what you want. My dad would kill for a daughter like you. I'm nineteen and still haven't got a clue.'

But Ava wasn't done with me yet. Next, she pestered me for my five-year career plan.

I rambled along, quoting my favourite journalists, authors and, pathetically, my high-school English teacher. It was official: I was a brown-nosing tosspot who'd paid *way* too much attention to her teacher's classroom soliloquies. Ava soon grew bored, her eyes darting away from mine the moment I opened my mouth, so I finished with a mumbled 'And that's my plan,' even though I didn't have a plan at all. (Well, other than becoming a world-famous journalist ... and maybe falling in love with a smoking-hot prince.)

With the show-off career questions completed, we faded into silence. Ava pursed her lips, then recrossed her legs. Steph checked her phone, only to recheck it a moment later. I straightened my dress and took a deep breath.

I gazed around the room, taking in the bright posters covering the walls. The reception desk was stacked with magazines, folders and books. *Sash's* office, like a lot of things in the city, smelled like fresh coffee.

Three girls, three internships. Filly hadn't mentioned there'd be others here, too. The thought terrified me. How was I supposed to be the gold-star intern with such impressive competition? These girls were older and looked the part. I squashed my certificates further down into my tote, embarrassed I'd brought them.

Click, click, click, click. Click, click, click, click. For a moment, I thought the nearby clock was broken, but then I realised it was the sound of heels tapping along the hallway behind us. We all turned in unison to see *Sash*'s famous editor-in-chief, Rae Swanson, standing poised with her hands on her hips.

She wore a tight, knee-length dress with a cinched-in waist and stiletto heels. Her hair was cut in a straight black bob that fell to her shoulders, skimming them when she moved her head. Her laser-beam eyes traced my silhouette, then she nodded in approval at Steph and Ava.

'You must be the interns,' she said. 'Come with me, girls. Let's begin.'

She stalked toward her office. The three of us followed, swapping nervous glances. I wondered if, like me, the other two were on the brink of wetting their pants. They didn't seem like it. Ava's lips were swollen into a pout, while Steph snuck one last look at her phone as she slid it into her handbag. My hands were slimy with sweat but

I refrained from smearing them onto my dress; it had experienced enough stains for one day.

'I can't believe she's dealing with us directly,' hissed Ava. 'This almost never happens, especially with these types of mags.'

'What usually happens?' I whispered back. But I didn't get a chance to find out because we'd arrived.

Liani stood outside Rae's office, clutching a stack of magazines and notepads. She was flushed, but still smiling. She mouthed 'Sorry for the hold-up' to the three of us and opened the door. I hobbled into the glossy domain of one of Australia's most feared and admired magazine editors behind Ava and Steph, wondering what fate held in store for me.

Ava, Steph and I perched on hot-pink poufs in Rae's office, waiting for her to speak. Her desk was covered with tagged magazines, water bottles, beauty products and stationery. Empty teacups balanced on books and notepads. Vanilla candles burned on the windowsill, sending a luxurious, delicious smell through the room.

'Forget Hollywood,' Rae began, leaning forward in her office chair. 'You want glamour? Welcome to magazines. Cocktail parties, launches, freebies like you wouldn't believe, celebrities and a fashion store at your disposal.' She noticed my mouth widen in astonishment. 'Like the sound of that? Well, let's not forget a supply of beauty products beyond your wildest dreams, photo shoots, television appearances, ground-breaking interviews and contacts that can set you up for life.'

Rae stood up, strode over to the office wall, which was lined with shiny *Sash* covers, and slapped a ruler against one of them, causing all three of us to jump.

'Great photo, average coverlines.' She hit the next one. 'Gorgeous celebrity, gripping stories.' And the next. 'Bestselling issue of the past four years. Impossible to beat.'

She glanced at us, a crooked smile at the corner of her mouth. 'But that's the thing, girls, we have to beat it.'

We nodded, nervous grins frozen in place.

'This is *Sash*'s year,' Rae said. 'Forget online, forget apps, forget mobile phone magazines, forget *Marilyn* and their been-there-done-that high-end fashion. My baby is going to be so brilliant, everyone will want her.'

Ava's eyes lit up. Steph stifled a small yawn.

'But it won't be easy,' Rae continued. 'There'll be long hours, challenging work and pushing of boundaries. I want exclusives. Lots of them. The team's workload will need to double, if not triple, to get this done. And that, lovely new interns, is where you come in. It's no secret this is an opportunity that thousands of girls would kill for.'

Better invest in full-body armour for my next trip to the city, I thought. And a guard dog. A four-man bodyguard team wouldn't hurt either.

'Congratulations on getting this far. Your applications impressed me for different reasons. Who's Josie?'

I raised my right hand, too scared to speak.

'Your grades and writing are phenomenal,' Rae said. 'Well done.'

I blushed. 'Thanks.'

'Your lecturer speaks highly of you, although he did let slip that you applied for a newspaper internship first. Is that true?'

I gulped. 'Ah, yes. But I'm so happy to be here. It all worked out, you know?'

Rae cocked her head to one side. 'I hope so.'

Good one, Filly, I thought, staring into my lap with embarrassment.

Rae continued. 'And who's Steph?'

Steph gave a little wave. 'That's me.'

Rae stared at her. 'Clearly your father's daughter.'

'So I've been told,' Steph said, but I noticed she averted her eyes from Rae's.

'Welcome to *Sash*,' Rae said. 'I've been intrigued by you ever since he passed on your CV at a publishing conference last year. I only hope his handicap hasn't improved too much since he and my husband last hit the green. Apparently he stole the show.'

'I bet it hasn't,' Steph replied tartly.

Rae leaned back on her desk, showing off polished toenails, and turned to Ava, who tossed her hair. 'Your portfolio of work is stunning, Ava, simply gorgeous. But you know that.'

'Thanks, Rae. I look forward to showing you what else I'm capable of,' Ava said, lapping up Rae's compliment without hesitation. I was clearly not the only intern with brown-nosing experience.

'What a talented threesome,' Rae said. 'Now, there's something you need to know ...'

Oh no, I thought. In my life, nothing good had ever followed those words. There was the time Mum had said, 'There's something you need to know about Uncle Phil — remember him? Big head, smells like old cheese? Well, he got a job as your high school's lollipop lady. He can help you and your friends cross the street every day. Isn't that great?' Or my personal favourite: 'There's something you need to know ... Whiskers was run over by an ice-cream truck. We buried him in the backyard next to the hydrangeas. The good news is they're giving us a ten per cent discount on ice-cream.' I'd gagged at any mention of ice-cream for three months after that.

'Due to the impressive calibre, I've bumped up the stakes,' Rae continued. 'As you know, this internship goes for twelve weeks and will take you behind the scenes of the magazine. You'll spend time with professionals from every department, learning from them and practising their craft. Now there's an added bonus — specifically, a five thousand dollar bonus.'

The number rang in my ears.

'At the end of the twelve weeks, two of you will be thanked for your time and will take away an invaluable experience and a reference. The third intern — the best — will take home five thousand dollars to spend however they like; a gift from our most generous advertiser, Lint Hygiene Products.'

My hand leaped to my mouth in shock.

'And that's not all,' added Rae. 'The winner will also score her own column in the magazine, complete with head shot and by-line. This is the kind of opportunity every writer dreams of. So, any questions?'

I shook my head, stunned. I was lost in a dream sequence involving me swimming in a pool filled with gold coins, while Mum sipped diamond-filled cocktails and Kat danced in a hula skirt made of hundred-dollar notes.

'Okay. Take these goodie bags from Lint,' Rae said, passing us each an enormous brown paper bag. 'I'll let Liani fill you in on the rules of the internship. Have a good day, do your best and welcome again.'

She sat down in her office chair and turned on her laptop, signifying the conversation's end.

Clutching what seemed like a lifetime's supply of pads and tampons, we filed out into the hallway, where Liani waited for us. She handed us each a folder.

'So, the rules are inside, read them when you get a chance. Steph, you're with design today. Ava, as requested in your email, beauty is all yours this week, which leaves Josie with the fashion team.'

Fashion team? What was I meant to do there? I gazed longingly at the writing department, where five girls sat at computers. One had her head buried in a dictionary, while another was typing as she chatted away on the phone. The second girl hung up, swore and called out to the others for their thoughts on her story. They crowded around to brainstorm ideas.

One day that'll be me, I told myself.

'Josie, I'll take you to the fashion office,' said Liani, snapping me back to the present. 'Ava and Steph, someone from your departments will come to collect you.'

I followed Liani past brightly dressed, beautifully made-up women to a closed door plastered with fashion spreads. I heard giggling and talking from inside. Maybe this wouldn't be so bad. Maybe it was my chance to transform from fashion flop to fashion forward.

The fashion office was a disaster zone. Dresses were turned inside out, shoes were scattered across the carpet and jewellery spilled out of bags and boxes. The room was stuffy, cluttered and windowless; very different from the glamorous office of my imagination.

Liani introduced me to *Sash*'s fresh-faced fashion editor, Carla, who shrugged off the mess, clearly used to it.

'It's easy, really, just hang the up the clothes, sort the shoes into pairs and detangle the jewellery,' she explained. 'I mean, it can take a while to match up the pairs, but you'll get there. Eventually. Oh, and if you need anything, just yell out "Carla" and I'll come and help. But I have to sort out a model casting first.'

'Sounds good.' I forced a smile, wondering how tidying up was going to get me through university and into a successful journalism career.

'Thanks ... Jodie, was it?'

'Er, it's Jos—'

'Cool, you're the best. Oh, and if you get a sec, could you polish the boots in the other room? If you run out of stuff to do, Marg needs help with the steamer, Gen has something going on with bikinis, and Tina could use a hand calling in products. But, you know, see how you go, Jodie. Bye.'

Carla raced out the door, her boots clomping on the floor. I heard her squawking on the phone as she waited for the lift.

Left alone in the fashion office, I had a moment to think about Rae's announcement. Five thousand dollars; five freaking thousand dollars. Mum had tried to keep it from Kat and me, but I knew she was struggling financially since Dad had left. I'd overheard her on the phone to Aunt Julie, stressing about how she was going to pay the bills. Mum worked casually at the local library and also pocketed a small amount of money doing odd jobs — baking cakes, weeding gardens, walking dogs — but her bank balance was far from overflowing. With five thousand dollars, she wouldn't have to fret for a while. Ava and Steph were tough competitors — their groomed hair and clothes almost eliminated me on sight — but I could tell I wanted that by-line and five grand more than they did.

I turned to the mountain of clothes, ready to get to work. I didn't know where to begin, so I just grabbed the first top I saw, a bright-red tunic, and swung it onto a hanger. Easy enough. After that, I hung, polished, scrubbed, detangled, wiped, sorted and repeated for three hours. At lunchtime, I scoffed my sandwich and apple in the fashion office because no one came to tell me otherwise. Afterwards, I sorted some more.

I had a dramatic coughing fit after dragging down a box of shoes from the top shelf of the cupboard and releasing a cloud of dust. I saw a mouse scuttle away under the door and screamed like a banshee. I found jewellery, lost jewellery, broke jewellery and fixed jewellery. I realised how strange most clothes look off the hanger. I tried on a fabulous pair of boots, only to realise they cost more than Mum's monthly wages.

Finally, with everything put away or hung on clothing racks, I dragged out the internship rules. They were typed on a clean white page and read:

SASH INTERNSHIP GUIDELINES

1. *The internship takes place one day a week for twelve weeks (unless alternative arrangements are organised with a senior staff member).*
2. *Arrival time is 9.30 am, no exceptions.*
3. *Departure time is to be organised with a senior staff member.*
4. *Interns must use their best efforts to promote the interests of Sash.*
5. *Appropriate dress code must be adhered to. No thongs or gym gear. Interns will be sent home if dressed inappropriately.*
6. *The winner of the $5000 prize will be determined by Rae Swanson, editor-in-chief.*
7. *The prize money may be spent however the winner chooses.*
8. *Failure to meet these guidelines will result in immediate dismissal and cancellation of the internship, no notice required.*

The rules seemed fair enough, although I was surprised by number five. As fashionably challenged as I was, even I knew kicking around at *Sash* in trainers and trackies was a no-go. For now, I had other things on my mind: like how much longer I'd be confined to the fashion office.

I poked my head out of the room to look around. A twenty-something with a brown pixie cut and bright-red lips stood next to a buzzing photocopier, sucking on a lollipop and tagging magazine pages. She looked up and caught me snooping.

'Oh! Hey, you must be one of the newbies.'

'Yep, that's me. Er, Josie. Hi.'

'I'm Gen. Hey, do you have a sec?'

'Sure. Carla mentioned something about bikinis?'

'Yep, come with me.'

'Did you need a hand choosing some nice styles?' I asked as I followed her into a small, dark room. 'Or maybe I could get you a coffee?'

Gen found the light switch and my voice trailed off at the sight of two tiny sinks, a tall cane basket overflowing with bikini tops and bottoms and two shelves cluttered with cleaning products.

'It would be amazing if you could wash these bikinis for me,' Gen said. 'They're too delicate to go to the laundromat.'

I looked at the massive basket. 'All of them?'

'Is that okay? It's just that I'm flat out with photocopying and PR meetings today, so you'd be an absolute lifesaver. I'll pop in later to help, I promise. Well, if I have time.'

I swallowed. 'Yeah, okay, sure.'

'Thank you, thank you!' Gen raced out of the room, leaving me alone with the overflowing basket.

As I filled the first sink with soapy water and the second one with clear, for rinsing, my mind flashed back to Kat's and Rae's speeches about the glamorous side of the industry. I stopped counting bikinis at about eighty-nine.

4.

I fumbled the key into the lock of Tim's front door, opened it and waited for the blackness to melt into focus. It didn't. I took a step forward and my hip rammed into something smooth and sharp, causing me to yelp. I rubbed at my hip, trying to ignore the sting, and I ran my palm over the grainy walls until I found the light switch. Jackpot. I flicked it on and bright yellow light flooded the apartment hallway. I took a moment to soak up my new surroundings. Stacks of books, DVDs, vinyl records and CDs cluttered the limited floor space, forming teetering towers that flirted with the possibility of crashing at any moment.

I turned around to see what had struck my hip near the doorway and screamed at the sight of a human-size figure, before realising it was a mannequin. I shook my head in disbelief, laughing at the pink lei wrapped around its neck. Tim had failed to mention the mannequin in the scribbled note I'd found poking from under the doormat. All he'd said was to take his spare key from the rosebush at the main entrance (a prickly adventure in itself), use the fresh towel on the couch if I wanted a shower and to make myself at home while he was at a music gig.

I walked past the dummy into the living room, which had a pile of dust-coated boxes stacked in one corner. Posters lined the walls, some swinging off blobs of Blu-Tack. The couch and television looked new, not quite matching the shabby styling. The couch was my bed for the evening, so I was pleased it was clean. Based on what I'd seen so far, I was half-expecting to be greeted by a family of singing mice. I left my bag to be unpacked later and explored the rest of the place. The smell of musky aftershave tainted the air and got even stronger as I approached the bathroom. Fingers pinched over my nostrils, I peeked my head in for a look. Unsurprisingly, it was small. Very small. A broom closet would've felt spacious compared to this bathroom. But, surprisingly, it was clean, almost as clean as our bathroom at home. There was a neat stack of toilet rolls, toilet freshener poised on top of the loo, and a teeny-tiny corner shower and tub combo.

Less than one minute later, the water was running, bubble bath was bubbling, music was blaring from my phone and my clothes littered the bathroom floor. Tim was out, so I had all night to belt out bad pop songs in a bubble-bath fantasy land where the horror of my first day at *Sash* was a foggy memory. I sang along to the music, splashing the water with my toes to test the temperature. It was ready, so I lowered myself into the white, foamy bath.

Three short, sharp knocks on the bathroom door suddenly snapped me out of my karaoke party for one. I slammed off the volume on my phone and plunged beneath the water's surface, splashing bubbles the size of golf balls onto the floor.

An uncomfortable silence followed, until someone with a deep voice cleared his throat.

I resurfaced and called out a tentative, 'Tim? Is that you?'

Nothing.

Crap, I thought, dragging a washcloth up over my chest. I drew my knees toward me, rounding my body into a ball like a nervous hedgehog. But there wasn't anywhere to hide. I was trapped. And I couldn't remember if I'd locked the bathroom door. Or if the door even had a lock. Not that it mattered because a serious burglar could break through a rickety door like that in seconds.

'Tim?' I whispered.

I closed my eyes, waiting for a man wearing a balaclava to burst through the door, shouting orders at his crew of burglars, each burlier than the next. My mind flashed with Mum's warning about the city's weirdos. Why was that woman always right?

Once again, I heard a guy clear his throat. But this time, he spoke. 'Ah, excuse me, but who are you and why are you in my bathroom?'

It didn't sound like Tim. My cousin's voice was flaky and scattered, as though he was always daydreaming. This voice was deeper. Friendly, but self-assured.

'Your bathroom?' I said. 'Where's Tim?'

'Tim's my roommate.'

'Tim never mentioned he had a roommate.'

'Oh really? Well, he didn't mention I'd get home to find a stranger yodelling in the —'

'Yodelling? That was ... Oh, never mind.'

'Great. Well, that's sorted then.'

I looked around for a weapon just in case, Mum's know-it-all words ringing in my bubble-soaked ears. Everything I could see was soft, fluffy or cuddly. What was I supposed to do? Towel the guy into a coma? Shampoo him to death?

'How do I know you're not trying to lure me out?' I said. 'I've seen crime shows. I know how it works.'

The guy laughed. 'Okay. Test me, then.'

'What?'

'Ask me three questions about what's in the bathroom. If I don't get all three right, call the police. You do have your phone in there, don't you?'

My phone glinted on the washbasin, reminding me help was only a call away. And I'd always been a sucker for guessing games.

'Fine. Three chances.'

'Brilliant.'

His voice sounded closer. The door moved slightly and I imagined him leaning against it, waiting for my questions. I looked around the bathroom for something to test him on.

'Okay, here we go. First question: what colour is the washer hanging off the shower tap?'

He chuckled. 'Easy one. Green.'

I studied the washer. 'Are you sure?'

'It's green, definitely green.'

Now it was my turn to laugh. 'The answer I was looking for was lime green, actually. Hideous lime green to be exact, but I'll give it to you.'

My eyes moved to the scungy burgundy bath mat on the floor. 'Your bath mat's worse.'

He chuckled again. 'Hey! That's below the belt — and it's Tim's anyway. Come on, next question.'

'*Fine*. Second question: what's the brand of candles on the windowsill?'

Pause.

Here we go, I thought, I've got him. 'Well?'

'Trick question: we don't have candles on the windowsill. You're not even trying.'

Burglar or not, this guy wasn't messing around. 'Okay, lucky last question. Get this right and I'll believe you're not here to murder me and this may, in fact, be your bathroom. What scent is your handwash?'

'That's seriously the question? You know your life depends on it.'

'I do. And yes, that's the question.'

'Well, it's easy. Lavender — floral, flowery, take your pick.'

I grinned. 'I hope you look good in handcuffs, mister. I'm calling the cops.'

'But that's the right answer! I bought it myself!'

'The answer I was looking for was vanilla. That's V-A-N-I —'

'I should have known — Tim's swapped them. He said the lavender one smelled too girly. Come on, one more question.'

I pushed myself up out of the bath and wrapped my towel around me. 'The deal was three. You said it yourself, three out of three.'

'Look, I'm starving. Call the cops if you want, but I'm going to eat my pizza.'

'Pizza?'

'Yeah. Hawaiian.'

Hawaiian was my favourite. I'd been so swept up in the moment that I hadn't noticed the scent of juicy pineapple, melted cheese and ham teasing me through the door. Until now.

'You, ah, want some?'

My stomach growled, reminding me it hadn't been fed since lunchtime.

'No, thanks,' I forced out, almost drooling. 'I don't accept pizza from potential criminals. Besides, I have a phone call to make.'

'Just remember to tell the cops I'm charming *and* good-looking.'

I heard him pad away. My phone beeped and I leaned over to see Tim's name flash across the screen. His message read: *Sorry cuz, forgot to say my roomie will be home tonight. He's cool. Back later.*

'Bloody Tim,' I muttered.

I was in a strange apartment, wrapped in a strange towel with a strange guy down the hall eating pizza. I calculated I was only one more embarrassing incident away from morphing into a rom-com character.

I opened the bathroom door, peeked out to check the hallway was clear, then raced into Tim's room. Safe at last. But a quick glance around proved I'd planted myself in the wrong room. Based on the evidence — this guy cave didn't reek of dirty socks; it had wobbling stacks of vinyls and books on the floor; a bass guitar resting on the bed; and an ironed pinstripe shirt hanging from the doorknob — there was almost a 99.9 per cent chance that this was my new friend's room. And I was in it. In a towel. Without my clothes, which I'd forgotten to pick up from the bathroom floor. Seriously, world: are you kidding me?

A knock rattled the door and the roommate's voice piped up from the other side. 'Here's your bag, I'll leave it outside the door. Oh, and when you're ready, I've saved you a few slices.'

I bit my lip. 'Thanks. By the way, we're probably well past introductions, but I'm Tim's cousin Josie.'

Pause. 'I know. He told me you were coming.'

I erupted into laughter. 'Well, there you go.'

'Oh, and while you're snooping around in there, check out my music collection. It's pretty sick.'

'I'm not snoo — yeah, okay, I'll check it out.'

'I'm James, by the way. Pizza's getting cold ...'

I heard him walk away, then opened the door and pulled my bag inside. As I dragged on shorts and a T-shirt it hit me how far away I was from life back home with Mum and Kat.

I forced myself to join James in the lounge room for a slice of (by then, cold) pizza. When I shuffled in, red-faced, he laughed and brushed his shaggy brown hair out of his eyes. He was cute — hot, even — with an olive complexion, warm blue eyes and an athletic body.

'Want a beer?' he asked, gesturing for me to sit down.

I flinched, which must have cost me at least ten cool points.

James didn't seem fazed. 'Tea it is,' he said, then popped on the kettle.

Alcohol and I hadn't been friends since Suzy Heywood's eighteenth birthday party at the bowling alley. After a few glasses of champagne, I ended up sobbing in the toilets after missing out on a strike by one pin. I took it hard. Really hard, apparently. The time before that, too many drinks resulted in me wearing a chicken suit to a high-school dance. Nothing else needs to be said about *that* situation.

After James had fixed a pot of tea, he plonked himself on the couch next to me. My nerves simmered, but then something wonderful happened. He broke the silence and for the next few hours we talked until my throat was scratchy, my cheeks were aching and we'd powered through two pots of tea.

James told me about his IT degree, which he sounded as thrilled about as a kick in the crotch. He also shared lots of cool stories about his job at a nearby music shop: his boss who looked like a giant lizard; the fact that he watched movies on the sly on his laptop when no one needed help; and the customer who'd hooked up with at least three of the male staff (not him) and one of the female staff. My eyes widened at that, my innocence beaming from every pore of my body. He even revealed his biggest secret — that he hated IT and wanted to become a music producer, but his father didn't believe he could make a career out of it.

When James's blue eyes locked onto mine and he asked me about my plans, I stuttered and stammered that I dreamed of becoming a world-famous journalist.

'I've got an idea,' he said, pouring me another cup of tea. 'Let me interview you, test my journalistic skills. Then you can interview me and show me how it's really done.'

I repositioned myself on the couch. 'You're serious? An interview between you and me?'

'Yeah! Think of me as Oprah, Ellen or Doctor Phil.' He laughed at his own lameness and I couldn't help but join in.

'Fine,' I smirked. 'You know, you're super cheesy. Did anyone ever tell you that?'

'Only every day.' He grinned, showing off straight teeth and soft pink lips. 'Now, let's begin ... Wait! I need a mic.' As James leaned over to the windowsill behind us and picked up a half-empty water bottle, I searched his face for flaws — a crooked nose, tiny ears or bad skin. But he didn't have any (at least any visible ones). All I discovered were a couple of to-die-for dimples and a light powdering of freckles. I was a goner.

He raised the bottle to his lips, holding it like a microphone. 'Welcome to *James*, everybody, the show where I get to ask the questions — *wooo yeaaaaah*.' He feigned a crowd cheering while I laughed.

He turned to face me and my stomach danced with anticipation. There wasn't a real crowd, there weren't any cameras or directors or a million viewers watching from home, it was just me and him. Yet I couldn't have been more terrified.

'Josie,' he began, running his hand through his hair, 'this is your first exclusive interview so it's only fair we go back to the beginning. Way back. Tell me about your most humiliating childhood incident.'

'Wow!' I spluttered. 'Aren't you meant to butter me up with compliments and freebies first? Maybe I do need that beer.'

James smiled. 'You'll get your payback, remember.'

'You can bet on that,' I said, and paused to come up with a good answer. It was a toughie. My life was an ongoing series of humiliating incidents wrapped in a box of shame and tied with a bow of awkwardness. 'Well, there was the time I got chased around a shopping centre by Santa Claus. Or would you prefer the tale of the little girl who ate so many liquorice allsorts on a school trip that she, er ... Actually, that one didn't happen. Urban legend, I swear.'

James leaned forward, holding the water-bottle mic to my lips.

'We clearly need to hear about both,' he said, adding some more fake cheering. 'See the audience is gagging for it. They love it!'

James wanted humiliation, so I served it up for him on a platter, with a side of disgrace for good measure.

I revealed that the Santa who'd chased me and Kat through the shops was actually my sweaty excuse for an uncle who'd decided it would be fun to terrify us while onlookers screamed with laughter. I told him how my liquorice allsorts overdose had resulted in an unfortunate incident on the bus that bestowed on me the nickname Josie Brown-Pants for the rest of primary school. (Bless Mum for sending me to a high school where no one knew me.) I even 'fessed up to him about my love of writing, my dreams and my obsession with stationery. I didn't mention Dad leaving, though. I couldn't.

The craziest part wasn't that I handed over morsels of information I'd never even told my best friend, Angel. What blew my mind was that James listened, really listened.

And he laughed. When I told him about Kat locking me outside the house at age twelve in nothing but my training bra and baggy white knickers, he laughed so much his tea splashed all over the carpet and coffee table. But he didn't seem to care. He simply clutched his stomach, laughing, mouth wide open.

When the clock on the living-room wall chimed three, he jolted up and announced he had to go to bed. I'd been stifling yawns for hours, but hadn't wanted the night to end.

He walked toward his bedroom, stopping to say, 'Well, that's episode one of *James* complete. Can't wait for the first ep of *Josie*,' then disappeared, leaving me alone in the lounge room.

'James!' I whispered loudly. I wasn't sure why I was worried about noise; Tim still hadn't come home.

James poked his head around the door. 'Yeah?'

'Sorry again about that whole thinking-you-were-here-to-rob-or-murder-me thing.'

He paused, then smiled. 'Night, Josie.'

He disappeared again, signalling the end of a night that would go down as one of my top favourite experiences of all time. A gorgeous guy had sat next to me for hour upon hour, laughing at my jokes, flirting with me and flashing his baby blues. As I made myself comfortable on the couch, I couldn't help but smile. Life was giving me a break. A tall, shaggy-haired, hilarious break.

The sound of a truck screaming toward the apartment window woke me. I burrowed myself deep under the sheet and waited for imminent death. It'd be a dramatic way to go; I'd probably make the nightly news or at least a small filler article in the paper. I pushed away the fact I was going to (a) die a virgin; (b) miss my own eighteenth birthday; and (c) be found wearing hand-me-up Sesame Street PJ boxers with matching faded singlet. Hopefully the journalist covering my death would take pity on me and not mention that part.

Moments later, it was apparent death hadn't plucked me from the lounge room. There was no shattered glass. No broken furniture. My matching PJs would remain unreported, which pleased me most of all. I poked my head out from beneath the sheet and looked around. The living room was exactly as it had been the night before: two teacups on the coffee table; my bag open, its contents strewn over the carpet; the TV gleaming in the corner.

I hadn't been completely wrong. There was a truck. A loud one. But it was outside, which made sense, really, considering a truck would've needed serious Spider-Man powers to make it through a second-storey window. The truck's engine revved as it stopped and started in front of each building. Welcome to the city, it roared, scolding me for trying to sleep in. Throaty male voices cut through the noise, yelling to each other about rotting fish, folks who were 'too lazy to recycle' and arguing about whose wife had the best butt.

The garbage truck chugged away and the room was quiet for a moment. My phone beeped, bringing me back to the present. When I checked it, I found a text from Tim: *Can you come in for a sec? Bring juice.*

I shook my head, untangled myself from the sheet and walked to the fridge. The two-litre bottle of pineapple juice wasn't hard to spot; except for an out-of-date carton of milk and a half-eaten kebab there wasn't much else in there. I grabbed the juice, picked up a plastic cup from the counter and walked to Tim's room. I knocked on the door and heard a mumbled 'Come in'.

Tim was spread-eagled on the bed, staring up at an old-fashioned ceiling fan that whirred and rattled with every spin, his slim body encased in a pair of skinny jeans. His eyes were half-open and his hair was rumpled into a mousy brown mess. An untouched burger and half-drunk beer stood on the bedside table.

'Cuz, long time no see,' he croaked, as though he'd eaten a packet of cigarettes for dinner. Something told me he may have. 'Help. Juice. Mouth.'

I unscrewed the lid and reached for the plastic cup.

'No,' he murmured, pointing to his mouth. 'Straight in.'

I paused for a second, aware of the absurdity of the situation. Oh well, I thought, first time for everything. I hovered above Tim, pouring juice into his mouth. The yellow liquid splashed onto the bed around him. After what felt like hours, he held up his hand for me to stop.

'Lifesaver,' he said.

I breathed through my mouth to avoid smelling the BO-beer-burger cocktail again.

'Popeye has spinach, I have juice,' he said. 'Thanks. Normally James brings it in, but he ducked out early for work, I think.'

Damn, I thought. I'd wanted to see him again before I headed back home.

'Ah, man, what a night. I didn't wake you when I got home, did I?'

'Nope,' I lied, jolted back to 4.19 am when Tim had crashed through the front door, screaming with laughter on the phone to someone called Luca. He'd tripped over the mannequin as he stumbled around in an attempt to find his room, before mistaking the kitchen bench for his queen-size bed. I didn't have the heart to tell him I'd had to get off the couch to push him in the right direction.

'Cool,' he said. 'So, ah, it's nice to see you.'

'Yeah. You too.' If nice meant suffering sleep-deprivation.

'So, how was your interny thing? You CEO of the company yet?'

I sighed. 'Yeah, good. Pretty good. It was fine.'

'So it was bad?'

'No! Well ... the office was amazing, the deputy editor was nice ...'

'But?'

'But I felt like an ugly sore thumb all day. Plus, they forgot about me so I didn't leave the office until seven thirty. The other girls were all beautiful and ... Oh, who am I kidding? I stained my dress, they didn't let me near a computer and I had to wash bikinis. It was awful.'

Tim wriggled into a black scoop-neck T-shirt that he'd selected from the floor. 'So quit.'

'What? No, it's for uni. I can't.'

'Can.'

'Can't.'

'I can go all day. Can, can, can. Look, quit, don't quit — it's up to you.' Tim took another swig of juice. 'Anyway, it's been good catching up again after all this time, huh?'

I nodded, even though my catch-up with Tim had consisted of a hand-scrawled note, five minutes of chitchat and hand-feeding him pineapple juice. Coming to the city had been good. In fact, it had been great. It just had nothing to do with catching up with Tim.

'Er, maybe don't mention all this to our mums?' he suggested, waving a hand around his bedroom.

I laughed. 'Got it. Look, I'd better pack. I'll see you out there, okay?'

I walked back to the lounge room, stopping only to brush my fingers over James's closed door.

5.

My best friend from high school, Angela Michaels (or Angel as she'd asked to be called since discovering yoga, lentils and meditation), hated being ignored. In her mind, nothing said 'Stuff you' like a hot guy not noticing her edgy new haircut or, worse, not being invited to an incredible party.

'I can't believe Holly Bentley forgot me again,' Angel whined, flicking through a copy of *Sash* magazine as we lounged on my bed the night I got home from my first trip to the city. 'Everyone will be there except us. We have to get in.'

I rolled my eyes. 'Wasn't this all meant to end after high school?'

After years of countless rejections, I was used to not being invited to parties. Being six months younger than most of our year hadn't helped my social status. When my classmates were hooning around as P-platers, I was still getting dropped off to events by Mum, usually with

Kat in the back seat, waving me goodbye with her tongue poking out and a flash of her middle finger.

My social life took an even bigger step backwards when the eighteenths began and everyone could legally drink. On the off-chance I scored an invite, I'd have to head home around ten or eleven, when the others headed to the local pub or trashy nightclub. I'd be tucked into bed before the stroke of midnight, like Cinderella, although switch the ugly stepsisters for a popular little sister whose fake ID had already got her into at least two of the town's clubs. As my best friend, poor Angel was left with the unappealing choice of braving the pub without a wingwoman or calling it a night. Nine times out of ten, she chose option two.

As far as our year was concerned, we were still invisible — and Angel couldn't stand it.

She glared at me, her cropped black hair showing off her piercing hazel eyes. As much as she'd tried to re-create herself since Year Twelve ended, her eyes told a different story. Her haircut may have screamed 'I don't give a rat's' but underneath she was still my blonde best friend who'd wanted to be a vet before she just scraped through school with a pass. The same girl who'd had her heart shattered by one of the popular guys, who broke up with her at a school assembly because she was 'too weird'. Brutal.

'Angel, seriously? Isn't it time we stopped caring?'

'You do know Pete Jordan will be there?'

'So?' I shot back.

'The guy you've been obsessively pining for since Year Eight, even though he vom—'

'Don't say it.'

Angel pretended to zip her lips, but seconds later unzipped them. 'You need to hear this. Alana dumped him a week ago. He's alone. He's lonely. He's alone and lonely. You know what *that* means?'

I sighed. Angel hadn't given up. Not even close.

'Angela!' I hissed. 'Shut up. You could wake Mum.'

'First, it's *Angel*. And second, well, I'm just saying it could be fun.'

'Fine, I'm in. Can we change the topic already?'

Angel waved the *Sash* mag in the air. 'So, how was it, anyway? Lots of babes and stuck-up bitches?'

'Pretty much.'

'I knew it.' She shook her head. 'Any scrag fights over lipstick?'

'Shuddup, you.' I rolled my eyes and bit my tongue to resist telling her how much the first day blew. Little Miss Arts Student would just arch her eyebrow and say 'I told you so'. Since she started uni, Angel had been up on a soapbox, spouting her opinions to anyone who'd listen, and even those who wouldn't.

I didn't mention meeting James either. For now, I wanted to keep that lovely little memory to myself.

Especially because a small part of me suspected I may have hallucinated the whole thing. Guys like that didn't talk to me for hours on end. They just didn't.

Angel threw down the magazine. 'Wow, I can't read another page of that. Do you really want to write stories on how to make a guy moan in bed?'

I shrugged. This was just another outburst in a long line of outbursts. And she was partly right — I didn't want to write stories about how to make a guy moan in bed: (a) because it would be a death sentence if I ever wanted to be taken seriously as a journalist; and (b) well, I had no idea how to make a guy moan. Squirm, run and never call? Sure. But moaning? Not so much.

Angel stood up and smoothed down her hair. 'Anyway, I'm off to see someone about getting us two invites to Holly Bentley's party. Promise me you're excited.'

I made cheerleader hands. 'Promise.'

Angel glanced at herself in the full-length mirror. 'Urgh, when will yoga make my butt shrink already?'

'You have a great butt.'

'You're too kind. My butt and I thank you.' She grinned. 'Anyway, gotta run! Love you.' She pranced out, leaving me alone on the bed with *Sash* magazine. I picked it up and flicked through a few pages, wondering how I was going to make myself go back next week for another long day of domestic drudgery.

* * *

Mum charged ahead in the supermarket, scooping up apples, spinach and loaves of bread. Kat and I trailed behind, pushing the trolley. Mum muttered to herself, glanced down at her shopping list, checked the shelf, then tore off to another aisle. For Kat, this signalled pouncing time.

She turned to me, hands on hips. 'Well?'

'Well, what?' I replied, pushing the trolley past her.

Kat pulled at my arm. 'Why won't you tell me how *Sash* was? You've ignored me the last four times I've asked.'

'Like I said, it was fine.'

'Fine is Mum's attempt at stir-fry. Fine is going on a date with a cute guy with a boring personality.'

'Okay, it was more than fine. It was very fine. Uberfine.'

'You told them that story about pooing your pants after eating all that liquorice, didn't you?'

'No!'

'What, then? Did being that close to gorgeous magazine people cause your brain to implode?'

A screaming child at the other end of the aisle smashed a carton of eggs onto the ground. The mother was wearing stained tracksuit pants and looked washed out. She exhaled a sad, tired sigh that I translated to mean

'Here we go again'. With Kat pushing me for an answer, I felt like slamming a carton of eggs onto the ground, too. But the poor mother had enough problems without worrying about her child's tantrum being infectious.

Kat wouldn't give up; she just talked more, louder, faster.

She cornered me by the frozen vegetables for my interrogation. 'Seriously, what went down? I'm your sister. You're supposed to share these things. If you did spill the dirt on that embarrassing liquorice thing, I promise I won't tell anyone. Well, no one except Tye because, well, I've already told him. C'mon, Jose. You can trust me.'

I rolled my eyes. The last time Kat had said those infamous four words, she'd ended up lopping off ten centimetres of my hair and creating a fringe that resulted in an emergency trip to the hairdresser. Trusting Kat was about as safe as trusting a pickpocket with a cute smile. I never knew when she was going to strike, and by the time I realised she had, it was always too late.

'Mum's taking a while,' I said, ignoring her tirade.

Kat muttered, 'I'll find her,' and stormed off. Her speedy exit left me alone to daydream. Out of nowhere James's face appeared in my mind, sending a wave of heat through my body and causing me to blush. I focused on a tin of tuna to distract myself. Canned in spring water, great, I thought, but within seconds James had launched himself back into my brain. I wondered what he was doing at that moment. Watching movies on the sly at work? Listening to his jaw-droppingly large music collection? Having lunch with Tim? Definitely not daydreaming about a seventeen-nearly-eighteen-year-old called Josie. Or could he be?

My phone beeped and for a minute I thought the universe had answered my wishes. But no, not today. The message was from Angel.

Still waiting to hear back about the party, but it'll be so on. Petey baby better watch out. You're gonna be hot, hot, hot.

Confused, I scrolled down for more detail but there was nothing there.

Beep, beep! My phone went off again. I saw a pic of a teeny-tiny black miniskirt with the caption 'Can't wait 'til Josie wears me while making out with Pete.'

Makeover round two appeared to be in full swing and Angel was on a mission to reduce the centimetres of material I clad my body in. There was no way I was wearing that skirt. I'd worn bigger pairs of undies. I was halfway through a message to tell Angel where to shove the skirt, when —

'Found her,' Kat said behind me, dragging Mum by the arm.

'Sorry, love. Got distracted near the yoghurts,' Mum said, whisking the trolley away from me. 'Now, what do you want for dinner? Let me cook your favourite. Your big achievement deserves a celebration.'

'No, Mum, there's nothing to celebrate. Seriously, the internship's no big deal.'

'Oh quiet, love,' she said. 'How about beef stroganoff? You've always loved that.'

Mum trotted off in search of sour cream while I wondered whether I should remind her beef stroganoff was Dad's favourite dish, not mine.

I turned to Kat. 'Doesn't Mum remember that's Dad's —'

'Leave it,' snapped Kat. 'Just leave it.'

She plugged in her earphones and walked away.

What's with her? I thought. Sure, Kat wasn't exactly a dream to be around on her good days, but this was a whole other level of bitchy.

Mum reappeared holding a bottle of soft drink. 'That should just about do us for today,' she said.

'The sour cream, Mum?'

'I knew I forgot something,' she said, pushing her boofy, unbrushed hair out of her eyes. 'I'll just run and get it.'

I didn't think she realised she was humming her and Dad's wedding song as she headed off again.

A minute later, she returned with enough sour cream to feed a team of famished footy players. 'Half price, love! Isn't that great? Someone's looking down on me.' She punched the price into the handheld calculator she'd started carrying around to track our ever-growing expenses.

'Great, Mum. That's great,' I said.

'Now, we can have beef stroganoff all week. I bet you're dying with excitement.'

'Yep, I'm dying,' I muttered.

Part of me wished Dad would appear, sweep me over his shoulder like he used to and tell me everything was going to be okay. But he wouldn't. He was kilometres, towns, maybe even oceans away.

So much time had passed since I'd seen him that I wondered what he looked like now. Maybe he'd grown a beard, lost his pot belly, donned a pair of thick-rimmed glasses? Waiting with Mum at the checkout, it was hard to believe we were ever a tight-knit family of four.

'So I'm up in the helicopter, looking down at the clear blue ocean, and I think, this is the best day of my life. I could die happy. Glad I didn't, but seriously, I could have.'

'Totally, man. My day was wicked, too. I sat there watching the interview, thinking, this is it, I've practically made it. Living, breathing journalism, right before my eyes. I could smell the opposition leader's fear. It was sensational.'

My uni classmates Tony and Jeff were practically organising a parade in honour of their first internship days. I couldn't help but feel dejected. For the past five minutes Tony'd re-enacted how the pilot had let him steer the weather chopper. As for Jeff, political newshound in the making, he was still salivating over getting to sit in on an interview with one of the country's most prestigious journalists. They almost choked on their enthusiasm as they one-upped each other's stories.

Tony turned to me. 'What about you, Josie? How was your day at the paper?'

'Yeah, seen your by-line in print yet?' Jeff asked.

'I, ah, didn't go to the paper. All out of positions.'

Tony tilted his head. 'Oh, really? I heard Fiona McClay got a spot and she's already researched a piece with the news editor.'

My jaw dropped.

'So where'd you end up, then?' asked Jeff. 'The radio station? I always thought you'd be perfect for radio.'

'Er, thanks, I think.'

'C'mon, where are you?'

'*Sash*,' I muttered.

'Where?'

'*Sash*.'

Jeff shrugged. 'Never heard of it. Is it one of those independent mags? What did you get up to? Interviews, research, editing?'

My mind flashed back to the pile of dirty bikinis and being hidden away in the fashion office for hours with no one to talk to. 'Yeah, pretty much,' I said. 'That and, er, other stuff.'

Remember this moment, I told myself. This is what living a big fat lie feels like. Thankfully, Filly called me into his office just then. He'd asked us all to report back on our first internship day and I was only too happy to tell him *exactly* what I thought.

After I'd filled him in on the depressing details, Filly shook his bald, bulbous head. 'I'm sorry, Josie, there's nowhere else I can send you.'

'Really? There has to be something — *anything* — I can do instead.'

He leaned back in his chair, linking his sausage-like fingers behind his head. Sweat stains the size of dinner plates clung to each armpit. 'No, there's nothing.'

'Not even *Cats Quarterly*?' My desperation was as obvious as a yapping puppy.

'Not even that. Look, as far as I'm concerned, you have two options: finish the internship at *Sash* and make it work, whatever it takes — because that's what professionals do. Or, stay here in my office complaining for the next hour, then join the list of wannabes who never made it because they gave up on their dreams. Well?'

Filly's no-nonsense approach shocked me, but I managed to whisper, 'I'll do the internship.' Giving up on my dream of becoming a journalist wasn't an option.

Filly smiled, his face softening. 'A fine choice. Josie, you're a great student and a hard worker, but you've got to pull your finger out. Show those magazine girls how it's done. You think washing a few bikinis was hard? Try doing that for a lifetime. This isn't school, you aren't going to be surrounded by friends all day. You can give up if you want, but that's not going to earn you a high distinction. Besides, I hear there's quite the bonus up for grabs at *Sash*.'

'I know,' I croaked out. 'Thanks, Filly.'

I collected my books and turned to leave his office. When I reached the doorway, he spoke again.

'Oh, and forget about Jeff's and Tony's bragging. Between you and me, Tony shrieked for his mummy for half the helicopter ride.'

I snorted with laughter.

Walking away from his office, I felt lighter and happier than I had for days. I was ready for my next visit to *Sash* HQ. I just had to bring my A-game. After all, there were five thousand big ones on the table. Five thousand big ones my family could put to great use.

6.

'Stephanie, pass the box,' ordered, Ava, who was standing a mere metre from it herself. 'Yes, that mauve one. No, not the lilac one, the mauve one!'

Steph passed Ava the box without a word, then returned to sorting dog-eared back issues of the magazines, forming teetering piles on the shelf.

Ava had unofficially crowned herself the leader of the interns, barking orders at us like a glossy dictator. She didn't complete tasks; she just pointed, waved and flicked her hands, no doubt conserving energy in her patent leather heels. Apparently a half-finished online interior design course gave her all the styling skills required, although Steph and I weren't convinced.

Maybe Ava had sniffed too much hairspray before work and missed the memo that we were about as important to *Sash* as the mail boy. In fact, the mail boy was *Sash* royalty compared to us. We were the plebs, the scum, the bottom feeders. Exhibit A: we'd been sent to a musty room where air conditioning was a pipe dream to sort thousands of magazines. But somehow Ava thought we mattered. Or, more to the point, *she* mattered.

Not satisfied with Steph's lacklustre response to her bossiness, Ava turned on me. 'Have you worn that dress before, Josephine? It's not that I want to make a big deal or anything, it just looks so familiar. Glad you managed to get the stain out, too.'

My face flushed red. I was wearing the same dress as last week. I'd run out of time for another shopping trip, so I'd borrowed a pair of Kat's heels and mixed up my jewellery and hairstyle and hoped no one would notice. Normal people wouldn't have noticed, or if they did, they wouldn't have cared. But I wasn't dealing with normal people, I was dealing with Ava, who apparently could sniff out a repeat-outfit offender faster than a police dog could sniff out a drug-crammed backpack.

'Not sure, maybe,' I said, returning to my sorting.

She sniffed. 'Well, you'd better be careful. I doubt Rae wants people showing up in the same clothes time and time again. You know, for the sake of *Sash*'s image. Just something to think about.'

Steph slammed down a magazine, causing us to jump. 'Ava, what's your problem?'

'What's my problem?' Ava snapped. 'Nothing. What's yours? Why are you even here? You clearly don't want this as much as me or Miss Grade As over there.'

'What would you know?' Steph turned her back on Ava to face me. 'Hey, Jose, I've had it with this sorting. Want me to paint your nails?' She held up a bottle of silver polish she'd pulled from the shelf.

I waved my hands at her — the nails were still a soft pink from last week.

Steph sank to the floor and wriggled over to me clutching the polish. 'All good. I'll do your toes.'

'Okay ...' I replied, aware that Ava was shooting dirty looks at the back of Steph's head. I prayed to whichever god or goddess was on duty that Steph wouldn't notice my weird feet. 'Clown's feet,' Kat called them, and shoe sales people always came out with a version of 'Yikes, they're awfully long.' But Steph didn't seem to care as she swiped the polish over my toe nails.

'Well, if you two children are going to play sleepover games, I'm out of here,' Ava spat out.

'Wait, Ava —' I started, but it was too late. Ava stalked out, slamming the door behind her.

'Good riddance,' said Steph.

It was the first time we'd been alone and I didn't know what to say. Steph was so cool and confident; the complete opposite of me. She painted my nails like a pro, layering on the polish until my toes became gleaming silver buttons.

'You bring your lunch today?' she asked.

'Yeah, just a sandwich and an apple,' I replied,

admiring my toes. 'Boring, but it was all I could scrape together.'

'I was going to see if you wanted to grab some Vietnamese with me. There's a place across the road that does amazing rice paper rolls, like super-authentic. Man, you wouldn't believe how good the food is in Vietnam — I lived on noodles. It was the best. I need to get back there as soon as Dad lets me off the leash for more than two seconds. I swear, that man believes taking me to over-priced restaurants and buying me new clothes will convince me to stay put. He thinks too much with his wallet. First-world problem, right?'

'Ha, right.' I laughed awkwardly.

'If *this* is the real world — all rules, and jobs, and mean girls — then I don't want it. Give me a hostel and a handful of strangers up for a laugh any day. So ... want to do lunch?'

'Oh, I thought you said ... um ... yeah, I'd love to,' I stammered.

I liked the idea of spending more time with Steph, and I was curious about the food. Back home, the closest we had to Vietnamese rice paper rolls were greasy spring rolls at the local Chinese restaurant.

'Will your sanger be okay though?' She grinned.

I blushed. 'It'll keep.'

The door creaked open and Liani peered in. 'Josie, got a minute?'

'Sure.' I'd just spent five minutes getting my toenails primped and pampered. I had all the time in the world.

'How would you like to help out in the features department? They're a writer down today. Keen?'

Lunch would have to wait. I nearly raced over to hug her, but managed to restrain myself. After all, I didn't want to ruin my fresh pedicure. I beamed. Kat would have been proud of me.

'Number thirty-four,' I muttered while click-clacking on the computer keyboard. 'He says he'll call you tonight but he doesn't, and then you catch him posting flirty comments online to that total babe from the coffee shop. Number thirty-five: you find a pair of undies that aren't yours in his gym bag —'

'Jordie!' a shrill voice piped up behind me. 'Can you drop that and come here, please? We need all hands on deck at the photo shoot.'

'Josie, I think she means you,' whispered the girl next to me, an olive-skinned features writer called Eloise.

I looked up from my typing to see a wide-eyed Carla standing at *Sash*'s office door and waving me over with a handful of coat hangers. Her left foot tapped over and over on the carpet, causing the hangers to jangle together.

'Jordie? Jordie!' she repeated, her voice getting louder.

Eloise nodded at me. 'You'd better go. Carla hasn't hit that decibel level for a while. Must be serious. Just leave that work until later ... *Jordie*.'

We both giggled.

For the past two hours, I'd been writing a piece for Eloise entitled '101 Signs He's *Not* Interested' (for which, unsurprisingly, I had plenty of ideas). I was a little peeved to be plucked from the features department and thrown back into the world of fashion, but intern beggars couldn't be choosers. I said goodbye to Eloise, saved my work and walked over to Carla, who by this stage was grinding her teeth with stress.

As we made our way to the photo shoot, Carla babbled through a list of the things she needed help with. I lost track after task nine and figured I'd have to wing it.

We arrived at a door with the words 'Studio 7B' printed in bold, black lettering. I opened it, excited and ready to experience my first magazine photo shoot. It was chaos. The room was full of people: dolled-up women pushing racks of men's clothing, weaving between guys holding trays spilling with coffee. A photographer wearing a jaunty cap was head-to-head with Rae in a corner, his arms flailing and gesturing. Rae nodded, and occasionally shook her head, while he ranted.

Nearby, Liani was chatting to four hot twenty-something guys who were sprawled in black chairs. They had self-confidence down to a fine art, keeping one eye on themselves in the mirrors and the other on Liani as she made awkward small talk.

'So you got here alright, then?' I heard her say.

'It would appear so,' one of the guys cracked. The others tittered.

'And, ah, you don't feel like a coffee?' she tried again.

'Not since the last time you asked, about two minutes ago,' one of the guys muttered.

'Rightio,' Liani said. 'Good.'

A few metres away, a curvy-figured woman with big lips and even bigger hair was playing with her phone, glancing over occasionally to check what was happening with the self-assured quartet; a protective mother hen in fire-engine red lippie and a power suit. 'You lads okay over there?' she hollered in a thick English accent.

One of them — a cute guy with brown hair — grinned. 'We're sweet, Claire.'

'Thanks, Billy, love.' She nodded and returned to fiddling with her phone.

Carla put me to work steaming clothes and sorting belts for the photo shoot. Initially, I didn't recognise the four guys — our 'models for the day' as Carla described them. But after about ten minutes of sorting belts (there were categories apparently: stylish, practical, statement and NFW — no freaking way) it hit me like a slap across the face. The arrogant foursome were Greed, the country's latest music 'it' boys. No wonder they looked familiar: their faces were always in the papers, on the sides of buses, billboards and social media. Especially Billy, their resident bad boy, whose hobbies seemed to consist of partying and being a player. There'd even been whisperings he had got a girl pregnant.

Even though we were kilometres apart I felt Kat hating me right then. The Greed boys were famous, which took them straight to the top of her list of what was important. And I was standing a mere metre from them. I wished I had a camera, or that I could get their autographs for her, but Carla had warned me three times to 'stay away from the talent'.

I was sent to a corner of the studio while the photography crew set up lights and hung white sheets. Adrenaline and energy buzzed around me. I watched Rae in another heated discussion, this time with Liani, whose arms were crossed over her chest. Claire hovered near the catering cart, shovelling mini quiches into her mouth.

Apparently 'staying away from the talent' didn't apply to Carla, who flirted with the foursome, tossing her hair and batting her lashes, before asking two of them — Chris and Jamie — to join her in wardrobe. The other two — Billy and Anthony — would be interviewed by the features department. Tough day at the office, right? 'What did you do at work today?' the writers' friends must ask. 'Oh, nothing much,' the features girls must reply, shrugging and looking bored. 'Wrote a bit, edited a bit, interviewed two famous dudes. You know. The usual.' Jealousy didn't even begin to describe it.

'Hey, you,' I heard someone call out nearby. I knew they didn't mean me so I didn't reply. The voice came again, louder this time. 'Hey, you, can you pop over here for a minute?'

I glanced up to see the photographer waving at me. Along with his jaunty cap, he wore sneakers, skinny jeans and an Astro Boy T-shirt.

'Sorry, am I in the way?' I asked.

He shook his head. 'No, no. Can I just get you to stand in front of the camera?'

This was it. My time to shine. If Kat could see me now.

'Oh, I'm not a model,' I replied, aiming for demure but professional.

'Yeah, I figured that. I'm testing the lights before it's time to shoot the boys. My assistant's nipped off to make a call.'

'Oh right, sorry,' I stammered, thankful my little sister wasn't there, after all. 'Just ignore what I said before. Of course I'm not a model. You must think I'm insane.'

He grinned. 'Just a wee bit. Don't worry, a little insanity helps in this industry. Now just stand there, Queen of the Catwalk, I have to adjust this light …'

I stood, channelling my inner supermodel. Elbows jutted, lips pursed.

'There you are, Josie,' Liani said. 'Jeremy, I'm sorry to

break up the party, but there's an emergency and we need Josie's help.'

I'd wanted to write, I'd wanted to interview, I'd wanted to be a real journalist and my chance had arrived in a big pop-star-shaped box.

The entire features department had been called into an emergency editorial meeting with Rae and Liani over a last-minute request from one of *Sash*'s biggest advertisers, leaving Billy and Anthony from Greed without an interviewer. That was until Eloise, impressed by my writing earlier in the day, floated my name with Liani. They decided I'd be perfect to fire off a few questions and keep Greed's manager, Claire — the walking power suit in heels — happy.

The only downside? I had three minutes to prepare.

'It's no biggie,' Liani assured me as I scribbled down questions and notes. 'Just ask them about their album, what they look for in a girl, what makes them happy. Forget they're famous and pretend you're chatting with your boy best friend — any nice, normal guy!'

My lack of ability with 'any nice, normal guy' clearly hadn't come across to Liani. Stammering, stuttering and accusing guys of potential burglary and murder were just a few sociopathic behaviours that occurred when I was out of my comfort zone. Which was always.

Especially today.

'What about all the drama with Billy in the papers? The girls? The partying?' I asked.

Liani placed a small black dictaphone in my lap. 'Those questions are probably in the too-hard basket for today. Keep it light and you'll be great.' And she rushed out the door, back to her emergency meeting with Rae and editorial.

I scrawled two more questions and an uneven heart in the corner of the page, then went back to the studio to find Billy and Anthony.

I was up.

7.

'So, what inspired the title of your latest album, *All The Riches*?'

I wondered if my question was even in proper English. Due to nerves, there was a chance it had come out as 'So, what contrived the teapot of my greatest alimony, *Stall The Glitches*?'

Billy smirked. 'First you wanted to know about our favourite foods, and now this? I suppose you'll ask about our childhoods next?'

'Er, sorry … um, let me …'

His tone softened. 'I'm only kidding. The album title came from our desire to get filthy stinking rich, retire by thirty and never work a day again in our lives. But you can't print that, can you?'

I felt my jaw drop to an embarrassingly low level.

Anthony burst out laughing and batted Billy over the head. 'B, she's just doing her job. Stop being mean to the magazine girl.'

The magazine girl. The girl from the magazine. I liked that. But Anthony was wrong: I wasn't doing my job. If I was, I'd be asking the real questions, the tough questions, the things that people wanted to know. The girls. The drugs. The partying. I remembered my mock interview with James and how he'd pressed me for uncomfortable details, which had resulted in a far more interesting conversation.

I cleared my throat, fighting nerves. 'Let's change the pace a bit.'

'Okay.'

'Billy, you've been spotted out and about with not one but seven different girls in the past fortnight. Who are they and what's the story with each of them?'

Anthony's eyes widened.

Billy, a perpetual smirker, shrugged his shoulders. He was clearly proud of his conquests. 'What can I say? I have a lot of friends.'

Claire, swathed in a fresh coating of perfume, sat on a couch nearby, glued to her phone as usual. She sniffed and looked over to make sure I wasn't asking anything inappropriate (I'd been warned against anything to do with rehab), then returned to her electronic plaything. I revved up for my next question.

'What do you say to the rumours that one of your, er, friends is now three months pregnant and you're the father? Especially when you've been spotted with other, um, friends since?'

Billy's face darkened. 'Ahhh ...'

'Is the baby definitely yours?' I pushed. 'What kind of involvement would you like to have with his or her life?'

Anthony's eyes narrowed. Billy had frozen and didn't reply. Claire was no help to him; she'd strutted off to bark orders at Carla about what brands of jeans the guys would and wouldn't wear.

Anthony broke the silence. 'Look, Josie, aren't you meant to ask one question at a time? Maybe we should move on to something else. Like, did you hear about Jamie falling off the stage in Paris two weeks ago?' He forced a laugh.

Anthony was right. I shouldn't have shot off the questions so fast, but that wasn't going to stop me from finding out the truth. No way. Not when I'd scratched the surface and realised there was so much further to go.

'Okay, let me rephrase that,' I said.

'Great,' muttered Billy, cracking his knuckles.

'What are your thoughts on the rumours that you're about to become a father?'

It was as though we'd all taken a collective breath. Not a word was uttered. Not a sound, not a sigh, until ...

'They're true,' said Billy.

'But don't you think that — wait, what?'

My head jolted up and I locked eyes with Billy.

Anthony murmured, 'Shut your mouth, bro,' and turned around to look for Claire.

'That's what you wanted to hear, wasn't it?' asked Billy. 'The truth? Well, you've got it. I'm going to be a dad.'

'And there goes our fan base,' burst out Anthony. 'Billy, this interview is over.'

'But please,' I said, aware things were unravelling fast. Liani was going to flip out if I lost this interview. I didn't even want to know what Rae was capable of. Torture with paper cuts? One thousand hours of photocopying? The woman wore heels that were higher than *me*, surely they could do some serious damage?

'No,' spat Anthony. 'We're out of here.'

Billy sat in silence with his head lowered while Anthony stormed over to Claire. Desperate to save the situation, I tried to reason with Billy.

'I'm so sorry. Can we please start again? The last thing I want is for you to leave. Please, say something. Anything.'

Again, our eyes locked. A shiver shot through me and I wondered if he felt it, too. But without a smirk, a smile or even a goodbye, Billy stood up and joined the others, leaving me alone to wallow in my first failed interview.

Claire glared over her shoulder at me, her butt as plump as a Christmas ham. 'Your boss is gonna hear from me. You better believe it, girly.'

The band exited the studio, leaving a stunned crew wondering why the celebrity shoot had ended before they'd snapped a single frame. Carla sat on the floor, legs crossed, her head in her hands. The others whispered together, exchanging dark looks.

Jeremy, the photographer, separated from the pack and plonked down next to me. 'So are they coming back or what?'

'Doesn't look like it,' I murmured.

He looked over at the crew and shook his head. People started moving again. Carla packed suits into dark, black bags, while Jeremy's assistant pulled down props and switched off the huge hanging lights on the other side of the studio.

'What are you going to do now?' Jeremy asked me.

I didn't know. Changing my identity and flying to the Caribbean sounded like a plan.

'I, ah, guess I'd better see Rae and come clean,' I finally murmured.

He sighed. 'I don't envy you. The last person who "came clean" to Rae now works as the night-shift manager at Happy Burgertown.'

I cringed. 'That's pretty bad.'

'Wait, did I say manager? I meant cleaner. How are you with a mop?'

I looked at Jeremy. 'On a scale of one to ten, how dead am I? Honestly?'

'I just hope you've packed a bulletproof vest, kid.'

Pretty dead then, I decided. Pretty freaking dead.

I waited outside Rae's empty office, trying to ignore the churning, whipping anxiety in my stomach. I willed it to go away, but it only whipped harder.

With a ladylike clearing of her throat, Rae strode past me into her office. As always, Liani hovered a few paces behind her. She paused in front of me. 'Ready, Josie?'

I managed to squeak 'Yes' and followed Liani inside, my stomach thrashing with every step.

This situation had the potential to become a Code Vomit. And from my previous experiences with Code Vomits (there had been plenty), I knew they weren't to be messed with. Not throwing up on Rae's four-thousand-dollar office couch became my most pressing goal.

Rae clicked her nails on the desk and stared at me with big, smoky eyes. 'Well, you've had quite the morning,' she said. 'Let's start with what you think happened.'

I swallowed. 'Okay,' I said. 'Well, I asked them basic questions about the band, which seemed to bore Billy, so I decided to bump up the pace, you know? I heard about the baby rumours a few days ago — my sister loves Greed. She's got all their albums, including that awful Christmas one with the kitten wearing a hat on the cover. I was reading one of her —'

'The *point*, Josie.'

'I asked Billy about all the girls he's been dating.'

'And?'

'And the pregnancy rumours.'

Rae's eyes flickered for a moment. 'Then what happened?'

'The other guy — Anthony — cracked it and ended the interview when Billy admitted it was true, he was having a kid. Rae, Liani, I'm so sorry. I mean, *so* sorry. I don't know what to say or do.'

Of course I didn't. I'd never been responsible for a bunch of pop stars fleeing from the set of a photo shoot before.

'Josie, it's no secret this will stuff up the magazine's budget, which, according to the suits in finance, is meant to be locked down,' Rae said.

'I know, I was an idiot —'

'Not only that. Greed's manager has flames coming out of her ears, the crew lost a great shoot opportunity and Carla's wasted a week calling in designer clothes.'

'Are you going to fire me?' I wished Rae's office floor would morph into a black hole.

Rae sat up straighter. 'Well, to be honest, Josie ... I couldn't be happier.'

I wasn't sure if I'd heard her right. 'Happier?'

'Every one of our competitors wanted that story — and you got the exclusive.'

'I did? An *exclusive*?'

'You did.'

I turned to Liani, who beamed at me. I felt as though I was floating, blissed out on a cloud of happy. Even Rae was smiling — a small one, but a smile nonetheless.

'That was great work, Josie,' Liani said. 'Our own editorial team have been trying for weeks to get a juicy quote from Billy — or any of the boys — without success. That's why I didn't encourage you to push him. I thought they'd just serve up another puff piece. How wrong I was.'

Rae leaned forward. 'Josie, I'm giving you the chance to break this story. Three hundred words. Keep it short, sharp, snappy. Nail it and you'll get a by-line.'

A by-line. My first by-line. Stunned didn't even begin to describe what I felt at that moment. 'Oh thank you, Rae. I don't know what to say.'

'Say, "Yes, Rae", then get to work. I need it in thirty minutes, max. This story needs to go live on our website before Greed's publicist has time to issue a press release.'

'Okay,' I replied. 'I'm onto it.'

'Take a long lunch once it's done. And Josie?'

'Yes?'

'Try not to scare away anyone else today.'

'Yes, Rae.'

I left her office accompanied by an imaginary troupe of munchkins, rainbows and singing animals. Cloud Nine had never felt so good.

* * *

Later that afternoon, once my feature story was handed in and published online, I was free to leave. As I waited by the elevators, a whiff of rose perfume wafted past my nostrils. I turned to see Ava behind me, looking poised and striking as always. Her usual flowing curls were pulled into a fierce bun on top of her head. Her lips twitched in what may have been a smile but came across as a grimace.

'Josephine, on your way home?'

'Yep.' I smiled back. A real smile.

'Busy day?'

'I suppose you could say that.'

I swallowed nervously. Ava clearly knew about my interview with Greed. The entire office had whispered about it all afternoon. The silence was becoming painful so I clogged it with nonsense, as usual.

'So how was helping out the beauty editor? What's she like? I bet it was really great seeing all that amazing beauty gear. Beauty booty. Booty. It's a funny word, isn't it? So how did you sort it all out? Boxes? Piles? Piles in boxes? Or did the boxes go into piles then into other boxes?'

'Jerms mentioned he was really, *really* disappointed that he didn't get to do the celebrity photo shoot today,' Ava said, her head tilted to one side. 'Such a shame.'

I took a sharp breath at the sudden change of subject. 'You spoke to Jerms ... er, Jeremy?'

'Yeah, for ages. Sia — that's the beauty editor — and I got everything sorted quickly, so there was all this extra time to kill. That's when Jerms asked me to be in a photo shoot. He'd called in three male models, too, and it was *fabulous*.'

'Oh?'

'Well, Carla had worked so hard, and we couldn't let those suits go to waste after … well, you know. What am I saying — of course you know. You must feel awful,' she rattled on. 'I'd be so embarrassed, I probably couldn't show my face here again. Oh, but don't listen to silly old me. They understand you're just a child, and everyone knows children make mistakes.'

I bristled at her use of the C-word. As though I were a toddler with pigtails who'd smeared apple puree over the office walls. 'Actually, Rae said it all worked out —'

'Sorry, got to run,' Ava announced, clearly not sorry at all. 'I'm getting my make-up touched up again. Jerms is going to squeeze in an extra shot of me for my modelling portfolio.'

She spun on her heel and walked away. Her perfume lingered, stinking out the foyer and confusing my thoughts. Ava had said Jeremy was 'really, *really* disappointed'. I didn't want to be on Jeremy's bad side. He'd probably use my lighting test shots as a dartboard. Or toilet paper. And as for Ava just wanting to say hello? Yeah, right. *Sash* magazine's office had become a gladiator arena, and only the best intern would win.

Despite my nerves and apprehension, maybe this

was my time. My time to feel like a budding journo, to have a fantastic internship, to get one step closer to winning five thousand dollars and a regular by-line. The promise of such glory was made even sweeter by the thought of snatching the prizes away from a nasty person like Ava.

I stared at the metallic grey of the lift door, willing it to open. Moments later, the lift arrived, whirring and grinding. I'd just slammed my finger onto the ground-floor button when someone cried out behind me, 'Hold the lift.'

It was Carla, wheeling the rack of men's suits. I held my arm out to keep the door open as she squeezed in.

Once she was safe inside, she breathed out loudly and yanked her hair into a messy ponytail. 'Thanks, Jordie.'

I nodded, too embarrassed to say anything after what had happened earlier.

'Or is it Jodie?'

'Josie, actually.'

'Sorry about that. When it comes to names I've got a memory like a goldfish. I called Rae "Fay" last week.'

A snicker bubbled up inside me and erupted before I could stop it escaping. Carla laughed, too.

'Carla, I'm so sorry about all this,' I said, gesturing to the suits. 'Far out, I feel like I've spent the whole day apologising. "I'm sorry I'm a terrible interviewer, Billy", "I'm sorry for ruining your shoot, Jeremy", "I'm sorry for wasting *Sash*'s money, Rae". And I am sorry, I really am. Maybe I'm not cut out for this whole magazine scene.'

Carla shrugged. 'What's to be sorry about? Rae is going off in there. Apparently your story's already had more than eight thousand hits and it's only been up for twenty minutes. Suits or no suits, Greed will sell our magazine. And as they say, when Mama's happy, everyone's happy.'

Ding! We'd reached the ground floor. Carla waved goodbye and legged it toward the courier dock with her rack of suits.

As I stepped out onto the street, my phone beeped. It was Angel with 'devastating news': we hadn't scored invites to Holly Bentley's party, which meant no Pete Jordan make-out session for me. It looked like my pash drought would probably continue forever, but I wasn't worried. I'd impressed one of the biggest magazine editors in the country today and nothing was going to bring me down.

8.

A phone was ringing, but I couldn't be sure if it was in real life or in my dreams. Too sleepy to care, I rolled over on Tim's couch and buried my face in the pillow. It'll stop eventually, I told myself. But it didn't. It just kept ringing. And it was my ringtone.

Eyes clamped shut, I stumbled up from the couch in search of the culprit. I lunged in the direction of the noise, which seemed to come from the carpet in the hallway. Stubbing my toe on a box, I swore loudly and picked up my phone. It was an unknown number, but I answered it anyway.

'Hello?' I croaked. A quick glance at the clock on the wall showed it was just after 6.30 am.

'Hi, Josie?' a woman's voice chimed.

'Yeah?'

'I'm so sorry to bother you. It's Liani. From *Sash*. Did I wake you?'

'No, not at all.' Yes, yes, you did, I sleepily slurred in my mind. I knew roosters that didn't wake this early.

I sat back down on the couch, straightening my hair and wiping under my eyes, as though Liani could see me. Luckily, she couldn't. I was in a T-shirt with rainbows on the front.

'Josie, I have some good and bad news.'

'Oh?' Forget coffee. A phrase like that was an effective way to wake me up.

'The good news is your exclusive on Billy has gone off even more overnight. Rae's phone is ringing off the hook. Everyone wants to know more — more from Billy, more detail about his reaction. Rae wants a second story, written up as a feature this time.'

'I'm speechless. You're saying Rae wants me to do it? Me specifically?'

'Yes, you were the only person there, and Rae wants to keep it authentic. The bad news is,' continued Liani, 'Rae wants it done today.'

'Today?' I glanced at the clock again, stifling a yawn. 'Okay, I guess I can pop in midmorning before I head home.'

'Ahhh, just a small problem, tiny really … Rae's version of today means now.' I could almost hear Liani wringing her hands down the phone line. 'Now as in right now, not a second later. She wants to get the feature up before Billy caves and gives another magazine more detailed goss. I'm probably pushing my luck, but is there any way you can come into the office now?'

I hesitated. I had planned to meet up with Angel to mourn our lack of party invitations, not to mention a uni lecture that afternoon and the fact I wanted to catch up with Mum and Kat. But this was important. The way Liani spoke, it sounded like my future career depended on it. If I didn't write this feature, I may as well give up on becoming a journalist and take up garbage collection instead. Or apply to clean toilets at Happy Burgertown.

'Of course,' I said. 'I'll be in as soon as possible.'

'You're a star. See you soon.' Liani hung up.

I slouched on the couch, my mind racing over my unexpected to-do list. I had to bail on my lecture, find my way to the *Sash* office at this yawn-worthy time of morning and, most importantly, tell Mum I was going to be late home so she didn't think I'd run away forever. But she wasn't the only person I needed to sweet-talk: Angel would be annoyed that I'd ditched our plans.

'Everything okay?'

Alarmed, I looked up to see James standing in the doorway in boxers and a singlet. I jolted upright and crossed my arms over my chest in a poor attempt to hide my T-shirt.

'How long have you been standing there?' I asked.

'Long enough to see your top has rainbows on it. What's that about?'

I blushed and ignored the question. '*Sash* just rang. They want me to go in again today. Right now. Do trains even run this early?'

'Yeah, but I can take you in on my scooter, if you like? My work's in that direction and I need to get on top of some stuff before I open the shop.'

'Oh no, that's okay.'

'It's fine. Just don't tell your mum about the scooter, she'd probably kill me.'

'Thanks,' I said. I didn't think Mum would care too much about the scooter; she'd just be excited to hear I was in the same breathing space as a cute guy like James.

'Sweet,' he said. 'Just chuck on some clothes and we'll —'

'Oh no! Clothes! What am I meant to wear? I didn't bring anything else nice with me.'

James paused, then grinned. 'I've got an idea.'

I stared at my reflection, gobsmacked. Somehow James had transformed me to look ... *cool*. My hair was slicked back into a high ponytail, showing off my neck and collarbones. I'd slipped James's old leather jacket over another of my embarrassing T-shirts (this one had a teapot across the front) and it was slim-fitting and hugged my body in all the right places. Not to mention wearing it made me feel safe; somehow protected. On my bottom half, I sported a pair of Tim's skinny jeans, which I'd found drying on the balcony. A quick sniff test

(James had braved it, not me) had confirmed they were clean. To finish off the outfit, I slipped into Kat's heels. The rock-chick Barbie look worked, at least enough to get me through another day at the office.

I couldn't believe I was going into *Sash* again. I gave Mum a quick call to let her know, sent an email to my lecturer to ask for that afternoon's notes and fired off a text to Angel to cancel and apologise (and promising to make it up to her).

After one last glance in the mirror, I knocked on James's door. He opened it and his jaw dropped at the sight of me. I blushed, unsure what to say.

Luckily, he filled the silence before I ruined the moment. 'You look great.'

'Thanks, stylist.'

'Those magazine girls won't know what's hit them.' He picked up two helmets off his bedroom floor and passed me one. 'Ready?'

Minutes later, I was perched behind James on his scooter, my arms wrapped around his waist, my hair whipping from beneath the helmet. The roar of the wind was deafening, so I swapped small talk for daydreaming and watching the scenery. We passed high-rise buildings, each taller than the next, power-walking elderly couples wearing matching sweatbands, too many homeless people walking barefoot to count, and police officers sipping coffee as they patrolled the streets. I caught a glimpse of myself and James as we shot past a building with glass walls: our bodies were pressed together — a perfect fit. We were straight out of a romantic Italian movie, two love interests enjoying a spin through the cobblestoned streets before tucking into a giant bowl of fettuccine. I was finally living a storyline that didn't end with 'pooed her pants in public', 'hasn't been kissed for years' or 'was dumped on Valentine's Day'. My heart raced, as though I'd overdosed on candy canes, fairy floss and soft drink.

James pulled up around the corner from the *Sash* office to let me off. I dismounted and handed him the helmet. 'Guess I better give this back, right? Doesn't really match my outfit.'

'I think it does,' he said, stowing my helmet in the top box of his scooter. 'The jacket, the jeans, the helmet. Pretty bad-ass.'

'That was cool of you, swooping in all knight-in-shining-armour like that.'

'I guess that makes this my noble steed,' he said, patting his scooter. 'You know, that leather jacket looks far better on you than it ever did on me.'

'Oh, um, thanks.'

'Yeah. So, I better head,' he said. 'I've got paperwork to do, stock to unpack and shelves to pretend to clean. See you later.'

A quick wave goodbye and he was gone, but his words continued to pound in my head like early-morning council workers drilling holes into cement. I knew he was just being polite and friendly, but a small part of me — a niggly, pushy part that believed in Prince Charming and happy endings — ached for his compliments to mean something; that he was laying the groundwork for something else. Something *more*.

My enchanted morning came to an abrupt end when a beady-eyed security guard at the building's entry demanded to see my security pass. I showed it to him and babbled that I was an intern there to see Liani from *Sash* magazine.

'This early, huh?' he said, raising an eyebrow. 'Wait there while I give her a call.'

He punched Liani's extension into the phone, yawning as he waited for her to answer. 'Morning. I've got a real eager beaver here to see you … Yeah, that's her. You sure? Rightio then … Bye now.'

I swallowed. 'All good?'

'Off you go,' he grunted, buzzing me through.

I hobbled to the lift, my feet already blistering in day two of Kat's heels.

My fingers danced over the computer keyboard as I watched words, sentences and paragraphs arrange themselves on the screen. Rae wanted a tell-all feature story on Billy, packed with details about how the truth unfolded — and she was going to get one. I wrangled words like a master, positioned them in line like a pro. I was doing it, I was writing for a national publication, and I never wanted to stop.

But then I had to. Because a voice said in a tone that could only be described as fuming, 'You're in my seat.'

I spun around so fast I almost jarred my neck. Esmeralda, the features director, was standing behind me, hands on hips. I recognised her from the magazine's 'Meet the Team' page: short, edgy platinum-blonde hair that framed her face, statement hot-pink lipstick, and steely blue eyes that made me shrink back into the chair. This woman was fierce, there was no denying it.

'Um, I'm just writing a story —' I started, but Esmeralda had marched off, calling 'Liani' before I could finish the sentence.

Eloise and the other features girls shot me sympathetic looks but turned back to their computers when they saw Esmeralda storming over, this time with Liani in tow. I was on my own, defenceless as a mouse being lowered into a python's cage, waiting for Esmeralda to swallow me whole. That, or get me booted from the office. But then a wonderful thing happened.

'Es, please apologise to Josie, our extremely talented intern,' said Liani, mistress of diplomacy and queen of ego-boosting.

Esmeralda sighed. 'Oh, she knows I'm sorry. I didn't know you'd said she could sit there before I got in.'

I didn't know Esmeralda was sorry. In fact, I was pretty sure she'd belt me with the dictionary the moment Liani returned to her office, but I accepted her attempt at an apology and stood up, gesturing to the empty seat.

Esmeralda sat down in a huff. 'Oh, everything's in the wrong place now. Where did you move my pen?'

I pointed to her pen, which was in exactly the same place she'd left it, in the pen holder.

'Okay, well, what about my notebook? The one with the red cover?'

'You mean the one next to the computer?'

'And who left these pink lipstick marks on my coffee cup?'

'What?' I said. 'I think they're yours —'

'Esmeralda, *you're* wearing pink lippie, remember?' Liani cut in. 'Come with me, Josie. You can work in my office. It's still early so I'll edit on the communal table.'

Clutching my USB stick, which held my half-written story on Greed, I followed Liani to her office, leaving the clearly off-her-rocker Esmeralda to get into a paranoid panic over the beauty products and stationery littering her desk.

Liani set up her computer for me. 'Okay, you've got about forty-five minutes before Rae gets in for a staff meeting. Better get to work.'

* * *

With one minute to spare, I handed Liani a printout of the feature.

'Perfect timing,' she said. 'Can't wait to read it.'

She wasn't wrong: Rae had just walked into *Sash* HQ, coffee in one hand, an oversized designer handbag in the other.

'So, how long have you worked here?' I asked Liani, unable to keep quiet while she skimmed her eyes over my piece.'

'Feels like a lifetime and then some,' she said with a laugh. 'Coming up to five years, including a year of maternity leave for Dylan.'

'Wow.' The other girls I asked had all been there for less than two years.

'Rae and I are a rare breed these days,' Liani went on. 'Most girls race in with plans bigger than their credit card bills, and race out just as fast after their next career dream. Up, up, up, they go.'

'You're high up,' I said shyly.

Liani smiled. 'I'm doing okay.'

I remembered something Ava had said on our first day in the *Sash* office.

'Liani?'

'Yes, Josie?'

'Ava mentioned that it was, um, different for you and Rae to be dealing with us directly. Is that true?'

Liani nodded. 'Usually our ed coordinator would be managing you, but a special prize calls for special circumstances. If we're giving away five thousand dollars we need to make sure it goes to the right girl.'

Rae poked her head into Liani's office. 'Meeting?' she said, although it sounded more like a command than a question. We nodded and she disappeared again.

'Better wrap this up,' said Liani. 'Come on, let's find a spot out there. By the way, love your outfit.'

Within seconds, girls from each department had flocked into the central area, all sporting notebooks, pens and semi-terrified expressions. I buried myself at the back of the crowd, excited to see my first group meeting unfold.

Liani passed my story to Rae, who skimmed it and said, 'Change that to "smouldered" and that to "desperation" and get it online, now.'

Liani rushed into her office to make the changes. A few seconds later she was on the phone, pleading with the online producer for it to go live immediately. She must have been successful because we all heard her cry, 'Thank you, I owe you a banana cake,' before she joined the rest of us for the meeting. I caught her eye and she gave me a thumbs-up.

The next thirty minutes were a blur. Rae talked, staff members butted in, Gen told the story of how she pelted a pizza slice at her girlfriend's head due to chronic PMS,

Rae vented, and Esmeralda argued with at least three people, one of them being Rae.

After Rae closed the meeting and everyone snaked back to their desks, Liani called me over. 'Josie, I'm sorry for dragging you in again, but if it's any consolation your story is going well. Really well. We've had advertisers demanding to be positioned near it for the next twelve hours.'

'Wow, that's good, right?'

'It's incredible, and we sure needed it ...' She paused. 'The public's enthralled with Billy, they want to know everything, but I can't understand why. Okay, he's attractive, but he's a cheater, a liar ... Sometimes the world boggles me, Josie.'

I had a thought. 'I know he's a cheater, which is awful, the *worst* — but he's having a baby ... I hope I haven't, you know, ruined his life or anything.'

'Not at all,' she said. 'You were just doing your job.'

'I guess so.'

Just doing your job, I repeated to myself. You were just doing your job. But it didn't feel right. I imagined a mean bank manager telling herself the same thing after denying a struggling family a loan. Or a hired assassin sinking a beer after a hit and telling himself, 'I can sleep at night because I was just doing my job.' On the scale of things, writing a tell-all tabloid piece wasn't the worst, but I couldn't shake the feeling I'd screwed Billy over.

9.

My unease must've been evident because Liani chose that moment to introduce me to Sia, *Sash*'s beauty editor, a curvy brunette with smiling red lips and a rockabilly vibe. 'Now, Liani told me you can't stay all day,' said Sia, 'but before you leave we have a special surprise for you.'

I nodded, intrigued. Home would have to wait. Moments later I discovered the 'special surprise' was to sort through the day's beauty couriers. Translation: help Sia go through all the cool free stuff she'd been sent since the day before. And there was a lot of it. Sia's area was reminiscent of a department store cosmetics floor during sales time. Bright, colourful bottles lined the shelves above her computer, while her desk was cluttered with plastic containers, glass jars and woven baskets holding lipsticks, bronzers, lip balms, eye shadows and foundations. There were even false eyelashes and hair extensions strewn over her keyboard.

Sia didn't seem concerned about the mess. 'Coconut lip gloss?' she offered, passing over an unopened tube. 'Take it. I was sent three.'

'Three?'

'And about four others last week.'

'Wow,' I said, opening it. A gorgeous coconut smell wafted into my nostrils. 'Is your day always like this? Playing with make-up?'

'Sure is,' Sia said. 'When I'm not organising photo shoots, going to launches, interviewing beauticians, arguing with advertising and being dragged into ten meetings a day with Rae, Liani and Esmeralda.'

'Oh, right … sorry.'

Note to self: remove foot from oversized mouth before talking.

'No worries,' she said, then lowered her voice. 'Between you and me, there is a lot of playing with make-up. Hey, has anyone told you about the beauty sale yet? It's coming up soon and, sweetie, it's going to rock your world.'

'Beauty sale?' I had no idea what she was talking about. 'Do you mean at the shops? Or online?'

'Neither, it's here! We sell all our leftover beauty goodies — you know, the stuff the PRs have inundated us with — to ourselves. At *amazing* prices, I may add. I haven't had to buy shampoo from a salon or supermarket in years. Most of the money raised goes to charity, so it's pretty cool.'

'Are you serious?' Only in magazines, I thought. A beauty sale in an office? Now I'd heard everything.

'Oh yeah,' she said. 'We do keep a small amount of cashola to throw a party or two for the office, though. Who knows, if you're lucky, Liani might let you come along to the sale.'

We'd only just met, but Sia seemed different to the rest of the staff. The others flitted around the office like nervous butterflies, ready to fly away at any sudden noise — such as Rae throwing a tantrum about a late story or an overpriced cover image. But not Sia. She was loud and proud.

'And don't get me started on the eating!' She laughed. 'Oh, the eating.'

'What do you mean?'

So far I'd only seen people nibbling on salads and slurping green smoothies that looked too much like slime for my liking.

'The beauty PR girls are always sending me food with their products,' she explained. 'Every day, the bags arrive — lollipops, yoghurts, chocolates, biscuits. Their current favourite is cupcakes. Adorable cupcakes with five centimetres of icing that blow my mind, and my waistline, every time. And I wonder why I've stacked on six kilos since starting here. Oh well! A girl's gotta eat, right?' She held up a pretty blue perfume bottle and spritzed the air with it. I smelled the fresh scents swimming around me and relaxed for a moment.

When I finally left the office that afternoon, I was laden with two bags brimming over with beauty products from Sia — it had been a 'special surprise' indeed. I couldn't wait to see Mum's, Kat's and Angel's reactions when I shared the swag.

I climbed the steps to Tim's flat, put down my bags and fumbled for the key. When I finally found it and jiggled it into the hole, the door wouldn't open. It was jammed.

I needed to pack my suitcase and get to the station in time for the next train home. I'd already stayed longer in the city than I'd promised Mum. I jiggled the key again. Nothing.

I banged on the door. 'Hello! Can someone please open the door? Tim? James? Anyone?'

Moments later, the door swung open, revealing a grinning James wearing a 'Kiss the Cook' apron. 'I'm here, I'm here. Come in.'

I don't know whether it was his cheeky expression or the ridiculous apron, but I suddenly forgot I was in a rush. My stomach did a backflip. Or maybe it was a somersault. Who was I kidding? My poor guts were performing bruise-inducing bellyflops on repeat at the sight of him. Luckily James seemed oblivious to my nerves. He rattled on about another dull day at work while I beamed like an idiot, silently wondering whether he liked kayaking, tenpin bowling and eating Caramello Koalas from the bottom up or top down.

'So, how was your day anyway?' he asked, turning on the oven. 'Hey, you've still got my jacket on. Looks cool.'

'Thanks, I really owe you one,' I blushed. 'I couldn't have pulled off this morning without you and —'

I stopped talking as someone else walked into the room. A girl. A very attractive girl with long, wavy blonde hair and tanned skin. Not a cringe-worthy fake tan either — this girl was a sun-kissed surfer babe. She looked like she could catch a wave, teach an ashtanga yoga class and whip up a fresh orange juice all before breakfast.

'James, babe, is everything alright?' she asked, before turning to me.

'Yeah, just making us an early dinner. Spinach lasagne sound good?'

'Sure. I'll get a snack for our guest then, shall I?' She joined him in the kitchen, her hair swishing as she walked.

'Okay,' shrugged James, chopping onion as she rifled through the fridge.

'No, that's fine,' I insisted. 'I don't want to interrupt your plans and I'm just about to leave anyway, so ...' My voice trailed off as she assembled cheese and biscuits on a platter. 'I'm Josie, by the way.'

'Of course. I'm Summer, James's girlfriend. You're Tim's cousin from the country, right?'

I nodded.

'James has told me all about you and your fancy internship. Nice work.'

Funny, I thought, he hasn't mentioned you once.

Girlfriend. James had a girlfriend. And she was stunning.

'You'll have to forgive me for being a little flaky,' Summer went on. 'I'm still in holiday mode after being away with my friends, so I just swung past to see what my boy was up to. Loaning you clothes by the looks of it?'

I forced a laugh, ate a few cubes of cheese to be polite then excused myself to pack, leaving James's old leather jacket hanging on his bedroom doorknob.

'Trish Martin got one and so did Hannah Jones. I totally reckon Stephanie Simpson did, too, but she's keeping it a secret to surprise Akmal for his birthday,' said Kat.

I was lying on my bed listening to my sister rattle off the list of girls in her year who'd had Brazilian waxes. Okay, I wasn't actually listening — I was moping. I nodded along to her chatter while my mind drifted off again. I still couldn't believe James had a girlfriend. And not just any girlfriend: a stunning, blonde girlfriend who served cheese and biscuits, ate spinach lasagne and probably wore his faded leather jacket all the time.

Kat sighed. 'Did you hear what I said?'

'Yeah, um …'

'About the Brazilians?'

I paused, forcing myself to concentrate. 'I guess ... I ... What were those girls thinking? It sounds kind of desperate to me.'

'They like it.'

'They like their *you know what* looking like a red, plucked chicken?'

'Gross, it doesn't look like that.'

'And you know this how?'

Kat raised an eyebrow.

'Oh my god.'

'Nick dared me,' she said.

'Right. That's okay then ... Wait, who?'

'My boyfriend.'

'What happened to Tye?' I asked.

Kat shrugged. 'I heard he was about to break up with me so I got in first. Couldn't let him ruin my run of no-dumps.'

'Does Mum know?'

'As if.'

I shook my head. 'Brazilians are so wrong. Like, wearing-leggings-as-pants wrong.'

'You're just scared,' Kat said.

'I'm not.'

'Go on, then, do it.'

And there it was: the challenge. Kat had coerced me into doing a bunch of stupid things over the years, most ending with me regretting the day my little sister was conceived. There was the time she dared me to jump off the five-metre diving board at the local pool. I did and she cheered. But when I hopped out of the water, I saw the lifeguard holding up my bikini top, which had untied itself on impact with the water. There was the minor shoplifting attempt at age fifteen (I got busted for stealing a pencil sharpener, burst into tears and handed over the money) and the time I let her straighten my hair. With an iron. On an ironing board.

'Hey, your phone's ringing,' Kat said, pointing to my handbag, which was vibrating.

I lunged for it, but it had already rung out. Seconds later a message beeped through from Angel: *Forget that tosspot Holly's birthday. Better invite. Party tonight, wear something hot. Pete Jordan will be there. You in?*

A picture of James with Summer flashed across my mind.

'Kat, where did those girls get their Brazilians done?'

She grinned.

Angel gave my hair one last yank, pulling the thick, long strands into a fancy updo, then spun me around to take a look in the bathroom mirror. 'Oh Josie, you minx.'

I stared at my reflection. The severe hairstyle resembled something usually seen on a ballerina or catwalk model. It made my eyes look bigger and showed off my eyebrows, which Sia had neatened for me the other day. It also made my forehead look massive.

'Are you sure I look okay?' I said.

Angel rolled her eyes and tousled her own hair. 'Shut up, you look hot. Oi, Kat, get in here for a sec.'

Kat's face popped up behind us. Angel turned to her. 'Well? Approval rating? It's a ten, right?'

Kat rifled through our new beauty stash from Sia, withdrew a bold berry lipstick and waved it around. 'Wear this, and you'll be an eleven.'

'Urgh, really?' I cringed at the strong colour.

'Really,' said Kat. 'You should hear yourself. Really? Really, am I pretty? Really? Yes. Just do it.'

Kat, All-powerful Sister and Controller of the Universe, had spoken. I rolled on the lipstick — both Kat and Angel swooped in with a tissue to blot — and I was ready.

'You're a twelve,' said Angel.

'Hey Angel, did Josie tell you what she did today?' asked Kat, barely containing her laughter.

'No, she didn't ... well, go on,' pushed Angel.

'A Brazilian,' Kat announced with glee. 'Josie got a Brazilian!'

Angel's jaw dropped. 'And you forgot to tell me that?'

'Well, yeah,' I said. 'It's embarrassing and I ran out of time ... Anyway, let's forget it.'

'I can't believe it, this is huge,' Angel's voice was getting louder by the second.

'Shhhhh! Mum'll hear you and seriously, it was no big deal.'

And it wasn't. Because the truth was, I hadn't gone through with the wax. Well, not properly. The beautician, Olga, had told me to take off my knickers and, after fifteen minutes of umming and ahhing, I let her wax off one strip of hair. But it turned out one strip was enough for me. I yelped in pain, wriggled into my undies and fled the building. The worst bit? I was left with a bald patch in a very awkward place. Not that Kat and Angel needed to know that.

'Who *are* you, Josie Browning?' said Angel. 'This is so cool. I mean, do you feel any different?'

'C'mon, let's go,' I said, ignoring the question. 'And Kat, don't you dare breathe a word of this to Mum.'

Angel and I walked into the lounge room where it was clear the party vibe didn't extend to Mum, who was reading a book on the couch. I tried to ignore the stab of guilt I felt for leaving her again, but it didn't work. She was socialising less and less these days — I couldn't even remember the last time she went to a movie with a friend or invited guests over for dinner.

'Mum, are you going to be okay?' I asked.

'Yes, love.' She smiled and nodded toward the coffee table next to her, loaded with a cup of tea, a few biscuits and her phone. 'Kat's here. We'll be fine. Josephine Browning, I order you to go to this party and have a good time,' she added, half-joking, half-serious. 'If you don't, you're … you're grounded.'

'Can't argue with that,' said Angel, dragging me out the door. 'Bye, Mrs B!'

I tried to feel poised as we walked to the party, which was only around the corner. Out the front stood packs of girls in heels and teeny-tiny skirts. A sprinkling of guys dotted the lawn, clutching six-packs of beer or bottles of vodka. Loud, thumping music lured us up the garden path and through the front door. Inside, it was even louder. The hallway was jammed with sweaty, laughing people. We squeezed through, ignoring pinches on our butts, finally spewing out of the pack into an empty kitchen.

'Wine, my lady?' asked Angel, pulling a bottle from her massive handbag.

'Who are you? Mary Poppins? I'm not sure if I'm up for it tonight.'

'Don't you worry your pretty head. Just grab us some cups, would you?' she said, waving her ring-covered fingers toward the kitchen bench.

'Okay, but just a glass.' I grabbed two plastic cups and Angel filled them, spilling wine onto the benchtop and the floor.

'Oops.' She laughed.

'Josie Browning, is that you?' I spun around to see a short girl, Phillipa, from my old high-school English class. 'Wow, I almost didn't recognise you with your hair pulled up,' she said.

I gave a little wave. 'It's me.'

'How are you? Heard you're in the city a lot these days.'

'Yeah, well, on and off. I'm doing an internship at a magazine there.'

'A magazine, hey? Sounds flashy. A few months outta school and you've already outgrown this dump. Who needs a town like this when the big smoke awaits, huh?'

'No, it's not like that.'

'Whatever. The other girls from school have been "too cool" for this place for ages. It's inevitable that you caught up and found something better. Good for you.'

Phillipa disappeared into the crowd.

Stunned, I turned to Angel. 'Did you hear what —'

'Forget it,' Angel said. 'She's just jealous 'cos she'll be slicing salami at the deli for the next thirty years. Now, let's check your lipstick. Hot. Okay, wait here while I find Pete.'

Angel's transformation into a matchmaking Cupid was firing along and I could barely keep up.

'Wait, Ange.'

'Yeah?' she said, scanning the room for Pete's trademark shaved head.

'I can't do this.'

'You have to.'

'Why? Why do you care if I hook up with some random guy from school?'

Angel looked at me closely, so closely I could see the clumpy mascara on her lashes. 'I love you, Jose. You know that, right?'

'Yeah.'

'Then that's why. Can we leave it at that?'

'So if I lip-plant Pete it'll prove how strong our friendship is? I don't get it.'

She rolled her eyes. 'What do you want me to say?'

'Just tell the truth, woman.'

'Fine. I'm losing you.' Her words sliced the air.

'What?'

'Like I lost you last year. You know.'

'But I never went anywhere last year.'

'Exactly,' said Angel. 'You studied all the time, stopped calling me and bailed on coming around.'

'What about that night I came over for spaghetti and ice-cream?'

'You left halfway through because you wanted to finish your study notes. Look, Jose, it's great — I mean, look at you! You're doing exactly what you want, your life is going according to plan. Phillipa's right.'

I shook my head. 'No, no, she's wrong. Nothing's going to plan.'

'I know you don't think you're too good for this town, but you are … You're meeting all these people in the city with your internship, and who am I? Just some idiot wasting time on an arts degree at the local uni.'

'Dude, you're not wasting time — and I go to that uni too! Seriously, you're awesome. The best person I know.'

'Yeah, yeah, I'm awesome.' She rolled her eyes. 'So awesome I've spent the past five tutes sitting by myself. We had to pair up and I was the only one left out — the tutor made me third wheel to two French exchange students who played footsies under the table for the whole hour. It was like high school all over again.'

I pulled Angel into a hug. Despite her dramatics, I knew I'd been a slack friend — somewhere last year I'd forgotten how to have a conversation about anything other than getting good grades, nailing my exams and finishing my assignments. If anything, I was lucky she'd stuck around. Now she was right: we deserved to have some fun.

'Okay, you want to set me up with Pete? Fine. I'm ready.'

Angel grinned. 'Good, because he's here.'

My heart began to beat faster. 'Oh, really? I lied. I'm not ready. I'm the opposite of ready.'

'He's over there.' Angel pointed. 'Wait a sec — no, don't look yet!'

We both stood there, moronic smiles plastered to our faces.

'Can I look now, oh boss of me?'

'Yep.'

I turned and there he was, as tall and muscly as ever. His mates — two equally popular guys called Matt and Chris — were egging him on to scull a tequila shot. I watched him down one, then another, until the three of them were laughing louder than Kat on the phone with her friends. Pete didn't spot the overeager, underprepared nobody watching him from the kitchen.

'Now what?' I whispered.

'Allow me,' Angel said. 'I'll be right back.'

'Oh no,' I muttered as she strode over to the group. I didn't know how to talk to a guy, let alone be with a guy. I longed to be home, curled up with a novel, reading about a heroine being swept off her feet by a handsome hero. Instead, I was at a party, sipping cheap wine, while my best friend coaxed a guy to come and talk to me. The romance factor wasn't high.

I snapped out of my fantasy land to see Pete and Angel darting their way through the crowd and heading for the kitchen. I triple-checked there wasn't a leggy supermodel standing behind me. Nope. I was the only loser loitering by the dips and chips.

Angel slowed to a saunter so Pete reached me first. 'Thank me later,' she mouthed, then walked away, leaving me alone with my high-school crush.

Panic slapped me around the head. I wanted to press pause on the situation to consult an instruction manual on guys. How did these things operate again? My mind swirled with doubts and possibilities, leaving me completely confused.

In the end, that didn't matter because Pete took charge. He leaned toward me, his arms lolling by his sides. His breath smelled of tequila and cigarette smoke; his T-shirt wasn't much better.

'Hey Josephine,' he murmured.

'Hi Pete.'

He moved closer. 'So, ah, good party, huh?'

'Yeah, the best.' The *best*? Oh, be quiet, Josie.

'I, ah, like your hair. Looks different. And your lips look good, too.'

'Oh, thanks, my sister loaned me a —'

Pete lurched at me, smooshing his mouth against mine. Within seconds, his tongue had forced its way into my mouth, swirling and swishing with the subtlety of a washing machine. I tried to sink into the moment, to find a rhythm, but there was no moment or rhythm to give in to. I needed to cough. Or gag. Or throw up.

I pulled away.

'Hey baby, why you stopping?' he asked, his eyes still closed.

Baby? And that was the moment it clicked: that was the worst kiss of my life. Sure, we'd kissed once, years ago, and I'd never been able to shake the idea that he was amazing and crush-worthy. I'd planted him squarely at the top of my Guys To Lust Over pedestal. But I didn't really know him. And he didn't know me.

'Sorry, Pete, I've got to go.'

'No, wait — I haven't seen it yet.'

'Seen what?'

'It. You know … *it*.'

'I have no idea what you're talking about.' I really didn't. What was 'it'? My innie belly button? The small mole on my right shoulder? My one — and only — attempt at Irish dancing?

Pete moved in even closer and lowered his voice. 'Make me say it, then … your Brazilian.'

'My … Who told you that?' I blurted out.

Pete shrugged. 'Angela or Angel or whatever her name is. I didn't believe her — I mean, you, Josephine Browning, with a Brazilian? No way. But she convinced me.'

'She did, did she?' Angel was a dead woman.

'Oh yeah. I had to see for myself.'

Unbelievable. Years of pining after a guy only to discover he was a grade-A douche. And my so-called best friend wasn't much better. I grabbed my handbag off the floor and swung it over my shoulder.

'Josie, where are you going? Baby?'

'I'm not your baby,' I shot back, my skin still crawling from his slobbery, tequila-drenched kiss.

And with that, I stormed away from the party without saying goodbye to Angel. Fury and embarrassment boiled up inside me. What kind of person demands to see someone's Brazilian? Pete might as well have asked me to flop out my right boob and start a conga line at the party.

The lights were out when I reached home. I didn't bother turning them on. Like most nights, classical music echoed softly from Mum's room, while furious typing click-clacked from Kat's as she chatted to friends online. Exhausted, I crawled into bed fully clothed, the stench of cigarettes and alcohol seeping from my hair and skin onto the freshly washed sheets. My head thumped and pounded and buzzed, but I didn't care.

'Love, are you awake?' I heard Mum whisper from the hallway. 'How was the party?'

I wrapped myself tighter in the sheet as the door creaked open. Even in the dark I could feel her eyes staring. I faked sleep; silence would have wrapped around us if Kat's eager typing hadn't disturbed the gentle hum of the house. I heard Mum creep into the room and plonk down into my chair. It let out a slow creak.

'How was the party?' she repeated.

She already knew the answer; I'd been gone less than an hour.

'JB, I know you're awake. Your fake-sleeping is terrible. Your breathing patterns are all out and —'

'Don't call me JB,' I murmured, taking the bait. 'And my breathing patterns were fine.'

'Oh love, what happened?'

'Nothing.'

'Where's Angel?'

'I don't know.'

Mum perched next to me on the bed, rubbing my back while I snuggled deeper into my pillow.

'Talk to me, Josie,' she said. 'I feel like you don't talk to me any more. What's going on?'

'Let's go to sleep, Mum, save it for another time. I'm so tired.'

But Mum wasn't giving up. 'Tell me. I want to know everything.'

And so I did. The ups and downs of the internship at *Sash*, the amazing James and his surprise girlfriend, the hideous kiss with Pete, how I'd been a bad friend to Angel, and the fact I didn't know what to think about anything any more. What I didn't tell her was that *Sash* was offering one intern five thousand dollars and I was on a mission to win it for our family. We needed that money and I was going to do whatever it took to get it. I just needed to work out how to beat Ava and Steph.

I fell asleep with Mum's arms wrapped around me. When I woke in the morning I was alone, tucked in tightly, with an extra blanket over my legs.

10.

Steph shook the iron from side to side, then pressed its red and green buttons. 'Is this thing even on?'

'Maybe you have to wait for it to heat up,' I began.

Steam whooshed from the iron.

'Oh yeah, here we go.' She pressed another button, then held up a rumpled white shirt. 'This can be my first victim. Man, we're so not going to win Domestic Goddess of the Year awards, are we?'

'Guess not.'

'Keep an eye out for the fashion girls — I'm scared I'm going to burn down this whole place. I can't believe Ava got to "help Rae" today and we got stuck with the ironing!'

I didn't dare tell Steph that I'd never used an iron before in my life. Or a washing machine. Or a dishwasher. Mum ruled the domestic roost at home; my duties only extended to making my bed and packing a lunch box. When Mum didn't do it first.

'So, Rae told me you broke a crazy story about Billy

from Greed knocking up some poor girl?' Steph said. 'Is it true?'

My jaw fell open. 'Rae said that?'

Steph smirked. 'Well, not those exact words. But you broke a story! That's brilliant.'

'It was nothing.'

'Trust me, it's something. Still, Rae did tell me I looked nice today … for a girl with tattoos. I've taken it as a win. Oh, and did you see Billy's checked himself back into rehab for a week?'

'Uh, what? He has?'

'Yeah, his manager says he's cleaning up his act and preparing to be a dad. Maybe you helped him take a long hard look at himself.'

'Wow.' Stunned didn't begin to describe my reaction.

'From what I've heard, the mag really needed this,' Steph went on. 'No wonder Rae is losing her mind over you. Man, seriously, if I had your skills.'

I blushed. 'Is being a geek a skill?'

'Geek? You're seventeen and —'

'Nearly eighteen.'

'Nearly eighteen, then,' she smiled, 'and the whole world's waiting for you. Believe me, you're going to nail it.'

I blushed again. 'You're not that much older than me and you can do whatever you want.'

'Jose, all that's waiting for me is failure. My papa dearest is a man on a mission — to get his little girl a fancy job before she's shacked up with someone she met in an ashram in India or on an elephant farm in Thailand. You know, that ol' chestnut.'

I didn't, but I was fascinated and waited for Steph to continue. She ran the iron over the shirt, adding more creases than she took out. I didn't say anything; I couldn't have done any better.

Steph sighed. 'You want the goss on how I know so much about Rae? Well, it's no secret that she knows my dad, right? Well, let's just say in the past few weeks she's *really* got to know him.' Steph gave me a pointed look and raised an eyebrow.

'Ohhh,' I said as it clicked.

'Oh, indeed.' Steph shrugged.

'But your mum ... how does she feel?'

'Mum's doing the landscape architect.'

This time, my jaw nearly smacked the ironing board. 'What?'

'I know. She's a walking cliché.'

My reply tumbled out before I could stop myself. 'The gardener would've been more of a cliché.'

Steph snorted with laughter. 'Totally! Or the pool guy! Or her tennis coach.'

'And you know he'd be waving his big, bad racquet around.'

'Dude!' She laughed, then sighed. 'I really can't win, you know? Dad hooks up with Rae, complains to her about me having no direction, so Rae lets me come here and I *still* have no direction, Dad loses his mind, they hook up again and the joyous cycle continues.'

I still couldn't get my head around it. 'So Rae knows you know? About them?'

'In the past few weeks, she's been at our place every couple of nights. Mum and her probably get plastered together and talk about how Dad's a massive pain in the neck.'

Steph caught the confused look on my face. 'I know, it's weird. Somehow, I think it works, though. For them, anyway.' She held up the shirt, which was now stained brown and black in the pattern of the iron. 'I think I've stuffed this up. This is why I only buy clothes that don't need ironing. Bags not doing the next one. You're up.'

Unsure what to do but not wanting to admit it, I took over the iron.

'Okay, enough about my family,' said Steph. 'Have you decided how you'll spend your five grand yet?'

I blushed. 'No! Sure, it would be awesome, but I won't win.'

Steph rolled her eyes. 'Oh, please. The way Rae was rambling on the other day, it's yours.'

'But your dad and her —'

'Dude, if I won it, Dad would force Rae to put it in a trust fund or something. Nah, he's sent me here to keep me out of trouble. Rae wants to push me toward design, but I'd rather hang around and bludge.' Steph leaned over my shoulder. 'Jose, you are rocking this ironing biz.'

I held up the finished shirt. 'Done! Well, if you're not up for the prize, Ava will win it. Like you said, she's "helping Rae" — they're totally BFFs.'

'Ahhh, Queen Ava.' Steph rolled her eyes. 'I don't get her. I mean, she thinks she's this big-shot actress and model, but if that's true why work for free as an intern? No way, Jose, the prize is yours.'

I shook my head at Steph, but deep down I prayed she was right. I *needed* that five thousand for my family. Mum assured me and Kat we'd be alright, but for some reason, I struggled to trust in that. Perhaps it was because my innocent outlook on the world had disappeared the moment I saw Dad storming to the car and driving off last year. Mum wasn't coping. I'd overhead her frantic phone conversations with Aunt Julie too many times when she thought Kat and I were asleep. Five thousand dollars would kick some bills in the butt.

Steph snapped me out of my daydream. 'For argument's sake, what would you buy? A car? Holiday? Clothes? Throw a party that I can come to and forget about how much my life sucks right now?'

I paused, unsure whether to tell her the truth. 'I'd give it to my family. Lame, right? Mum's pretty stressed.'

Steph stopped polishing a pair of knee-high platform boots. 'Sorry, I had no idea ... So, what's your family like then? Perfect children, picket fences and all that? Or a cesspit of "coveting thy neighbour's wife" like my tribe?'

I laughed. 'No, we're not perfect. Not even close. But we used to be.'

Before Dad left, we had been a bit stereotypical: a classic suburban family, right down to the big backyard (just enough space for a pool that would never be built), washing line and friendly streets where kids played cricket until the sun set. Now, thanks to a runaway father, I felt like I was stuck in a soap opera and didn't know how to escape.

The door suddenly creaked open to reveal Ava holding her handbag. She was hunched over slightly, her hand grazing her stomach.

'Finished your secret women's business with Rae?' asked Steph.

Ava didn't flinch at the question. 'I'm heading off for the day. I've got a migraine.' Her hand moved to her head, but her hunched stance said otherwise.

'But you'll miss the beauty sale this afternoon!' I said. 'Want me to grab you anything? Sia said there's heaps of great stuff going for less than two bucks — and perfumes are only ten bucks!'

'Two-dollar beauty products? I'll be fine,' she said, rubbing her middle again. 'Josephine, didn't your mother teach you to iron? That looks awful.' With that, she closed the door behind her.

'She's clearly not sick enough to quit the bitch act,' said Steph. 'You're too nice to her.'

'Did you see her holding her stomach?' I asked. 'I don't think it's a migraine.'

Steph's eyes widened. 'Maybe she's pregnant. With a demon baby.'

'Or she could have food poisoning.'

'That would require digesting food. The girl barely eats.'

Steph was right: Ava nibbled on her lunch like a baby bird eating for the first time.

I pulled out another crumpled item from the cane clothes basket on the floor — a polka-dot dress. I laid it out on the ironing board, oblivious to everything but Steph's chatter about what she was going to buy at the sale and the soft fizz of the iron.

Liani and Sia stood in front of the meeting-room door, blocking everyone from entering the beauty sale a second before starting time. The corridor buzzed with chatter, and for a minute I forgot we were at a workplace. Right then, other people were chopping wood, fixing cars, changing bedpans or filing paperwork. We were lined up with our purses poised and game faces on, all in the name of nabbing a cheap brow brush. Forget surviving the daily grind of nine-to-five to make a crust; that afternoon felt like the mid-year sales, where everyone has seventy-five per cent markdowns on their mind — we'd been granted VIP access to the front of the queue. From what Sia had hinted, I'd need to toughen up if I wanted to score any designer-brand bargains. I wasn't blind: any moron could have spotted the other girls' eyes glinting with competition.

'If anyone sees volume-boosting mascara, can you grab it for me?' said Eloise to no one in particular, pacing on the spot.

'For sure. I'm dying for a replacement red lippie so keep your eyes peeled for that too,' chimed in one of the art-department girls, hoisting a giant tote bag over her shoulder.

Gen — another red-lipstick wearer — rolled her eyes, clearly coveting the same product. These girls meant business.

'It's almost time,' Steph said, nudging me in the side and pointing to the clock on the wall.

She wasn't the only one who'd noticed. The corridor's chatter reduced to a dull hum as everyone repositioned themselves like fired-up athletes taking their marks. Looking around at the determined grimaces, I wished I'd worn protective gear. Carla looked ready to snatch hair-treatment products from anyone who got in her way, and even Liani was clutching her wallet with a steeliness I'd never seen before. I wondered what products she was after; she didn't seem to wear much make-up. Rae was nowhere to be seen, but I imagined Sia had already put aside the best of the best for her. Let's be honest: wrestling her staff for reduced-price hand creams wouldn't be at the top of Rae's priority list, not with a magazine to run and editorial minions to terrify.

Sia whistled and waved her hand in the air. She wanted our attention and she got it.

'Okay, team, you have ten minutes in there before everyone — and I do mean everyone — from the rest of the company swoops in. All money raised goes to our beautiful sponsor child *and* our end-of-year party, so let's make it a good one! No IOUs, no bartering, and if you have correct change, I may just kiss you.'

Everyone laughed.

'Ready?' Sia asked. 'Happy shopping, beauties!'

She opened the doors and we spilled into the meeting room — a wave of perfume-pursuing, lip-gloss-liking, hair-product-hunting women with one mission only: to get our hands on the best beauty bargains before everyone else.

The first thing I noticed was the colour: the rosy hues of the blushes and lipsticks in one corner, the purple and blue of the eye shadows in another; a rainbow array of bottle after bottle of nail polish. The tables were lined with products, all squashed up against each other and divided into categories according to price and size.

Within seconds, I fell to the back of the crowd as the *Sash* team surged forward, throwing nail polishes and eye pencils, bronzers and tanners, hairsprays and serums into their bags. I'd never seen so many perfectly painted nails moving so fast before, snatching, shoving and grabbing. The girls muttered to themselves, weighing up their decisions quickly. There was no sympathy for slow thinkers — you needed gut instinct, fast reflexes and an eye for quality if you didn't want to get left with the goods that everyone else was smart enough to leave untouched.

Straining to reach the tables, avoiding swinging elbows and flicking hair, I yanked up supersized bottles of shampoo and conditioner and added them to my bag. I didn't care what brand they were — I was tired of my hair smelling like body wash, which was the only type of product left in Tim and James's bathroom.

Steph slithered into a small crack between Carla and Gen, who were rummaging through products faster than you could say 'shopaholics'. We caught each other's eye and shared a moment of excitement, although I was still a little dazed by the intense ferocity of the sale.

'Organic body butter,' mouthed Steph, waving an orange tub at me. 'It smells so good.'

'Nice,' I mouthed back, picking up a night cream and a waxing set for Mum, followed by a tinted moisturiser and lip gloss for Kat.

It was a fun afternoon, I couldn't lie, but the best bit? Thanks to all the hairspray, perfume and scented moisturiser being squirted and spritzed around the room, my brain cells had temporarily shut down so I didn't have the mental capacity to think about James and Summer and get upset all over again. I mean, sure, James was hot (and nice and funny, all wrapped in a neat, dude-sized package of awesome), and sure, I was ready to write a letter to the government asking that the season 'summer' be called something less beautiful and life-ruining, but seriously, it meant nothing.

I'm fine, I told myself, adding a metallic nail polish to my bag. Just fine.

Once the sale had wrapped up, Sia trotted out to attend a launch for new mascara. Or body lotion. Or toothpaste. I'd lost track of her endless stream of events. Half her days were spent 'fixing her face' at her desk before running out for the next appointment.

The art team packed up their handbags at 5.35 pm, heading off for drinks at a nearby bar. Not long after, laughter pealed from the fashion department, where Carla and Gen were telling dirty jokes in Scottish accents. They all strutted down the hall to the lifts, a tight unit glued together by matching heels and complementary hairstyles.

The editorial team — the ones who wrote and edited the features — were the last to leave at 6.22 pm, their reddened eyes and early-evening switch from heels to flats setting them apart from their more glamorous colleagues.

As the clock ticked toward 6.24 pm, I realised it was just me in the office, amid the buzz of sleeping computers and racks of shiny magazines. Heading home to Tim's apartment again wasn't an attractive prospect. It was dirty, gross and I had to sleep on the couch.

Except they weren't the real reasons I didn't want to go back there.

Apparently — surprise, surprise — I wasn't fine with the whole James-having-a-girlfriend scenario after all. I couldn't bear the thought of going to the apartment because James would be there, probably with Summer in tow — and no amount of cheap beauty goodies could distract me from that any more. In my mind, I saw them cuddling on the couch, feeding each other at the dinner table and splashing each other in the tiny bathtub.

I couldn't face them until it was closer to bedtime and I could feign tiredness and crash out straight away on the sofa. And so, instead of facing the dream couple head-on, I took advantage of being alone and pretended I was one of the lucky few paid to strut around the *Sash* office. It was fun, cleared my head and relaxed me.

But as it turned out, I wasn't alone after all.

I heard the sniffling first. Short, sharp sniffs coming from down the hallway, that exploded into sobs that echoed through the foyer. I edged toward the noise, almost frightened to see who — or what — could be emitting such painful wails.

And then I saw her. Alone in the office, her perfect bob now scruffy, her made-up face stained with tears.

Rae saw me, too. Our eyes locked, hers growing wider. She spun away from me in her chair (no doubt muttering 'That damn intern!'), grabbed a tissue, wiped under her eyes, then spun back around.

'You're still here?' she said in a stern voice, patting her bob into place.

'Ah, hi,' I said weakly. 'How's it going?'

Rae's face now showed no signs of blubbering. The woman was incredible; my eyes stayed red and sore for days after a cry-fest.

'You should have gone home hours ago, Josie.'

'I know, I know,' I rambled. 'I'm just happy to help out.'

There was something thrilling about being alone in the office with her. It felt illegal. Maybe it was.

'Well, isn't that nice,' said Rae. 'And if I believed you for one second, then I'd say thank you. But, Josie, this isn't my first day in magazines. I've seen enough girls hanging around the office and dropping excuses about late-night photocopying or internet trawling to know when something's up.'

'Oh?'

'Oh, indeed. And it's always for the same reason. So, tell me … who is he? Or is he a she?'

I opened my mouth, ready to deny everything. These days, I'd got used to repressing things, pushing them so far down toward my toes I sometimes wondered if my feet would bleed. They were aching now, but that was probably from cramming them into heels all day. Then James's face lurched into my mind and I couldn't bear to push him away again.

'He,' I said. 'James.'

Rae's tone softened. 'Is he worth all this? Staying back late? Feeling sad?'

'I'm not.'

'Josie.' Rae reactivated her I-wasn't-born-yesterday tone. 'Well, *is* he worth it?'

'Um, I don't know.'

But I did know. He *was* worth it. The way he told jokes about the weirdos at his work made me snort with laughter. His passion for music impressed me, I couldn't drag my eyes away when he tucked his shaggy mop behind one ear, and the way he teased me made me feel tingly and giggly, like I'd had champagne for breakfast.

'Maybe you should call it a night?' said Rae. 'Sounds like you've got someone to see.'

I couldn't look at her; my eyes had misted over. The speed with which she'd switched focus from her meltdown to mine was brilliant. She was three steps ahead every time, even when she was caught off guard. I wanted — no, needed — to be around her, to learn from her.

'Are you sure you don't need a hand?' I asked. 'I mean, if something's wrong, I could —'

'It's home time, Josie. I'll see you next week, bright, early and unburdened.'

I wanted her to clutch me to her bosom and tell me everything would be okay, despite it feeling so wrong. But, as Rae possessed the maternal qualities of a broken fridge, she didn't do that. Of course she didn't. I wondered whether I'd imagined her sobbing in the office. Maybe I'd experienced a mirage. But then I remembered those wails and knew Rae was repressing something of her own. Something she wasn't going to tell a lousy intern.

'Oh, and Josie?' she added.

I turned back to face her. 'Yes?'

'Before I forget, Billy's back from rehab next week. I can't believe I'm even saying this, but he's requested another interview. And he wants you to do it.'

I swallowed. 'How is that possible? Wouldn't Esmeralda prefer to do it?'

'Yes, she would,' Rae said. 'But he only wants you. I'm not convinced, but Liani's backing you a hundred per cent.'

'I don't know what to say.'

'Are you up for it?'

'Um, sure, of course,' I stammered.

'Great. Prepare some questions and we'll lock it in. Josie, this could be a game-changer for you, for me and for the magazine. Don't screw it up.'

11.

Muffled yells rang out from the bedroom: James's voice rising up and down; Summer's remaining at a constant higher pitch. I couldn't hear the words, but that wasn't for lack of trying. I wanted to press my ear against the bedroom door, but I knew that would make me a freak. And possibly a stalker. Instead, I wrapped myself in a blanket and snuggled into the couch. I pushed my fingers into my ears and pressed my eyes closed, but sleep wouldn't come. Not even counting one hundred fluffy white sheep helped. Summer's voice grew louder and louder, until, finally, I could make out what had fired her up.

'What is it about her, huh?'

Either James didn't answer or he muttered, because I couldn't hear a reply.

'Why are you looking at me weird, James? Do you hate me? Fine! I hate you too.'

There was silence. I held my breath for James's response, but still couldn't hear him. Only her. The back-pedalling began.

'Baby, I'm sorry. I don't hate you, I love you. Do you love me? Do you? I'm sorry, I'm so overwhelmed and then ... What? Fine, shut up, then. Stuff you!'

I heard the bedroom door open, followed by footsteps thumping down the hallway ... toward the lounge room ... where I was curled on the couch.

Summer and I caught each other's eye at the same time. Her hair was matted, mascara was smeared all over her face and she wore lacy pink lingerie. That was a surprise for both of us. She screamed and clutched at herself and raced back down the hallway to the bedroom. Cue: round two.

'Does she still have to be here?' she yelled. 'I mean, what's really going on?'

'Nothing. Just leave it,' I heard James say. His voice sounded stronger this time.

'Damn right, it's nothing. You even look at her again, I'll lose it. I don't care how many scooter rides she's begging for.'

'Geez, Sum, I did her a favour. One favour. Calm down, come back to bed and —'

'I've seen the way she stares at you!'

Gradually, the fighting stopped and, thanks to the rhythmic tick, tock, tick, tock of the clock in the living room, I eventually faded into a fitful sleep.

The next morning, somewhere around 5.30 am, I slipped a 'Thank you' post-it note under Tim's bedroom door and snuck out into the darkness of the city. My train wasn't due for a while, so I sat on the platform in silence staring at my hands. A strong sense of homesickness tapped me on the shoulder. Rubbing my temples, I turned my attention to the people arriving at the station: city workers in suits, checking their phones; a young backpacking couple arguing over the best train to catch; a twenty-something guy in sneakers talking into his phone about planning a party for the weekend. My eyes rested on a girl with sad eyes and brown hair. She wasn't doing much, just sitting and staring into nothingness. And then I recognised her mouth, her eyes, her pointy chin.

It was me, reflected in the glass opposite.

'Angela's on the phone for you,' whispered Mum, gesturing to the landline in the kitchen. 'Apparently she's been trying your mobile for a week and hasn't heard back.'

I sighed. 'Tell her I'm busy. I'm in the shower, in the bathroom, watching paint dry, I don't care.'

'Oh, love, I don't like lying to your friends.'

'Tell her the truth then — that she stuffed up and I don't want to talk to her.' The snarky words came out before I could stop them.

Mum ignored them. 'Fine, I'll tell her you're mowing the lawn.'

'Are you crazy? She'll never believe *that*.'

'The shower. I'll tell her you're in the shower.'

I heard her force out the words; Mum was a terrible liar. Her voice shook and she rushed through the sentences, eager to get off the phone. She came back into the room, the deed done.

'You can't ignore the girl forever, Josephine.'

'Mum, don't full-name me.'

'Love, she's your best friend.'

I hadn't felt like talking to Angel since the Pete Jordan incident, which still gave me horrible flashbacks. Angel knew my lack of experience with guys — she shouldn't have set me up like that.

Mum hugged me. 'I'm going to pick some herbs from the back garden to go with dinner.'

'Need a hand?' I asked, feeling bad for getting her to lie for me.

'No thanks, love. You can set the table, though. We're having pasta.' Mum picked up a cane basket and headed out the back door.

Despite the difficult circumstances, I knew Mum was doing her best to make things normal for Kat and me. This was my chance to do something for her. I walked into the kitchen and pulled the fancy cutlery set down from the top of the cupboard. I was fairly sure the set had been a gift from a great-aunt on Mum's side. As far as I could remember, it had only been used twice — once at a Christmas when long-lost relatives came to visit and then again at my sweet sixteenth birthday dinner. It was time to give it another run.

The box was heavier than I expected and it caught me off balance. It slipped out of my hands and the cutlery crashed onto the kitchen floor.

'Oops,' I muttered, dropping to my hands and knees. One by one, I placed knives, forks and spoons back into place in the navy velvet-lined box.

About halfway through, Kat strolled into the kitchen and watched me scrabbling around on the floor.

'You idiot,' she said, rolling her eyes. 'Why'd you get that out? You know Mum hates it.'

'Hates it?' That was news to me. I'd always thought she just couldn't be bothered getting it down from the top of the cupboard.

'Yeah, it's their wedding cutlery, remember?' she hissed, crouching to collect a couple of spoons that had escaped across the room.

'I thought it was a gift from Mum's great-aunt — you know, the sweet one with all the purple soaps and creepy frilly dolls?'

Obviously I wouldn't be winning any awards for paying attention to Extremely Sensitive Family Topics anytime soon.

'It *was* from her. For their wedding.'

'I can't believe I stuffed that up.'

'And can you call Angel back already?' Kat went on. 'She's stalking me on Facebook to try to get hold of you. I don't want to block her on there, but seriously, Jose ...'

'I'll call her when I'm ready.'

'Is this about Pete Jordan?'

'Shut up, Kat.'

''Cos I heard Mum talking to Aunt Julie about it, and it sounded awwwwkward —'

'I said, shut up.'

'Josephine and Katherine Browning, why isn't the table set?'

We froze, then turned to see Mum standing in the kitchen doorway, her basket overflowing with basil. Her lips trembled at the sight of us surrounded by teaspoons and cake forks.

'Girls, what are you doing with that?' she asked, pointing at the cutlery set.

I swallowed. 'We can explain.'

But Mum didn't wait to hear it: she spun on her heel and bolted down the hallway to her bedroom. The sound of her door slamming echoed through the house.

'I saw tears, yep, definitely saw tears,' said Kat. 'Far out, you know what that means?'

I didn't, and felt bad that I didn't. 'Well, obviously she's upset and —'

'*Obviously*, but what it means is she won't be coming

out of her room tonight. Fine, I'm going to eat in my room too.'

'No, let's get her and eat together. We can fix this.'

Kat rolled her eyes. 'Whatever. I'm eating in my room.'

She heaped an enormous serving of pasta into a bowl, covered it in parmesan cheese and walked off without uttering another word. Kat may have given up but I hadn't, so I filled another dish and carried it to Mum's bedroom.

Knock, knock.

'Dinner, Mum.'

Nothing.

Knock, knock. Knock, knock.

'Mum? The pasta's ready,' I tried again. 'It'll taste great with that basil.'

Still nothing.

'You need to eat, so I'll leave it outside your door, okay? Just in case you get hungry later.'

Defeated, I returned to the kitchen to eat pasta sauce straight from the pot. But later that night, on the way to bed, I snuck a peek at Mum's door and was thrilled to see my plan had worked: the bowl was no longer there.

'The marks for last week's essay are available online, so you can view them at your leisure,' announced Filly to a roomful of sleepy students. 'A special congratulations to Lisa Hantz, who scored the highest mark in the class. Great work.'

She did? I'd given up sleep and sanity to finish the essay and had been confident I'd smashed it. Too confident, it would seem.

Lisa blushed and slid down further in her chair, embarrassed. As a fellow over-achiever, I was at the other end of the spectrum: I wanted the glory; to receive the crown, certificate, trophy or praise. Not that I'd ever received a crown. I was still working on that one.

'Okay, that's it for today, folks,' Filly continued. 'I've got a fishing trip to get to.'

Everyone cheered at the early mark, collected their bags and shuffled toward the door. Filly claimed to thrive on a work–life balance, although he favoured life over work nine times out of ten.

I heard him call my name. 'Josie, can I grab you for a minute?'

I waited until the last student had straggled out the door, then asked, 'What's up?'

'Just one sec, it won't take long,' Filly said, gesturing to a brown chair on my right.

'Okay …' I said, taking a seat. It expelled a long creak that made me giggle.

Filly rubbed his head with his palms. 'So, I couldn't help noticing your essay was handed in a couple of days late …'

'No, I handed it in on Friday,' I said. My jaw tingled, signalling that my body was seconds away from being swamped by anxiety.

'I know that,' said Filly, 'but it was due last Wednesday.'

'I'm sure that can't be right, I wrote it down and everything,' I muttered, pulling scarves, pencils, lolly wrappers and mints out of my bag in search of my diary. 'I'm positive you said Friday.'

I found my diary and swiftly turned the pages. And there it was, among the other scribbled notes, reminders and due dates for uni, life and *Sash*, written in bright red marker: *Journalism essay due*. And, like Filly had reminded me, it was due last Wednesday.

'But I don't make mistakes like this,' I said. 'I don't.'

'Josie, you seem to be carrying a heavy load at the moment — and I don't just mean your handbag,' Filly said. 'Is there anything you need to talk about?'

Did a soap-opera-style family crisis count? Or what about unrequited feelings for someone else's boyfriend? Surely being terrified by a magazine editor would score me sympathy votes?

But for once I kept my mouth shut on the details. 'I'll be okay ... Wait, does this mean I fail the assignment for handing it in late?'

He smiled. 'No. You've never broken the rules before, have you? But I had to deduct ten per cent from your overall mark — five per cent for each day it was late. If you'd handed it in on time you would have beaten Lisa by two marks.'

'Oh man.' *Oh man!*

'Think of this as a lesson,' he said. 'Keep writing, work hard, remember the correct due dates and you'll top this course.'

'So I haven't failed? Oh, thank you,' I sighed. 'I kind of want to hug you right now.'

'Probably best not to,' he deadpanned. 'Oh, and don't think I haven't noticed your work on the *Sash* website — Liani's flicked me the links. I'm glad to see things have picked up on that front. Now, I'm off. Those fish aren't going to catch themselves.'

The bitter smell of coffee wafting from my cup made my nostrils ache. I glanced around the uni cafeteria and saw students of all ages enjoying large mugs of the stuff. A few even had enormous thermoses. I sniffed my cup again, hesitating, then took a sip.

'You really have changed. I thought you didn't drink coffee?' a voice piped up behind me, causing me to splutter over the table.

I wiped my mouth with a serviette and turned around to see Angel, alone as usual. She flicked me a small, awkward wave. Her dyed hair was fading and she looked pale, as though she'd been hiding in her room (which wouldn't have surprised me).

'Ah yeah, just testing it out again.' I leaned in for another sip. 'Urgh! It really is awful. It tastes worse than Mum's chicken casserole.'

Angel let a small laugh escape, then pointed to the empty seat next to me. 'May I?'

I shrugged. 'Sure.'

'So … what have you been up to?'

I played with the coffee cup, circling the rim with my finger. 'Oh, this and that.'

Somehow, our friendship had arrived in a scary land where small talk was the order of the day. May I? This and that? Who *were* we? Despite being a bit frustrating, Angel was my best friend. Love her or loathe her, I'd never gone this long without talking to her. It had to stop.

'I'm sorry,' we yelped at the same time, then laughed.

Angel got in first. 'JB, I've got to give credit where it's due. There's been no call, no text, no Facebook, no tweets, no love. Seriously, you take out first prize in the Ignoring Your Best Friend Olympics. Your certificate's being laminated as we speak.'

I smirked. 'Good to know.'

'So … about the Brazilian and Pete Jordan thing …' Angel forged on, blunt as always. 'I was an idiot, desperate and stupid and trying too hard and —'

'Yeah, you were. All of those things and more. Major friend fail.'

'I'm sorry. I'm so sorry.'

'Look, we're all good, okay? Forgiven.'

'And forgotten.' Angel hugged me.

'For you, maybe.' Nothing could scrub the memory of Pete's awful kissing technique from my brain.

'So, you better give me a life update. What have I missed?'

I took a deep breath and told Angel everything. We talked 'til late in the afternoon, ignoring the cafeteria staff packing away chairs. We talked 'til they flashed the 'Closed' sign and stood moaning by the register, waiting for us to clear out. We talked on the way to the bus stop. We talked on the way home, in Angel's driveway, at her front door while she fumbled around for her keys. We talked as her brother stumbled to the door to let her in because, as usual, she'd *forgotten* to bring her keys.

We talked, we talked, we talked.

We were back.

12.

I wheeled my suitcase into the guys' front hallway and took a deep breath. After Summer's outburst, I'd considered not coming back, but I couldn't afford a hotel so I'd skipped out on staying the previous night and caught the early morning train from home instead. The less I had to be around Summer and James, the better.

I looked around the silent apartment. Sunshine beamed through the window, casting bright, light shapes on the lounge-room floor. I counted to three in my head and waited for something, *anything*, to happen: attack dogs to be set on me; a trapdoor to open beneath my feet; a net to drop from the ceiling and capture me. Nothing happened. I was safe, for now.

'Tim? James? Anyone here?' I called.

'Just me,' Tim yelled out from his bedroom. 'James crashed at Summer's.'

'Hey, no probs,' I said, wheeling my suitcase over to the couch and pretending Summer and James were the furthest thing from my mind. They weren't. In addition to our family's financial and emotional woes, they'd been the only thing clogging up my brain lately. Well, other than the fact I'd be face to face with Billy from Greed again in a few hours.

I poured myself a glass of pineapple juice and sipped it while leaning against the bench.

'Hey, can I grab one of those, cuz?'

I turned to see Tim behind me, yawning with his mouth stretched wide and wrestling himself into a stained grey T-shirt.

'Sure.' I reached for another glass. Once filled, I handed it over.

'Thanks.' He gulped it down. 'Actually, can you pass me the carton?'

As I watched him chug from it, I reminded myself to avoid drinking his juice from now on.

After he'd emptied the carton, he looked me up and down. 'You got eyeliner on? Big day ahead?'

'Something like that.'

'Are you meeting Oprah? Interviewing the prime minister?'

'Not quite.'

He let out a deep sigh. 'Ahhh, what am I going to do with you?'

I tilted my head to the side. 'What do you mean?'

'Don't act like you don't know what I'm talking about.'

My mind raced. He's read me like a book. He knows everything. He knows about my feelings for James and the imaginary voodoo doll of his girlfriend that I've been sticking pins in. He *knows*.

'Tim, I have no idea what's going on,' I managed.

'J-Brown, you're turning eighteen in, like, a day or something and you haven't even organised a party. Your mum told my mum you're "keeping a low profile", whatever that means.'

I breathed a sigh of relief. Of course Tim didn't know. He couldn't read me like a book. In fact, I'd never seen him pick up a book, despite supposedly being at uni.

'Oh yeah, the big one-eight. I'm thinking maybe a small dinner with the family next week.'

His jaw dropped. 'That's it, we're officially not related because that is the lamest thing I've ever heard. Stuff that, I vote you party in the city with *me* next week. You'll be eighteen then, right?'

I would. In fact, I'd be eighteen in a few days, but things were so strained at home I wasn't going to make a fuss. Mum had enough going on. 'I don't know ... it sounds a little —'

'Awesome? Rad? Potentially the best night of your life? C'mon, what did you do for your birthday last year?'

I didn't dare tell him. Our whole family had been recovering from a nasty flu so we'd kept things simple with baked-bean-and-cheese toasties and a game — well, half a game — of Monopoly. From memory, the night ended with me flipping the board over in anger (I tend to get a little competitive with games) and Kat slapping me on the arm with the fake paper money for 'ruining the night'.

'Fine, count me in,' I said.

'Yes! I'll round up my mates.'

'Okay. Wait, what mates?'

'Just a few guys who like a laugh. You'll love them.'

I instantly felt 10,031 times more nervous about turning eighteen.

'You can crash here, but you have to bring some people, too,' Tim went on. 'I vote "hot girls". Yep, you've definitely got to bring some friends.'

'Is that so?'

I could bring Angel, for sure, this was something she'd want to be a part of. But who else could I ask? Kat was hardly an option, even if she did look older than me.

Tim wasn't finished. 'Oh, and whatever you do, don't tell —'

'Mum or Aunt Julie. I know.'

Tim yawned. 'Okay, bedtime. Better crash.'

'Didn't you just wake up? It's morning!'

'I only got home a few hours ago. A nap calls.'

Tim dawdled back to his bedroom, while I carried my gear into the bathroom to get ready for another day at *Sash*. I slid into a new green dress (thank you, designer factory outlet sale); the silk breezed over my thighs and made me feel glamorous. Smoothing out my hair was the final touch. I looked in the mirror and tried to convince myself I looked older, sophisticated, worthy of interviewing a celebrity.

I spun on my heel to admire the back of the dress and saw a strip of Polaroid photos lying on the floor. I picked it up for a closer look: James and Summer, laughing together like a toothpaste commercial. In the first one, Summer was pulling James's ears out like a monkey. In the second, she was showing off hot-pink lips in an exaggerated pout. The third was a blur of her hair being whipped around. It was the fourth that made me want to stick my head in the toilet bowl. They were sharing a passionate kiss, her hand pressing his face into hers. I shuddered and put the photos back on the ground, avoiding the urge to toss them in the bin.

Tim pounded on the door. 'Cuz, you nearly finished in there? That juice ran right through me.'

I straightened up and stared in the mirror. 'I'm done.'

And I was.

I was done with liking a guy who clearly had other things on his mind, like seeing how far his tongue could reach down someone else's throat (which, based on the evidence I'd just seen, was quite far). Summer seemed psychotic and awful, but James still looked happy.

I wished it was a week from now so I could legally drown my sorrows with Tim and his mates and forget all about James. But I couldn't. I had an interview to do. An interview that could put me exactly where I wanted to be: in the top spot for winning five thousand dollars.

The wall had thirty-seven scratches on it, two paintings, one broken clock and a calendar that was three months behind. I noticed all this as I sat in the meeting room's high-backed business chair and waited for Billy and his entourage to arrive.

No longer content with counting things to soothe my nerves, I resorted to tapping my right index finger on the table. Tap, tap, tap, tap, tap. Tap, tap, tap, tap, tap.

I re-read my pages of questions (this time I was prepared), triple-checked the battery in my dictaphone and clicked my pen to see if it still worked. It did. Of course it did. I scrawled on the top of my notepad, signing my name, scribbling hearts and stars. Bored, I switched back to clicking my pen.

'Well, that's annoying,' a voice drawled behind me.

I spun around, almost falling off the oversized leather chair, to see Billy in the doorway. He was scruffy, in a black jacket and tight jeans. He looked fantastic and, by the smirk on his face, he knew it.

I leaped to my feet, almost tripping over my heels, and shook his hand.

He laughed. 'What, no kiss? After everything we've been through.'

'Oh.' I leaned in and we attempted to peck each other's cheek, but mistimed it. 'Ah, hey, how are you?'

'Great, fantastic, brilliant ... dying for a ciggie.' He laughed again. 'And how about you, Miss I Broke A Big Story About A Sleazy Muso And Got A Pay Rise? How are things?'

'Ah, pretty good,' I said. 'But no pay rise.' No pay, I added in my head.

'Sucks to be you, then. You picked the wrong industry.'

'Maybe.' I said. 'Not all of us can be rock gods.'

Billy laughed again, then took off his jacket and swung it over the chair. 'You know, I never got the chance to thank you.'

I wasn't sure if I'd heard him right. 'Thank me? For what?'

'Let's just say that article you wrote forced me to confess to a few things, and ... well, thanks, I guess.'

I swallowed. 'Any time.'

'If it weren't for you, I don't know where I'd be ... Probably off my head and up to no good. Instead, I've finally got myself together and Kara and I are going to give this parenting thing a real go.'

'That's great.'

'So if there's anything I can ever do for you, just ask. I mean that.'

I smiled. 'Okay, I'll remember that. Well, shall we do this, then?'

Billy nodded. 'You bet. The fans have been begging for this, apparently. My Twitter's gone off so hard, my publicist can't keep up.'

'Let's begin.' I gestured to a chair, sat back down, flicked my dictaphone to 'record' and, without a single stutter or hint of nerves, asked the first question.

I'd done it. Two hours of interviewing Billy without stammering or sweating (or worse, sending him fleeing from the building). And it had been magnificent. Even though I was a newbie features writer, this time I felt the part. I'd controlled my nerves — they hadn't controlled me.

I'd probed and prodded into his personal life and he'd been great: offering polished, entertaining anecdotes; tears in the right places; laughter when it called for it. His publicist had clearly spent more time rehearsing lines with him than with an Academy Award winner, but it had worked. He'd spoken about becoming a father — his fears, his dreams, his excitement. He'd admitted he'd fallen for the baby's mother, Kara, and they were working together to build love and trust. He'd confessed about the latest rehab stint — the toughest week of his life, but worth every struggle, as he was doing it for his unborn child and girlfriend.

When the interview was over, Billy pulled me in for a hug and kissed me on the cheek. His embrace went for longer than I expected so, unsure of journo-and-celebrity-post-interview-cuddling protocol, I pulled away first.

'Damn, Josie, you turn me into such a motormouth, it's like you've slipped me a truth serum or something,' he said, shaking his head. 'I guess that's what they pay you for, right?'

I wish, I thought, thinking of the five-thousand prize at stake.

'Anyway, good luck with the article,' he continued. 'Make me sound good, yeah?'

'Of course. Bye Billy, thanks again.'

It wasn't until he left that I realised I was busting to go to the toilet. I shouldn't have been surprised: we'd gone through a pot of tea, two jugs of sparkling mineral water and a fresh juice each. If anything, I was lucky my bladder hadn't burst during the interview. I rushed to the ladies' bathroom and, without a second to spare, entered the closest stall.

Just as I sat down, I heard someone come in and go into a cubicle to my right. A few seconds later, I heard the choking, gasping hideousness of someone being sick.

I've always been a sympathy spewer. I hear someone throwing up and two seconds later I need a bucket myself. This was no different. In fact, this was worse than the time I chucked up my scrambled eggs on a business-class flight. (Mum had won tickets in a raffle.) *Waaaay* worse.

Back then I was child, so I could get away with it. But this time I was at work. This time I had to hide it.

I tried to block out the noise with rapid toilet-paper-unravelling and peeing louder, but nothing worked. I gagged once, then twice, and thought, here we go, but then the sick noises stopped. And the sobbing started. Long, deep, painful sobs.

I sat there in my cubicle, listening to the mystery girl crying, holding my breath so she wouldn't know I was listening. Finally, I couldn't handle it any more.

'Are you okay in there?' I asked, and immediately wanted to hit myself. Of course she wasn't okay. No one hid in a bathroom vomiting and crying if they were okay.

No response, other than more sobbing.

I tried again. 'Do you want me to call someone for you?'

Silence. Not even a sob.

'Um, I'll go and find Liani. Maybe she can send you home and —'

'No, don't. Please, just go away.'

The girl's voice grated through me. It sounded familiar.

'Do you want me to get you some water?' I asked.

'Josie, just go away, would you?'

And then it hit me. The harsh tone. The dislike.

'Ava? Is that you in there?'

The silence told me everything I needed to know.

'What's wrong? Have you got a migraine again?'

'Go away. Please.'

'Is it something you ate? Once I had this huge bowl of soup and then I —'

'Just go.'

'But you're sick. I can't leave you.'

The toilet flushed and I heard the clip, clop of Ava's heels as she climbed to her feet, no doubt pausing to smooth down her hair before she came out. Following her lead, I flushed, too, and opened the cubicle door. Ava's eyes were red and she was dabbing at the corners of her mouth with a paper towel.

'Josie, I'm fine,' she said. 'Please stop worrying. I wasn't feeling crash hot and I got sick, okay? You're right — it was something I ate.'

'Was it pork? I've heard dodgy things about pork.'

'Look, I feel much better now, I promise,' she replied, ignoring my question. 'Let's just leave it.'

I noticed her gleaming diamond band wasn't threaded onto her finger. 'Ava, you're not wearing your ring. It didn't fall down the toilet, did it?'

'No, I'm ...' She faltered. 'It's at the jewellers, actually. They're giving it a polish for me.'

'Do they do that?' I said. 'Nice.' But I still couldn't shake the idea that something strange was up. 'So you're okay then? You're looking a bit pale and —'

'How dare you comment on how I look,' she snapped. 'Who do you think you are? Maybe you should learn to mind your own business.'

'I'm sorry, I was worried. I didn't mean anything —'

'You're right,' Ava interjected, her tone softening. She took a deep breath. 'I'm just tired, that's all.'

'It's fine.'

We both stood in silence, staring at the floor. I was ready to fire off another awkward question (tossing up between 'So, have you ever had a Brazilian wax?' and 'How tall are you?') when Ava beat me to it.

'So, got any plans on the weekend?'

It was the first time I'd heard her attempt small talk with a lesser being like me.

I wished I had something interesting to share, like, I'm learning trapeze, or going on a picnic with a hot guy, or travelling to an expensive beach house with a group of babes to bake brownies and ride retro bikes, but I didn't. My calendar was bare. Boring and bare. 'Not really. What about you?'

'Nothing too exciting.'

'Oh, cool.' It wasn't really, but I didn't know what else to say.

'Probably working on some ideas to show Rae, you know, for the internship.'

'Yeah. Yeah, for sure.'

Oh boo, I thought. Steph may not give a rat's about the internship prize money or by-line, but Ava's claws were hooked in deep. I didn't stand a chance.

Ava yanked the bathroom door open. 'Anyway, thanks

for the chat. Let's keep this embarrassing pork incident between us, okay?'

'You promise you're well enough to work? And I mean that in the nicest possible way,' I stammered, backtracking.

'I'm fine. I'll see you back in there.'

Ava stalked out before I could reply, leaving me alone at the basin.

The blank screen glared at me and I willed it to fill itself. It didn't. I closed my eyes, took a deep breath and sighed, wriggling my nose at the rich smell of coffee overpowering the office. The cursor flickered, menacing me with its slim, black line. Flash, flash, flash. My words had fled the building, probably to escape from my run-in with Ava, and I wanted to follow them. Instead, I was frozen in Esmeralda's chair while she was at a launch for compression pants or something equally bizarre. I couldn't get Ava throwing up out of my mind. Something felt wrong with the whole situation — I just didn't know what yet.

'How's it going? Nearly done?' Liani appeared at my shoulder. A glance at the computer showed her I wasn't nearly finished. Not even close. I hadn't even started except for the working title at the top: 'Josie and Billy interview'.

'Um … not quite.' I could barely make eye contact with Liani, not when she'd convinced Rae I was up to the task of interviewing Billy for the magazine.

'Not quite? Please tell me that blank page isn't the story?'

'Ahhhh …'

Liani crouched down next to me. 'What's going on? You're normally so quick.'

She was right. I was usually set to lightning speed whenever anything to do with writing was asked of me. I'd persevere until I got the job done, fuelled by nothing but passion (and sometimes an energy drink). But this time, I was deflated. I couldn't see past the cursor, let alone to the potential five thousand dollars and column by-line teasing me from the finish line.

Ever the mentor, Liani tried again. 'Josie, what's the matter?'

'I, ah, I don't know.' I stared at the computer. 'Sorry, I was just distracted. It's all good, I promise.'

'Tired after a long night up with your baby? Oh wait, that was me.' Liani smiled, then pulled up a chair next to me and sat down. 'Let's start it together, shall we?'

I pulled myself together. 'Thanks.'

For the next few minutes, Liani helped me to nut out the article's heading, introduction and first sentence. It seemed so easy with her by my side. She rallied the words together and ordered them into line. And when she rallied and ordered, they followed without a fuss.

'Great, Josie. You keep churning away, and pass it over as soon as you can.'

I kept writing after Liani left and, before I knew it, the feature was complete. A few re-reads and it was clean, tight and ready to show her.

I walked to Liani's office, knocked on the door and entered. She was reading a story on a website called *indi* (I established that from the bold red headline). I waited for her to notice me hovering, but she didn't, so I cleared my throat. Her head snapped up and she minimised the screen.

'Oh, Josie, hi.' She collected her thoughts. 'How'd you go? Need another hand?'

'Nope, all done.'

'Even better. Alright, hand it over.'

I passed it to her. Liani had a quick scan and beamed.

'Oh hon, the detail is fabulous — did he really say that about buying blue and pink baby booties, just in case?'

'Yep, they're not finding out the sex. They want it to be a surprise.'

'Brilliant. Rae will love it.'

Praise was addictive. I wanted more and I wanted it now.

'Is there anything else I can help with?' I asked, crossing my fingers for a fun assignment like choosing the half-naked models for the Hottest Guy of the Year photo shoot I'd heard Sia drooling about.

'Now that you mention it, a coffee would be great. Check with the rest of the team, too, okay?'

'Okay, will do.'

'Grab Rae a skinny cap; it's her favourite. Steph's helping Sia today, but Ava should be around if you need a hand carrying them back.'

I flinched at the mention of Ava, but Liani didn't notice; she'd already turned back to her computer. The sound of Ava's sobbing in the bathroom rang in my ears and, despite her asking me to keep what happened a secret, I couldn't bite my tongue for another moment. I needed to speak up. If it came to it, I'd deal with the fallout later. Besides, she'd probably be grateful if Liani let her take the rest of the afternoon off to get better.

'Um, Liani?'

'Mmmm?' She didn't glance up from her typing.

'I'm not sure how to say this, but there's something I need to tell you about Ava.'

I held my breath, wishing I could take the words back. But it was too late now. My confession hung in the air, reminding me I was officially the worst secret-keeper in the world. Probably in the universe.

Liani looked at me, her eyes locking on mine. 'Of course. Tell me everything.'

13.

The coffee run hadn't been too bad. I'd waited in line for seventeen minutes, got into a feisty debate with the barista over skim versus low-fat milk on Carla's behalf, and knocked over not one but two pots of decorative coffee beans on the way out. Who was I kidding? It was a disaster. But when I got back to *Sash* HQ it appeared I had everyone's orders right, after all. People nodded, smiled and sipped from their matching foam cups. Unless they spat their drinks into the bin when I turned my head, everything was on target.

The teary designer fleeing Rae's office should have been the first clue for me not to bother Rae. The shouting should have been the second. Standing outside her closed office door, her skinny cap clasped firmly in my hand, I could hear her forceful, raised voice.

'No, they just changed their minds,' she spat. 'There was nothing I could … It just happened. What was I meant to do, walk over to their office and force them to sign?' By now it was clear she was on the phone. 'I tried.

I more than tried, okay? It's this market. Look, we still have one more brand and I've got the paperwork ready to go. Forget the others, forget it ever happened ... Why? Because what's the point otherwise? Look, I'm doing my best, what else can I ... Okay. Okay. Okay. Fine. Sure. Bye.' She slammed the phone down. 'No, no, nooooo.'

She leaned back, flicked her bob and sighed. A long, drawn-out sigh that didn't match her power-woman persona. That kind of fed-up exhalation usually came from creatures further down the magazine food chain. Creatures like the mail boy, who got blasted for putting the domestic mail in the international mail crate. Creatures like me.

Rae looked up and our eyes met through the glass. Taking that as my cue, I opened her office door, wincing at its loud creak. Rae didn't say a word, which prompted my usual bumbling, stumbling need to fill the silence.

'Skinny cap. I got you one. A skinny cap, that is,' I blurted, palms sweating. 'Liani thought you might like one, so I went to get you one and, ah, well, here it is. Your favourite. It's a bit cold, though, I've been waiting for a while out there, so it might taste like rubbish. Actually, do you want me to get you another one? I'll get you another one.'

Rae's expression didn't change. 'That's fine, bring it over here, just mind the proofs.'

'The what?'

'Proofs. The shiny magazine pages on my desk? Forget it.'

I walked toward her, readjusting the cup in my hand for better balance. Then, in what seemed like slow-mo, I stubbed my toe on a leafy green plant in a bright yellow pot and tripped forward. The coffee cup lurched from my hand and its contents drenched the mountainous stack of proofs on Rae's desk.

'Oh crap!' I tried to blot the pages with a coffee-shop serviette. 'Let me help. If I just dab this and —'

'Stop it!' Rae said. 'Put that thing away and get out of here. You're making it worse.'

'I'm so sorry, one minute I was holding it, the next —'

'The next, *what*? What am I supposed to do? I have a presentation with these pages in fifteen minutes.'

'I think —'

'You know what I think? This internship program is more trouble than it's worth. Do you understand what you've done? Do you understand the hours that went into those proofs? The time and energy?'

My jaw tightened and I fought the urge to bite my fingernails. 'I swear it was an accident. The coffee slipped. If you'll let me help you —'

'I think you've done quite enough for today,' she spat. 'I learned a long time ago that if I want something done right around here, I have to do it myself. Now get out of my office.'

'Once again, Rae, I'm so sorry.' I lowered my head and walked toward her door.

'Josie?'

I turned hopefully. 'Yes?'

'Your Billy feature is weak and needs rewriting. Fix it before you leave today. I don't know what you were thinking. Well … clearly, you weren't.'

I walked out of her office feeling as though I'd been slapped in the face.

I made it to Sia's desk before bursting into tears. She wrapped her arm around me and whisked me away from prying eyes into the stairwell, waving Steph over, who was filling coloured bags with beauty products.

They didn't ask questions; Sia just rubbed my back and whispered, 'I know, she's a witch,' while I whimpered. I wanted to quit then and there. Damn uni requirements, I thought. The excitement of celebrity interviews and beauty products had lost its shine. But I needed the internship at *Sash* to pass the subject. And I needed the subject to pass the degree. And I needed the degree to become a journalist. I had to toughen up and plough on through the internship whether the editor hated me or not — and boy, she really hated me.

'Seriously, what's wrong with Rae?' I asked. 'Is she insane? It was an accident!'

'Insane, no; stressed, yes,' said Sia, her arm still

around me. 'The hawks are circling and they've got their eyes on her.'

'Hawks?'

'The bigwigs upstairs,' said Steph. 'They're crunching the numbers on *Sash* and they don't like what they see.'

'Why? What's not to like?'

'Our reader numbers are dropping, which can be a death sentence,' Sia said. 'And we're losing ads. Money's everything in this business, so when the bigwigs aren't happy, Rae hears about it. And when Rae hears about it, we hear about it. Circle of life.'

I still didn't understand. 'How do you guys know all this stuff? Does Rae tell you?'

'No way. I heard her bitching the other night while she was cooking dinner,' said Steph. 'Then she ate a bowl of carbolicious risotto the size of your head and *cried*. Until she realised I was in the next room and the I'm-practically-perfect-in-every-way facade went up again. She even tried to dish out some tips on organic living — 'cos shopping at an overpriced health store makes you a real greenie, apparently.'

'Maybe she was trying to bond with you?' I said.

'Maybe … but I wish she was more honest. If you're sad, be sad. If you're happy, be happy. Pissed off? Let it out. I can't handle her whole ice-queen thing. It's like she missed the memo that it's okay to show real emotions. You know what I mean?'

'Yeah.' I did. More than Steph realised, I thought, remembering Rae's late-night breakdown the other week.

'You know, J, you look like you could use a drink after your close encounter of the magazine-editor kind,' said Steph. 'And I'm not talking about apple juice.'

I smiled. 'Got any plans next week?'

Kat poked her head into my bedroom. 'Hey, birthday biznitch. Feel older since I last asked?'

I smiled. Despite our many, *many* differences, Kat always made a big deal out of birthdays. Earlier that morning, she'd woken me up (brave woman) to present me with a swag of helium balloons with 'I'm 18' printed on them, then she'd climbed into my bed with me and we'd shared chocolate cake.

Now, hovering in the doorway, she'd reverted to her usual bossy self. 'Jose, come into the kitchen.'

'Why?' I yawned, snuggling deeper under the blankets. 'Have you planned something?'

Kat scoffed. 'In your dreams. It's 10 am, time to move your lazy butt.'

I hopped out of bed and followed her into the kitchen, to be greeted by Mum singing a pitchy rendition of 'Happy Birthday'. The smell of fried bacon, eggs, roast tomato and hash browns had me salivating. Three glasses of orange juice sat on the counter top.

Kat began piling a plate with bacon and eggs.

'Darling daughter, let me say something first,' Mum said to Kat, rolling her eyes.

Everyone was beaming, laughing and giggling together. Just like we used to. You know, *before*. It felt wonderful.

Mum raised her glass of orange juice in a toast and Kat followed suit. I drifted off into a happy place as Mum talked, so only heard snippets of her speech — words like 'lovely', 'my favourite eldest daughter' and 'so very proud'. When she'd finished, I grinned at her like a goon.

Mum leaned across to kiss me on the cheek. 'Happy birthday, love,' she said.

'Thanks, Mum,' I said, squeezing her hand. I had a feeling there'd be another speech coming. And boy, I was right.

'Ohhh, love, it feels like only yesterday when I brought you home from the hospital. You were so small — my god, tiny — and wrapped in that pale green blanket which you didn't let me throw out 'til you were eleven —'

'Mum, I wasn't eleven and —'

'I was like a baby myself. I couldn't believe those nurses with their fancy clipboards and answers for everything trusted me to look after you.' Her eyes glistened. 'But here you are, my big girl, and I couldn't be more proud of you. Editing a magazine and —'

'Mum, I'm not the editor,' I said. 'I'm an intern. I don't even get paid!'

'Eighteen, I can't believe it.' She pretended to swoon, not listening to a word I said. 'Is this the age where you flee the nest?'

'Not quite ready to flee, Mum,' I said. 'You're stuck with me for a little while longer.'

She wrapped an arm around me. 'Happy to hear that. So you're not the editor?'

'No!'

'Oh, you'll have to explain it again later. It's all too glamorous for me to get my head around. Anyway, love, I'll serve us up a big brekkie, hey?'

Mum bustled off to the stove, straightening a square platter on the way, which looked fine to me. I grabbed Kat's hand and pulled her toward me.

'Mum seems better,' I whispered. 'I haven't seen her this excited for ages.'

'Yeah, she has her days,' Kat replied, chomping on a hash brown.

I raised one eyebrow, confused. 'What does that mean?'

'Sorry, that came out wrong,' she said, trying to back-pedal. 'I meant, yeah, you're right, she does seem better.'

Except I could tell that wasn't what she meant at all. I didn't get a chance to find out what was going on because Mum appeared next to me holding a small pile of colourful parcels.

'Preeeeeseeeeents,' she announced.

'They look awesome, but I told you not to worry,' I said. 'We're not exactly rolling in money right now.'

'Oh, don't be silly. Every birthday girl deserves presents.'

'Yeah, it's just a few books and a bracelet,' said Kat. 'Don't worry, they didn't cost much.'

Mum bristled. 'Kat, would you please —'

'But they didn't!' Kat laughed. 'Whatever, just open them, Jose.'

I reached for the first present.

14.

Angel, Steph and I were huddled into Tim's pint-sized bathroom. Angel was pressed up against the mirror, pouting and posing while she slathered her face in make-up; I was perched on the edge of the bath, wincing as Steph, standing in the tub, played with my hair. The room was soaked in perfume, a fitting scent for my first night out in the city. Steph's iPod pumped dance tracks, which sounded to me like fingernails being scratched down a chalkboard to a doof-doof beat.

'So what's your cousin's name again?' asked Steph.

'Tim.'

'Tim, Timmo, Timmy,' butted in Angel, swiping on an extra coat of mascara. 'He has a nice … name.'

We all laughed. 'He's only in the lounge room,' I said. 'His head will explode if he hears all this.'

'All done,' announced Steph, tapping me on the arm. 'Look in the mirror.'

I stood up to peek at my reflection over Angel's shoulder. Thanks to Steph's styling prowess, my hair now looked beautiful, not scruffy. She'd fashioned it into a half-up-half-down hairstyle: the top layer was pulled into a feminine fishtail braid that fell loosely over the rest of my hair, which Steph had curled into soft waves.

'Wow,' I gushed. 'If I could marry this hair, I would. Like, I'd frock up and walk down the aisle so we could be together forever.'

'It's stunning,' beamed Steph. 'I'll teach you how to do it sometime — it's so easy. Okay, I better do my make-up now. I don't want to look like a troll next to you two.'

Yeah, right, I thought. Steph was that rare breed of person who could wear a dress made of empty milk bottles and still look incredible.

Three quick knocks sounded on the bathroom door. For a moment I was taken back to the night when I'd met James and accused him of being a burglar. Then Angel snapped me back to reality.

'Is that Tim?' she mouthed.

'Shhh,' I hissed, then turned to face the door. 'Tim?'

'Cuz, can I grab you for a sec?'

I squeezed out of the bathroom and huddled with Tim in the hallway. 'What's up?'

'Nice dress,' he said, admiring the yellow fabric. 'Looks sweet.'

'Thanks. Kat loaned it to me.' Not that she knew it.

'So, ah, are you girls nearly done in there or what?'

'Yeah, nearly. You guys ready to head?'

'Er, there's been a slight change of plans.'

Tim led me into the lounge room. It stunk of boys, aftershave and alcohol — a potent mix. The guys — two skinny-jean-clad party boys called Luca and Tran — were asleep. Luca was on the couch with his mouth wide open, while Tran was curled up on the floor in the foetal position.

A snort of laughter exploded from me and I clasped my hand over my mouth. 'It's not even nine. What happened?'

Tim scratched his head. 'Dunno, they were just talking, then I guess they got comfortable, then fell asleep. That couch is damn comfy.'

I raised my eyebrow.

'Okay, they may have overdone it last night.' Tim swigged his beer. 'My bad. I'll get rid of them before we leave.'

I noticed Luca was drooling on my pillow. 'Oh, brilliant.'

'I'm still up for it and that's all that matters, right?' Tim said. 'Oh, and James can't make it either.'

My throat tightened. 'You invited him?'

'Yeah, roommate one-oh-one. But he's staying at what's-her-face's joint again.'

'All good, doesn't bother me.' Oh, but it did.

'We'll have a wicked time, especially if Stella can get us into that club,' he said. 'I've heard it's epic.'

'Steph, her name's Steph. Yeah, I think her brother's mate works the door.'

'I hope you're braced for the best night of your life, cuz.'

'I'm braced, Tim. I'm braced for anything.'

Lights pulsed and the crowd heaved. The four of us were packed into a corner of the dance floor, bumping into everyone who squeezed past. A couple nearby were grinding and kissing, almost losing their tongues down each other's throats. A lone older man in a navy suit bopped and swayed to the music while every woman in the bar avoided eye contact, lest he took it as an invite. A drunk redhead sloshed wine down my dress. Another guy blew cigarette smoke in my face.

'I thought smoking was banned in clubs now?' I coughed to Steph, trying to ignore the wine trickling down my back.

'Yeah, it is, but anything goes here,' she yelled. 'Chill out, birthday girl. Relax and dance.'

And so I did. I danced, I twirled, I popped my butt out like I was a girl in a video clip and only fell over once. Okay, twice. The second time I was trying a complicated move with Angel, but our legs got interlocked and I crashed to the floor. Luckily, the lights were so dim no one could see. Well, that's what I told myself.

A circle of girls danced next to us, their handbags piled in a heap in the middle of their group. One girl wore a tiara that flashed with the words '18 today'.

'Aww, Jose, we should've got you one of those,' said Angel. 'Friend fail number two.'

'I'll sort this,' said Tim.

He wandered over to the pack of dancing girls, and veered toward the one in the tiara. We watched Tim pull her aside to whisper in her ear. She listened, laughed, listened again. Then she took off her tiara, walked over to me and planted it on my head.

'Happy birthday to you, too,' she slurred, then grabbed my hand and dragged me to the bar.

My trusty trio scurried behind us, cheering.

'Birthday shots!' yelled Tim.

The girl, who I later found out was called Rachel, cheered when the bartender lined up our bright-blue drinks. Every time she woo-hooed, the nerves in my stomach clamped tighter. I'd never been a good drinker. The time I'd downed a shot of rum and impersonated Beyoncé in front of the most popular girls at school came to mind — if 'impersonating Beyoncé' meant falling over and gaining two bruises the size of butter plates on your butt cheeks. But there wasn't time to worry about that. Both groups — Rachel's girlfriends and my friends, who seemed to have formed a demented rumba line — egged me on.

'Drink, drink, drink,' they chanted.

I threw the fiery liquid down my throat and felt it burn and tingle. I let out a chain of swear words, then realised

I had another shot in my hand. Rachel grinned, clinked her glass with mine and we downed them.

I can't remember what happened next.

Well, that's not quite true. I'd love to say I excused myself, thanked Rachel for the drinks and went on my way, successfully ringing in my milestone birthday without injury or folly.

Ha! What actually happened next began as a simple dance with Steph and Angel. I flopped around, screaming along with the lyrics at the top of my lungs. In our minds, we were rock stars. In reality, we were three drunk girls and one extraordinarily loose guy gyrating around the dance floor.

It only seemed like minutes, but when I stumbled out of the crowd for a drink break, I was as thirsty as if I'd danced for hours. I slapped my palm on the bar and asked for water. Lots and lots of water. The bartender rolled his eyes and pointed to the end of the bar where empty glasses and a jug of water sat. I yelped with delight and snatched up the jug, splashing water everywhere. Enough made it into the glass and I drank from it as though I'd been deprived of liquid for a week. Water had never tasted so good. I went back for another glass. This time, I sent a wave of water flying over a stocky balding man who was standing next to me.

'Oh, sorry,' I blurted out. 'Here, let me help you.'

I reached over to brush at his shirt with an already-sopping napkin but he swatted my hand away.

'Rack off, kid,' he said, and stormed off, muttering to himself.

'Don't worry, his shirt looked cheap anyway,' a guy said behind me. I turned around to see Billy smirking in his usual annoying way.

'Billy!' I said, my voice rising to chipmunk levels of squeakiness. I wondered how much he'd seen. It didn't matter. It was clearly enough: the tiara, the drink stains on my dress, the way I was clinging onto the bar for dear life. Billy had arrived just in time to witness the Josie-turns-eighteen-like-an-idiot sequence. And there was probably enough footage for a sequel.

'Let me help you with that,' he said, leaning across to pour me another glass of water.

'Thanks.'

'So, eighteen, huh?' he said, pointing at the tiara.

I sipped my water. 'Yeah, I'm all grown up apparently.'

I swallowed, not sure what else to say. I found myself looking everywhere but at him. I stared at the bartender, who was shaking a cocktail; I eyeballed the poster-clad pillar in the middle of the club; I gazed up at the fluorescent light pulsating above the dance floor until I was almost sick with nausea. My head spun; the blue shots had clearly seeped through my system. I sensed

Billy's eyes tracing me from top to bottom, lingering on my face before moving further down.

'You look good, Josie.'

'Oh, I don't know about that,' I mumbled, tucking a sweaty strand of hair behind my ear.

'So, did you get enough info from our latest chat?' he asked. 'It was fun.'

'Thanks,' I said.

'I do hundreds of interviews with journos around the world — you're up there, trust me. Usually I struggle to stay awake because so many of them just drone on about themselves.'

I laughed. 'You're lying. I'm a total nobody! If you really knew me, you'd —'

'No way,' he interrupted. 'Your work's good. Fans have been printing off your articles and asking me to sign them.'

'Serious?' I couldn't believe it.

He shrugged. 'True story.'

And then it hit me. 'Speaking of fans, shouldn't you have a bodyguard or crew with you here?'

Billy pointed to a smoky roped-off area on the other side of the room. 'They're over there. I saw you by the bar and wanted to say hi.'

'Oh ...' He did? I almost blushed.

It was hard to see what Billy's entourage were up to — especially in my state — but I could make out a few details. A tall barrel-chested guard manned the rope, only lifting the bright-red cord for the sleekest of the club's visitors. I watched him let in a twenty-something woman in a blue minidress and silver platforms. She tossed her blonde hair and kissed the guard on the cheek before taking her place among the group. I was so out of my depth.

Suddenly, we were interrupted by three hyper-ventilating women shrieking Billy's name. Twin brunettes muttered, 'It's him, it's him' repeatedly to each other, while a redhead in a sparkly black dress pawed at his shoulder. 'Billy, I love you so much. Can I grab a signature?'

He laughed. 'Sure, darling. What's your name?'

'Hillary,' she said, breathing heavily. 'Can I get you to sign … here?'

Before anyone could stop her, she'd pulled down her dress and thrust a naked boob in his face. I repressed a snort of laughter while Billy played it cool.

'Darling, on second thoughts, maybe not today,' he said to Hillary and turned his back on the women. He clicked his fingers high in the air and two bodyguards appeared out of nowhere to drag the women away. The redhead's cries of 'But he didn't sign my boob' rang in my ears.

'So …' I said, trying not to laugh. 'Just another day in the life of Billy, huh?'

'Let me buy you a drink to make up for that,' he said. 'I'm used to being hassled, but I didn't wanna drag you into it.'

'It's fine, really, I'm not a big drinker ... usually. Anyway, I thought you couldn't drink any more after ... well, you know.'

'I can't. But you can. Seriously, I owe you. You've been good to me, you and *Sash*. Especially you. Plus, it's your birthday. I'm buying you one.'

This time I definitely blushed. 'Um, fine then — but not the blue shots. Anything but them.'

Billy smiled at me. 'I know just the drink. And I was wrong about saying you look good tonight ... you look great. Gorgeous, actually.'

He leaned over the bar and ordered my drink while I stood awkwardly behind him, flushed as red as a ripe tomato. Moments later he spun around holding a cosmopolitan cocktail. I hadn't seen any money change hands; the bartender had simply winked.

'Alright, you coming?' Billy gestured to his group sitting in the VIP section. 'We'll be able to hear each other talk better in there.'

'I better not, my friends will —'

'Probably not give a damn.'

I scoured the room and spotted them dancing in a large circle of excited Japanese businessmen. 'Okay, but just for a minute ...'

'Great,' said Billy.

As we walked over to the VIP section, his palm moved down onto my lower back, sending small tingles through my body. The guard lifted the red rope and, for the first time in my life, I was partying with the cool kids. Every second person had a cigar resting between their fingers. Bottles of champagne littered the low tables. If Holly Bentley could see me now, I thought. I recognised some of the other band members, either sipping wine or cuddling up to a hottie on a couch. Smaller groups of stunning (probably hand-picked) girls perched neatly on the couches, too, taking pouty photos of each other as they waited for their turn to chat with the guys.

Anthony — the other band member I'd accidentally annoyed mid-interview — made a beeline for Billy.

'Mate, what's going on?' he asked Billy, glancing at me. I knew he really meant, 'Mate, what are you doing bringing a random girl in here after everything that's happened with your pregnant girlfriend?'

'We're cool, bro,' Billy said. 'Just chill.'

Anthony sighed. Billy ignored him and led me over to a spot on one of the couches. It was black leather and gorgeous; it smelled of luxury and rich people.

'So, here we are.' Billy smiled. 'Cheers to us and a very happy birthday to you.'

'Why, thank you,' I replied and sipped on my cosmopolitan.

The couple to our left were getting increasingly caught up in their make-out session: the girl moaned softly while the guy pushed his body against hers. For the trillionth time that night, I blushed. And Billy noticed.

'So you know I think you're great, right?' he said.

I didn't get a chance to reply because suddenly he was pressing his lips against mine. The kiss was soft, unlike the kiss with Pete Jordan, and I felt myself give into it for a moment. But then I slapped him away. Hard. He had a girlfriend. A pregnant girlfriend.

'What are you doing?' I said, my words slightly slurred. 'What about Kara?'

'Is it because there are people around? Are you shy? Come back to my hotel then,' whispered Billy, nibbling on my earlobe.

'No, just ... no.' I pushed him off me. 'This never happened.'

I stood up and stormed out of the roped-off area, my head blurrier than ever. And that's when I saw him — James, standing at the bar, staring at me. He tipped his drink in my direction and gave me a small, stiff smile.

Oh crap, he must have seen the whole thing.

I didn't know whether it was the mix of drinks, the cigar smoke wafting through the room or the fact that a gorgeous-but-taken pop star had kissed me in front of James, but the urge to vomit hit me hard. Operation Find A Toilet Before It's Too Late was in full swing.

I lurched toward a darkened room, where I hoped to find the bathroom. Instead, I stumbled into a cocktail lounge with antique emerald-green lounges, vintage birdcages hanging from the ceiling and a stuck-up, well-groomed crowd. There were no fangirls in this room.

A waiter saw me with my hand clasped over my mouth and pointed in the other direction. 'Run,' he hissed.

I did.

I made the toilet stall, but the three milliseconds it took to get my head over the bowl were three milliseconds too many. There, in a five-star nightclub, I vomited down the back wall of the toilet cubicle.

Happy birthday to me.

15.

I'd done my best to clean up the vomit explosion on the bathroom wall, but apparently the definition of 'my best' differed greatly after a few shots. Drink-free Josie would have scrubbed, wiped and regrouted the tiles. Booze-hound Josie slapped at the wall with a tissue, then called it a day.

Walking out of the toilet cubicle was more embarrassing than the time Mum made Kat and me wear Stackhat bike helmets in the car after watching a disturbing news item on road fatalities. (There's more: she wore a neon yellow safety vest. And we passed Holly Bentley's family in their vintage Mercedes at the main streets' intersection.) But this was worse. Much worse.

When I'd entered the bathroom, it'd been empty, but as I hobbled out of the stall I was greeted by a queue of glamorous women with long hair and short dresses filing in the door. There was no escaping it. Someone was going to use that toilet. I searched for a good excuse to explain the avalanche of vomit within, but had to settle for stumbling over to a gorgeous red-lipped girl and slurring, 'Someone's been sick in there.'

I walked out to cries of 'Oh yuck' and 'I think it was her' but I didn't dare look back. When I spilled out into the club, dazed, I found James waiting for me. I glanced around, but the others were nowhere to be seen.

'You okay?' James asked, wrapping his arm around me.

I wasn't. My head was thumping, my stomach churned and my eyes were red, but I nodded anyway.

'Where to now, birthday girl?'

Wishing I had a mint handy, I leaned away from James and pursed my lips to prevent him from smelling my breath. 'Home.'

'Oh, okay. It's probably too late to head to your mum's but —'

'I meant your and Tim's place.'

He smiled. 'Our place it is.'

He led me through the crowd toward the exit. Tim and the girls were still dancing, this time with a group of cute hipsters rocking oversized glasses and cardigans. Arms flailing, Tim looked like an Energizer Bunny who could go all night; the other two weren't far behind him.

James waved Tim over, while I leaned against a pillar. 'Mate, I'm taking Josie back to ours,' he yelled over the music. 'She's not in a good way.'

'You serious? Her mum's going to kill me. And mine's going to celebrate at the funeral.'

'You coming?'

'Um …' Tim paused, soaking in the sight of Steph and Angel dancing. Even through my drunken stupor I could tell he was up to something.

'Hey, are you two staying at ours?' he called to the girls. It was impossible to tell which one he liked more.

'Do you have a bed for us?' Steph said cheekily.

'And clean sheets?' chimed in Angel.

'Yep,' Tim said. 'Green, grey or brown — take your pick.'

I hoped he and the girls shared the same definition of clean.

'Okay, we're in,' Steph said.

Tim beamed, no doubt planning an elaborate seduction back home. I was too tired to care. Too tired to worry about what might or might not go wrong. Too tired to do anything but let James lead me to the train station. The others walked behind us, shrieking with laughter at Tim's impersonations of Elvis Presley.

My feet had exploded with fiery red blisters, so when we got on the train I removed my heels and placed them on my lap. The last thing I remembered was mumbling to James, 'I really didn't think you were coming tonight,' then nodding off on his shoulder to the soft, rocking hum of the train.

* * *

The couch dug into my back. I tossed, turned and rolled around, but couldn't find a comfy position. The air was thick and stuffy; we'd forgotten to open a window when we got home. I'd only been lying down for an hour and my mind still raced and buzzed, pounding to the faint memory of the dance floor's beat. I lay flat on my back, wondering if I could be hungover if I hadn't gone to sleep yet. A hazy montage of the evening's events flashed across the ceiling like an old-fashioned slideshow. I saw the four of us laughing on the dance floor, Rachel giving me the tiara, the shots. Oh, the shots. I saw Billy smile at me, I saw Billy flirt with me, I saw Billy kiss me. I saw James see Billy kissing me.

And then, I just saw James.

For a second, I thought I'd slipped into one of my standard dreams (where I'd morphed into a six-foot babe and Summer ceased to exist), but then I realised I really was seeing James. He was hovering at the end of the couch holding a packet of lollies.

I sat up with a start. 'Hey!'

'Hey, how you feeling?'

'Okay, bit blurry. I thought I was … Never mind.'

'You did mumble something about a tall, hot guy called James.'

'I *what*?'

Oh crap, oh crap, oh crap. Maybe I had drifted off for a second? After all, that sounded *exactly* like something I'd say. Especially when I was still tipsy. Or hungover. Or somewhere in between.

James grinned. 'I'm kidding.'

'Funny.' I threw a pillow at him, then pulled myself further upright on the couch. 'I can't sleep.'

'Lolly?' he asked, offering the packet.

My big birthday night had caught up with me. Every fibre of me wanted to snatch the lollies from his hands and devour them. And a chocolate cake. With whipped cream. And a side of roast potatoes and corn slathered in butter.

Instead, I took one lolly. 'Thanks.'

James must have noticed the animalistic look in my eyes because he passed me the packet. 'Go on, birthday girl. I'll get you some water.'

As much as I wanted to play it cool and resist, who was I to decline him the pleasure of seeing me hoe into the lollies. I plunged my hand deep into the packet and licked the sugar off my fingers. 'Mmmmm,' I mumbled, content at last.

Without even realising, James had found the way (well, yet another way) into my heart. A Guy Who Brings Me Yummy Food was number six on my ideal-boyfriend wish list, followed closely by A Guy Who Makes Me Laugh Until I Cry Or Snort at number seven.

James came back with the water. 'So, you know what I realised about us?'

I wrapped the blanket around me, fireworks crackling and fizzing in my stomach. 'Umm ...' My usual verbal diarrhoea was zapped and I had no idea what he was going to say. More to the point, there was an *us*? I hoped whatever he said didn't end with 'That you're a total weirdo, Josie'.

'No, what?' I asked, afraid of the answer.

'We never did do the next episode of our show. You know, where you quiz me.'

I swallowed. 'That's true. Hey, can you pass me the water?'

James handed me the glass. 'So do you feel like slipping on your TV-host hat?'

'Now? I guess I could ask a question or two.'

'Awesome.' James sat down close enough for me to see every fleck of colour in his irises and the slight flush of his cheeks.

I held up a thick black marker to my lips to use as a microphone. 'Welcome to *Josie* ... Wait, I forget how to play this game. Do I ... or do you ... My head hurts.'

James laughed. 'Okay, maybe we should do it some other time. You need sleep.'

You're pushing away the hot guy, silly, my brain cried. I snapped myself to attention. 'Wait, no, I'll be okay,' I stammered. 'I promise.'

'Yeah?' He didn't sound so sure. And why would he? He'd seen my decline from geeky schoolgirl to trashy drunk girl.

'Yeah,' I said, sitting up straight. 'See … Okay, folks … Okay … Tonight's guest is a lovely, kind hero who rescues girls from themselves and brings them lollies when they're in distress. Ladies and gentleman, let's welcome the man of the hour … James.'

He threw his arms up in the air, pumping his fists and flexing his biceps. 'Thank you, thank you.'

'So …' My mind was blank.

'So …?'

My eyes rested on a pile of his vinyl records scattered in the corner of the lounge room. 'How many do you own?' Okay, not great, but I didn't know what else to ask.

'All up? Including the ones at Dad's place, one thousand two hundred and thirty-five. Three are missing, one's signed by the artist and seven are scratched.'

'Serious?'

'Nup. Probably more are scratched.' He winked.

'You really love your music, don't you?'

James paused. 'Yeah.'

'That's cool. I've heard you fooling around in your bedroom, you know?'

'What?' James blurted.

'I mean with music! Fooling around in your bedroom with music and equipment and … You know what I mean.'

James grinned and shook his head. 'Aren't you meant to be asking questions?'

Yes. Yes, I was.

'Okay, question … So if you're so into music, why are you studying IT? I mean … *IT*. I've never seen you at a computer. Do you own one?'

'Yes,' he laughed, pointing to a closed laptop under a pile of newspapers on the counter. 'Um, IT … well, it's Dad's dream, I guess. Safe bet and all that. Everything's online these days.'

'Yeah … that's what my dad said too,' I muttered.

'Really?'

'Yeah, among other things. Not that he'd buy me a laptop, even though I'd have loved one for my writing … But this is about you, remember,' I said, quickly steering us back on track. Despite sharing everything else with James, I wasn't ready to go into the details of Dad's disappearing act just yet. Luckily, James was too swept up in his own dad drama to notice.

'I mean, what are my chances of becoming a successful music producer, anyway? Like, honestly. One per cent or something?'

'Maybe.'

'I want it, but … I don't know. Dad planted a toxic seed in my head and I can't shake it. I figure I'll work at the music store, do this stupid degree, then join the rat race like everyone else.'

'I just can't see you as an IT geek spouting one-liners like "Have you tried restarting your computer, ma'am?"' I teased him.

'"Are you sure it's plugged in properly?" is another favourite,' he added. 'High-tech stuff, I know.'

I laughed. 'So, James,' I put on an over-the-top American accent, 'I think it's time we got down to business.'

'Okay,' he grinned. 'Bring it.'

'What would you say is your deepest, darkest secret? Any secret marriages or love children we should know about?'

James paused and, for a second, I swear my heart stopped. 'No, nothing like that. But now that you mention it, I do have a secret.'

'Oh? Care to share it?' I said, gesturing to our imaginary TV studio audience.

'It's pretty controversial.'

The possibilities pelted through my brain: he's into pottery; his favourite colour is dusky pink; he's a born-again virgin.

I swallowed. 'Well? What is it?'

'Here.' James stood up and held out his hand. 'I'll show you.' He pulled me up from the couch and spun me around, wriggling his hips.

'What's going on?' I asked, trying to keep up, but with no idea which foot should go where. The touch of his hands grazing my body almost made me forget my head was hurting, my throat was drier than the Australian outback and my toes were blistered. Almost. 'Seriously, what are you doing?'

'*Dancing*, birthday girl. You wanted a juicy secret — well, my mum's a salsa teacher and, ah, I've picked up a few moves.'

There was no music, just the soft breathing of us keeping up with each other and the tick, tick of the clock. And then James began to hum a beat and slowly, surely, I caught up with him, meeting him in the moment. We danced around the lounge room, and even though I tripped over fallen cushions, and stray shoes and, once or twice, James's feet, I didn't care. All that mattered was the humming, the dancing and James.

'You're pretty good,' I said.

I was so comfortable by now that I was resting my head on his shoulder. He didn't flinch, push me away or tell me to rack off. I don't know whether it was the excitement of feeling James's heart pounding through his chest against mine or my natural bad timing kicking in, but I ruined the moment by saying, 'So, does Summer like dancing with you, too?

I felt James's hands and body stiffen. 'Ah, no, not really,' he said, his voice trailing off. 'It's not her thing.' He dropped my hand and took a step back. 'Um, you know, I'm pretty tired … I should probably get to bed.'

'Oh, okay.'

'Sorry to pike, but you know ... big night and everything.'

'All good. I was counting down until sleep, anyway.' Liar.

'Yeah, you've had a long day — night — what with the dancing, that famous dude —'

'No, that was nothing. It meant nothing.'

I wanted to shake him until he believed me. More than anything, I wanted to press rewind on tonight and start over.

'Happy birthday, Jose.' He pecked me on the cheek. 'Sweet dreams.'

'Okay ... thanks for everything and, ah, say hey to Summer,' I said weakly, but James had already disappeared into his bedroom, leaving me alone again.

So far, eighteen wasn't feeling too different from seventeen: my clothes were a little more stained, boy dramas were a little more complicated and my mind was just that little bit fuzzier.

I managed to sleep until the sun pushed its way through the blinds and beat down on me. I had no idea what time it was, so I fumbled for my phone to find out. It wasn't next to the couch, hiding under the coffee table or tucked away on the kitchen bench.

I'd better not have lost it, I thought, but it was a possibility. A big possibility. I only hoped I hadn't dropped it into the nightclub's loo. Or left it on the train after the seedy ride home. Or on the table in Billy's VIP section. I didn't know which would be worse.

I couldn't even borrow someone's phone and call the club to see if I'd left it there, because I'd flaked on its name. It was the Lemon Tree. Or the Lemon Treehouse. Or Lemon Treacle? It definitely had 'lemon' in the title, I knew that much.

Despite the buzz of the city outside (not to mention the buzzing inside my head), the apartment felt still. The only exception was Tim's snoring rattling from his bedroom. I wondered if the girls were asleep in there, and if they were, how? He sounded like a rusty lawnmower trying to rev up on a summer's day.

Yawning, I turned on the television and flicked through the channels. I clicked past the Greek news, Italian news and Chinese news and landed on Channel 3, which was halfway through its morning news and lifestyle program, *First*. You know the type: attractive female host, cheesy male host. I nestled into the couch for some mindless viewing with a dash of napping thrown in.

The hosts, Cynthia and Arch, bantered with each other and every now and then a phrase or a giggle would stir me awake. I drifted in and out, until a deeper voice said 'Next up, our new favourite segment, "A Woman's

World". Let's welcome to the studio the lovely Rae Swanson, editor-in-chief of *Sash* magazine and guru on all things celebrity, relationships and fashion.'

Rae Swanson? *Sash* magazine? My eyes snapped open to see Rae on the screen, colour-blocking the hell out of a burnt orange blouse and deep purple pencil skirt. She looked outstanding.

'Pleasure to be here, Arch,' she said, pouting. She'd flicked her personality to charm-the-pinstriped-socks-off-the-TV-host mode today.

'Now, Rae,' chimed in Cynthia, 'we want to gauge your thoughts on something that hits the media time and time again: celebrity relationships and marriages. Can they ever work? Chelsea Mancini from Melbourne has written in saying yes, while Georgi Craft from Kalgoorlie says a big fat no. What do you think?'

I watched in awe as Rae nailed her answer. She said there were many high-profile people in loving, happy relationships but they worked hard to stay strong and took nothing for granted. She gave examples of celeb couples who'd survived through tough times, even adding that it took real commitment to stay together under such nonstop media scrutiny.

'But it's not all roses and happy days, is it?' butted in Cynthia. 'Many experts say infidelity appears to be on the rise. In fact, based on the photos taken of Billy from Greed last night, we'd have to agree.'

'Photos?' asked Rae, sitting up higher in her seat.

Oh no, I thought, my heart pounding. I could already tell this was *not* good.

'Billy was caught on camera last night with his tongue down a young brunette's throat at Limestone nightclub,' chimed in Arch, while Cynthia tutted loudly. 'Meanwhile, as we all know, he has a pregnant girlfriend at home.'

Limestone nightclub? So much for Lemon Tree. Although limes and lemon were both in the citrus fruit family.

'In fact,' continued Arch, 'here are the photos now. This is a *First* exclusive.'

Please don't be me, I willed on repeat in my head. Please tell me Billy made out with some other poor sucker after I left, even though that would make him an even bigger ass-hat.

A slideshow of pictures flashed across the screen: Billy with his arms wrapped around the 'mystery brunette'. His lips were pressed against hers, so her face wasn't clear; in fact, all I could see was a hint of nose and flushed cheek. Her hair was thick and wavy with a fishtail braid and her dress was bright yellow, tight at the waist and covered in what appeared to be splashes of something. Probably water. Or wine. Or shots.

Arch and Cynthia had no idea who the mystery girl was, but I knew for sure, absolutely, without a doubt in my mind, that it was me.

Rae had done a double-take when she saw the photos. I waited, barely breathing, for her to reply.

'Well,' Rae said, 'you've caught me off guard with this. I'm shocked. I can truly say I thought Billy was a changed man.'

'So did we,' said Cynthia. 'After that last exclusive interview in your magazine he had the nation fooled. But this shows, once a cheater always a cheater. My heart breaks for the mother of his future child.'

'So, Rae, what do you think this means for Billy's ongoing appeal in Australia?' asked Arch. 'And any thoughts on the identity of the mystery girl?'

Rae pursed her lips. 'I don't think it matters who the girl is, Arch. What I think matters is that Billy has done this again, after claiming that he'd turned over a new leaf.'

'Absolutely,' agreed Cynthia.

'It's going to be a tough day for everyone in the Greed camp,' continued Rae. 'This is bad, bad news for his image ... and for the girl if the media find out who she is. Hopefully she's smart enough to stay out of the limelight and not repeat her mistakes.'

I couldn't help wondering if she was speaking directly to me. But maybe that was just the overwhelming guilt screaming in my ears.

Suddenly, I heard my phone ringing. Brilliant, I hadn't left it at the club. The ringtone sounded muffled, like the phone was trapped under something. I hopped off the couch and hunted for it. I followed the noise across the carpet, into the kitchen, opened the fridge and there it was: buzzing and beeping on a block of cheese. What happened here last night? I didn't want to know.

Kat's name was flashing on the screen. I answered.

'You little tart,' she said.

'Hello to you, too,' I spluttered.

'You made out with Billy and you didn't even tell me?' she hissed in a loud whisper. I took that as a good sign; at least she wasn't shouting down the house and neighbourhood. Although, if I knew Kat, that would probably come later.

'I, ah … what?' I mumbled.

I was a terrible liar, just like Mum. If only I'd taken those acting classes she'd bought me when I was eleven to improve my confidence. I'd bailed at the last minute; ironically, I hadn't felt confident enough to go.

'Dude, don't lie to me,' whispered Kat. 'I saw you on *First* — they had a photo and everything.'

'Oh, that?' I said, my voice squeaking into borderline rodent territory. 'I saw that too. It was so … blurry. I wonder who it was. I'm thinking the girl who hosts that afternoon kids' cartoon show, or maybe —'

'Josephine Browning, I'd recognise that yellow dress anywhere. Cinched waist, low back, smoking neckline … and currently missing from my wardrobe.'

'I can explain,' I said, although I wasn't quite sure how.

'You better start talking, Jose. You better start talking right now.'

16.

I've seen some awful things in my time. There was the Saturday afternoon when the neighbours' puppy, Twinkles, darted, skipped and squealed through oncoming traffic and only just made it safely to the other side of the road. The night when Kat and I — by mistake — busted in on Uncle Reg reading the paper on the loo (I've knocked every time since). And let's not forget the scarring experience of seeing Mr Stevens, my Year Nine geography teacher, scratching his junk with a ruler under the desk when he thought no one was looking. But nothing could have prepared me for what I found when I went online after my phone conversation with Kat.

I borrowed James's dusty laptop and opened Google. In the short time since *First* had broken the story about Billy cheating with a 'mystery girl', the internet appeared to have exploded with hate toward me. There were blog posts, tweets and comments, each more passionate, brutal and angry than the next. Most of the news websites' entertainment sections carried a cobbled-together story accompanied by a blown-up photo of Billy kissing me. I read every article I could find and realised that eighty per cent of them were filled with flat-out lies. According to one report, 'a source close to Billy said it was a huge misunderstanding — the girl threw herself at him and he was caught off guard by her passionate kiss'. Um, no. In another, 'the girl reportedly propositioned Billy, who has a child on the way, for a one-night stand at a nearby hotel'. *What?!*

Kat had warned me against going online, and now I could see why. I — or rather, 'mystery girl' — was denounced as a skanky tart who'd tried to steal the vulnerable pop star away from his pregnant girlfriend.

Everyone had an opinion. People who didn't know the real me. People who didn't know I was just a nerd who placed way too much emphasis on getting good grades. People who didn't know my little sister had to dress me for my first big-city interview. People who didn't know I never got invited to parties, had never had a boyfriend for longer than five days and had the scheming seductress abilities of a drunk slug.

The online trolls called me everything from an 'ugly moll — he deserves better', to a 'stupid scrag with a body like a ten-year-old boy'. I tried to laugh at the ones with typos ('Your a dikhead'); however, the grammatically incorrect death threats made that harder. A few people jumped to my defence ('I'd pash him too'), but overall society seemed to have banded together and decided that I, Josie, aka 'mystery girl', was a terrible human being with a surfboard chest. (More posts than I care to remember mentioned my lack of boobs.)

The truth was, part of me had always wanted to be famous. I'd imagined a book launch with crowds of loving fans showering me with flowers and chocolates and begging for my autograph. And now here I was: infamous.

I just wondered who else knew it was me in the photo.

Angel took charge the moment I busted into Tim's room to confess what was going on. She woke up Steph, who had been drooling next to her in the bed, and dragged both of us into the lounge room to debrief. Tim remained comatose on a pile of clothes on the bedroom floor, oblivious to the unfolding drama. James was still in his room — he hadn't come out since our embarrassing/ amazing/awkward encounter the previous night.

'So this could be worse,' started Angel.

Steph yawned. 'Agreed.'

Mascara was smeared over both of their faces. I was sure mine was no different.

Angel pointed at the photo on the website. 'You can barely tell it's you. I mean, *we* know it's you, obviously. But that's it.'

'And Kat,' I reminded them.

'Do you really think Rae could recognise you from this photo?' asked Angel. 'I don't think so.'

'Although,' muttered Steph, 'I'm trying to remember if I told Rae where we were going out for your birthday.'

I sighed. 'If she knows it was me then I'm screwed.'

'Calm down.' Angel patted my back. 'Look, is there any food here? I'll fix us something for breakfast. Maybe that'll help.'

Bless her — she knew that food was always the answer for me. She walked into the kitchen to explore the cupboards, fridge and freezer.

'I'm sure I didn't tell Rae,' said Steph. 'You're safe, I promise. Anyway, what's the worst that can happen if she does find out?'

'If the *Sash* editor-in-chief finds out that I hooked up with my interviewee, who happens to have a girlfriend and a baby on the way?' I said, my jaw aching with tension. 'I don't know ... what do you think? Give me an "F" for the uni subject? Fire me? Blacklist me from every publication in Australia? Judge me for being a terrible person?'

'Well, when you put it like that ...' said Steph sheepishly.

'I'm sorry, I didn't mean to snap,' I said. Being tired wasn't doing me any favours.

Angel popped up from behind the kitchen counter holding a loaf of bread. 'Maybe it's not that bad, Jose. I mean, maybe —'

'It's on all the gossip websites,' I blurted out. 'They've shamed me as the "mystery tart from Down Under". Their followers are chiming in with awful comments too. One troll called me "Slutty the bush skankaroo".'

Steph sniggered. 'That doesn't even make sense.'

'Okay, so that's not ideal,' agreed Angel, trying not to laugh. 'But it's still anonymous. And heaps of people are laying into Billy too — don't forget that. *He's* the cheater. No one knows it was you. Not Rae, not the media, not anyone. You're safe.'

'But what do I do at *Sash* tomorrow?' I bleated. 'Should I confess?'

'No,' said Steph. 'Absolutely not. Deny, deny, deny, baby. You've done nothing wrong, so keep those pretty lips shut.'

James's bedroom door creaked open and he stumbled out, dressed in nothing but boxer shorts. He pulled on a crumpled blue T-shirt, but not quickly enough to stop me from catching a glimpse of the light dusting of hair on his chest.

'Morning, ladies,' he croaked, before planting himself on the couch. I could barely make eye contact with him after the previous night. 'How are you feeling?'

Silence. The girls looked at me for guidance.

'Fine, a bit tired. Angel's going to cook up some toast,' I said, putting on my best faking-it-until-I-make-it voice. 'Want some?'

'Sure, thanks.' He yawned. 'Man, have you guys seen Tim's pics of you all last night? Hilarious.'

'Oh, I forgot about those …' Steph laughed. 'I have vague, very vague memories.'

'Tim's pics?' butted in Angel.

'Yeah, there's a few of Jose and Steph pulling faces, you doing the splits — that's nuts, by the way, Angel — and a few selfies of him. Poser,' he said. 'Hey, can I grab honey on my toast? Ta.'

I exhaled. 'For a second I thought you were going to say he had pics of … Never mind.'

The less James had to be reminded about Billy kissing me, the better.

'Yeah, they're on his Facebook — he's tagged you all so you can check them out,' he added. 'That dude loves a late-night tagging spree.'

'He tagged us?'

I hated those terrifying words. The last time someone tagged me I was dressed as Bugs Bunny, wearing fake buck teeth and chomping on a gnawed carrot. Not exactly the image I wanted to portray to five hundred and sixty-one of my closest so-called 'friends'.

'Yeah. So?' James said, looking puzzled.

'In these photos, Jose's hair's all pretty and braided, right?' muttered Steph. 'And she's wearing the yellow dress?'

'Yeah, I guess,' said James.

'And if I'm tagged in the photos, then all my friends can see them, too, right?' asked Steph.

'Yeah,' said Angel.

'Jose, I almost don't want to say this, but I'm friends with Rae on Facebook.'

'You can't be,' I said, my voice rising.

'I am — we added each other after she and Dad started ... well, doesn't matter.'

'Oh my god,' I stammered. 'She knows ... Rae knows ... she must.'

'Let's all take a breath,' said Angel, waving a tub of honey at us. 'It may still be okay if we take the photos down right now.'

'What's going on?' James's face showed his confusion.

I hung my head in my hands as the smell of toast filled the apartment. I wasn't going to be the one to explain. It was bad enough that James had seen the kiss in real life; he didn't need an encore performance.

After breakfast, Steph and Angel hid James's laptop because they didn't want me logging on and drowning in the madness of evil trollers. But they'd forgotten about my phone and I didn't remind them. Angel begged me to join her on the train trip home but, as much as I wanted to get back to Mum, it was my internship day at Sash the next morning. I was staying put, whether I wanted to or not.

Once the girls left, I scrolled through Twitter, shocked by how much venom people could inject into one hundred and forty characters. Not only were they firing off evil comments about Billy, the 'mystery girl' and Greed, but they'd even started the hashtag *#Billynastyhookup*, which was now trending worldwide. Brilliant. Reading through all this rubbish while lying buried under a blanket on the couch was my punishment. And what a punishment it was: some of the tweets were just plain cruel. 'I hope she dies from glandular fever — Billy's mine, bitch lol' was one that stood out. The fact that glandular fever fatalities were extremely rare didn't ease my pain.

I pulled the blanket over my head and buried my nose in the pillow. The aching feeling of tears rising took over until I couldn't hold them in any more. I sobbed, convulsing under the blanket, leaving a stream of day-old mascara on the pillowcase.

'Hand the phone over, Jose,' a guy's voice said, startling me out of my meltdown.

I lowered the blanket and looked up, wiping my face to remove evidence of my ugly-cry. James stood there with his palm thrust out.

'Hand it over,' he repeated. 'The others told me what's happened. Tim's photos have been taken down so you're in the clear. C'mon, you've punished yourself enough.'

I shook my head, lips trembling. 'Someone's even started a blog about the kiss. It's filled with pictures of stuff they'd rather see Billy kiss than me — or "mystery girl", whatever. There's a freaking grand piano on the list. And a half-eaten apple. What's wrong with people?'

'Man, some people have too much spare time,' said James, prying the phone out of my hand. I threw the blanket over my head once more, and he pulled it down to look me in the eye. 'Do you want to talk?'

I couldn't reply; if I did, tears would stream down my cheeks again.

'Jose … are we cool?' he said. 'I mean, I know I kind of rushed off last night …'

I nodded.

'You know, not that it matters but I saw the kiss and it looked like nothing to me. I mean … it meant nothing to you, right?'

'Yeah, totally, it meant nothing,' I said, finally finding my voice.

'And I saw you slap Billy away — you really clocked him one,' James added.

That made me smile. 'I did, didn't I?' I sat up on the couch and pulled the blanket around me. 'Must have been all the years of practising with Mum's tae-bo DVDs. Er, I mean … all those cool, super-tough boxing classes I've done.'

James shook his head at me. 'That's an image I won't forget.'

'Argh, I can't believe I'm back at *Sash* tomorrow,' I moaned, changing the subject. 'The last time I was there Rae ripped my head off. What if she knows? Like, *knows* knows? I'm so nervous I could puke.'

'Again?' he joked.

'Hey!' I blushed at the memory of my epic birthday chunder.

'You're going to kill at this internship, I know you will,' he said.

I just hoped he was right.

Outside the meeting room, voices rose and fell, making it impossible for me to catch a full sentence. The wall was opaque glass so I couldn't see who was doing the talking. I peeked at their ankles, visible through a strip of clear glass that ran across the bottom of the wall. Rae's stick-like ankles in red peep-toe heels were recognisable; there weren't many women with legs as slim as hers. The other shoes looked like Liani's black ballet flats. I hoped it was her.

This check-in meeting had been planned weeks ago, as part of the uni curriculum, but I couldn't shake the thought that I was about to get in trouble. I hadn't spoken to Rae since the coffee-spilling incident and I had no idea whether her detective skills had uncovered me as Billy's mystery girl. Steph assured me that Rae hadn't mentioned anything to her about Billy, the nightclub or me, so I was counting on that. My only backup plan if she did ask was 'deny, deny, deny'. I had to survive the next ten minutes without ruining everything. Simple enough.

My mind drifted to Billy. He'd be so used to scandals this would be barely a blip on the radar; just a minor anecdote to include in his memoirs. He'd already appeared on *News At Nine* to share his side of the story (translation: he spruiked lies about what went down) and rumour had it *Marilyn* magazine was trying to lock in a contract with him to secure the first baby photos. He'd flown the I'm-human-and-everyone-makes-mistakes flag for the past twenty-four hours. While he may have convinced the mum of his future child, I wasn't buying it. Not one bit.

The meeting room door creaked open and Rae and Liani filed in, holding folders, magazines and notepads. Rae's lips were pursed (Steph called it her 'constipated duck face'), while Liani was smiling and warm as usual.

Rae didn't say anything throughout the meeting. Her face remained impossible to read, probably due to Botox. Instead of talking, she glared: at Liani, at her phone, at me (of course), at the pot plant in the corner. Nothing escaped her evil eye.

Liani did most of the talking, about the history of *Sash* magazine (it had been going for thirteen years and counting), the changes it had gone through (from quarterly, to bi-monthly, to monthly) and the staff (Rae had been the editor for six years and had moulded the *Sash* brand to what it was today). She reminded me the industry was in a state of flux, that over the last few years many print magazines had closed down, which served as a constant reminder to perform at the highest level.

I nodded after each point, unsure what any of this had to do with my internship.

'Any questions so far?' asked Liani, flushed pink from talking so much.

'No, that's all pretty clear,' I said. I'd read most of it on the company website.

'Any questions about your internship?' she pressed. 'Are you enjoying it? Happy with what you're getting to do? Keen to try something else?'

'Um ... nope, yes, yes and nope,' I joked. Liani beamed back. Rae didn't. 'Look, I can't get enough of the writing side of things,' I went on. 'It's been amazing. But more than anything, I want to apologise again for the other week when I spilled coffee everywhere. I'm such a klutz and ... I'm working on it, I promise.'

'Oh, that's fine,' said Liani. 'We haven't thought about it since. You're doing great.'

I glanced at Rae out of the corner of my eye. Still nothing. The woman made ice sculptures look like warm cuddly teddy bears.

Liani continued. 'Anyway, Josie, we'll make sure you continue to spend plenty of time with the features department while you're here. Eloise hasn't stopped raving about your work, so that won't be a problem. Sia's been singing your praises, too.'

'Great. Thanks!'

'Anyway, enough from me,' she said, standing up. 'This meeting was a box to tick, really. I'll be sure to let your professor know that everything's on track. I'll, ah, leave you to it then. Any questions, you know where to find me.'

'Chained to your computer?' I said.

'Always.' Liani rushed from the room, no doubt off to another meeting or some kind of product launch. Or maybe a phone call from her husband asking where the baby wipes were kept. I followed her lead and started packing my things.

'Wait a second, Josie,' said Rae, breaking her silence. She leaned forward and rested her elbows on the table. 'Do you have a minute?'

'Sure ...' Half-confused, half-excited that Rae was talking to me again, I lowered myself back into my seat. But then fear swamped my body: she knew; *she knew about Billy and me.* I needed a lie-down.

Rae swished her bob. 'I've got a quick story that you may appreciate ...'

'Okay.' I hoped it didn't conclude with 'Now get out of this office and never come back'.

'Years ago — it doesn't matter how many — I was working as a sports journalism cadet for a major paper in the city.' She paused for effect. 'Ambitious wouldn't even begin to describe me back then. When I got the job, I was out of my depth: I knew nothing about cricket, netball, hockey, football, but I didn't care — I learned and I learned quickly. I wanted to make it as a journalist. I was hungry for it. I wanted to be the best.'

Her voice was dipped in nostalgia. I waited to hear more.

'And then I had an interview that changed my life,' she said. 'He was twenty-five, a famous footy player. It was a real win for the newspaper, and for me. You know the drill: gorgeous, athletic, rich — but he was also married with a child. Happily married, or so everyone believed. I only interviewed him once, but that's all it took. Another journo from a rival paper saw him squeezing my butt as I left the room. *Him* squeezing *my* butt.'

Rae trailed off. I realised I was holding my breath in anticipation.

'By the afternoon, the story had morphed into a nightmare. So-called sources claimed we'd slept together, my colleagues were disgusted, and the media branded me "Home-wrecking Rae". It was devastating, and got worse when the paper stood me down. I was on leave with pay, but I didn't care about the money. I was disgraced — and I hadn't done anything wrong.'

This was starting to sound eerily familiar.

'The player made it worse,' Rae went on. 'He gave interviews, made up stories about me, blamed me for seducing him. As if he had no control over his own actions.'

'What happened next? Did his wife leave him?'

Rae raised an eyebrow. 'Not straight away. But two years later she caught him cheating with his sports physiotherapist. She took him for everything he had. Last I heard, he'd gained twenty kilos and was living in his sister's spare room.'

My mind buzzed with questions. 'Who was he?'

'It's yesterday's news, Josie. It blew over. Just like Billy's story will … if you know what I'm saying?'

Rae was being about as subtle as a cricket bat over the head, but I gave her credit for not shrieking, 'You made out with Billy in public, you self-centred little brat!'

'I do,' I said, almost whispering. 'I know exactly what you're saying.'

'Good. Oh, and Josie?'

'Yes?'

Rae pursed her lips once more. 'No more clubbing with Steph for a while, okay?'

17.

'Well?' demanded Kat, slurping her milkshake. 'Details, Jose.'

I shrugged. 'There's nothing to tell.'

'Do you want me to say it? Fine. I'll say it. I've totally got over the fact you were a bit of a nothing at school and am deadset jealous of you right now. There, are you happy?'

'Bit of a nothing? Give me some of that milkshake.' I leaned across the table and grabbed Kat's glass. But my attempt to change the subject from my non-pash with Billy was short-lived.

'Seriously, what a guy,' she sighed. 'Now, what really happened between you two?'

'Can you lower your voice?' I whispered, gesturing around the cafe. Our old neighbour, Mrs Pratt, was sipping a cappuccino at a nearby table. She was renowned for her grade-A eavesdropping skills so I didn't want to take any chances. 'Nothing. Nothing happened, okay?'

Kat raised her eyebrow. 'Nothing's what people say when something happened.'

'Or maybe it's what people say when *nothing* happened,' I argued, my voice growing louder than I'd planned.

'But there's more to it than the one-second peck on the lips Billy's claiming, isn't there?'

I paused for a second too long.

'Oh my … what happened?' spluttered Kat, leaning across the table. 'You saw his thing, didn't you?'

'No! What do you know about … *things*?'

Kat rolled her eyes. 'Nothing yet. I'm waiting for you to tell me.'

'There was a kiss. A bit of a kiss. I slapped him away, that was it.'

'Tongue?'

I paused. 'Kat, you can never tell anyone this. Mum would freak. You've seen all that stuff online.'

'She'd just be stoked that a guy tried to … No way.' Kat's eyebrows furrowed into a frown.

I turned to see what had caused her reaction. It was obvious within seconds: Pete Jordan stood in the cafe doorway and he wasn't alone. His hairless, fake-tanned arm was wrapped around a blonde girl who was about the size of my pinkie finger. I recognised her from Kat's year — Stacey something.

They weaved their way through the cafe, squeezing past tables, dodging coffee-carrying customers. As they neared my and Kat's table I held my breath in anticipation of some kind of apology. Something along the lines of 'I'm sorry for treating you like a piece of meat at the party,' probably delivered on bended knee.

Instead, Pete walked right past, squeezing Stacey's hand and whispering in her ear. He saw me, for sure, but he simply stuck his greasy nose in the air and soldiered on.

'Did you see that?' I hissed at Kat, who was glaring at them.

They took a seat at a table in the corner, kissing, rubbing noses and cuddling.

My stomach lurched. 'Ergh, let's get out of here.'

I walked up to the counter to pay our bill. The staff were rushing around, bumping into each other as they served coffees, sliced bread and arranged muffins. They didn't function with the well-oiled efficiency of the city baristas and waiters. Finally, after suffering through five people's coffee orders, it was my turn. I handed over the money, and then I heard her. *Stacey*. She was whispering into her phone, but loud enough that I could make out every word. She may as well have come up and yelled in my face.

'Yeah, yeah, it's her, the frigid one. Yes, here in the cafe. That's what I said! I mean, clearly she's not all that. Exactly. I know, right? You should see what she's wearing, too — I mean, c'mon, get with it. Yeah, okay. Yep. I'll call you tonight.'

Teeth clenched, I took my receipt. I'd already slapped one person this week, and if I didn't leave the cafe in the next five seconds, I was about to boost that to two.

Standing on the driveway, Kat and I could hear Mum's raised voice thundering from the house.

'She must be on the phone to Aunt Julie,' Kat whispered. 'Quick, c'mon.'

'What now?' I muttered. Running into Pete and Stacey at the cafe was bad enough. Was Aunt Julie telling Mum about my drunken night with Tim and the girls? I didn't know how much more my nerves could handle.

Kat and I raced up to the house and burst through the front door. The scene that greeted us was so bizarre it would have been funny if Mum didn't look so distraught. Mum was blubbering into the phone and waving a frozen chook around in the air, holding it by its scrawny right leg. Our ratty old children's toys, clothes, books and CDs in cracked cases littered the carpet. I noticed a broken vase in the corner. It looked like the one Dad had bought Mum for their anniversary a few years ago.

'What's going on?' I asked, voice raised. 'Mum?'

'Yeah, what's happened now?' piped up Kat. 'The place looks like a dump.'

Mum looked horrified we'd interrupted her meltdown. 'Julie, I'll call you back soon,' she said and hung up.

'Mum?' I tried again.

'I was reading about getting closure, you know, so I started sorting through a few of your father's belongings to throw out, and … well … things got out of hand,' she murmured, glancing at the frozen chicken.

The phone rang, causing us all to jump in fright.

'Ignore it,' urged Mum.

Kat answered it and rattled through the usual polite replies to the person on the other end, then held up the phone. 'Josie, it's for you.' She rolled her eyes. 'It's uni.'

I took the phone from her. 'Hello?'

Filly's friendly voice came down the line and somehow I pushed everything — Mum, Billy, James, *Sash* and Rae — into a tiny, locked compartment in my brain for a moment so I could listen to what he was saying.

'Yep, I'll come in tomorrow,' I told him when he'd finished. 'Yep. See you then. Thanks, Filly.'

I hung up. Filly's news would have to wait. Mum's tear-stained face snapped me back to the present, which, unfortunately, hadn't turned out to be a nightmare.

Kat, her cheeks flushed a deep red, waved a torn photo in front of Mum's face. 'Why are you doing this to yourself?' she asked. 'You're punishing yourself. I'm sick of it, I'm so sick of it.'

'Put that down,' Mum said. 'Just … just … put it away, Katherine.'

'Don't call me that — it's Kat. And you're the one who got the photos out and ripped them up. Dad's not coming home. Yes, he's an idiot and he's ruined everything, but aren't you supposed to be the grown up around here?'

'Kat, cool it,' I said, shocked at the way she was speaking to Mum.

'You have no idea what you're talking about,' she snapped at me, eyes blazing. 'You're off in your world of magazines and rock stars in the city. Meanwhile, I'm stuck here dealing with this!'

'I've been here every chance possible!' I retorted.

It was true. And when I wasn't busy at *Sash*, it was because I was at uni. So why did I feel smothered by guilt?

'Katherine Browning,' Mum said, her voice shaking. 'I told you —'

'Can't we have one day without drama?' yelled Kat, before storming off and slamming her bedroom door.

Mum plonked the frozen chook on the kitchen bench then fled into the backyard. I knew I'd find her later sitting among the roses and mint.

I considered calling Aunt Julie to find out more, but decided against it in case she packed her mothball-smelling overnight bag and came to visit. I'd let things cool off and then I'd see. For now, I wandered around the house putting everything back in its place. The anniversary vase was too shattered to fix, so I wrapped the pieces in newspaper and threw them in the bin. Just like Dad had done to us.

Filly had hinted at what he had to tell me on the phone. But hearing it in person was even better.

'The *Weekly Mail* wants an eight-hundred-word opinion piece from you,' he said, passing me the typed brief. 'There's no money in it, but you'll get a by-line and, if you're lucky, a head shot. I know it's for free and it's not a national paper, but regional is a great place to build your portfolio. The topic's up to you — just choose something you're passionate about. They want the story to feel "real".'

I scanned the brief. 'They want me? Um ... why?'

Filly raised an eyebrow. 'Why not?'

Why not? I thought. I didn't dare list all the reasons in case he changed his mind. Off the top of my head, I could have rustled up at least seven: one of them being if he'd somehow discovered I was at the centre of the Billy media scandal.

'Um,' I said, 'why not? Well, my late essay for one, I was refused a newspaper internship placement and —'

'Josie, you're a great writer. I know it, the *Mail* knows it — yes, I've shown them some of your work. When are you going to start believing that you've got what it takes?'

I wanted to believe it, more than anything. But a niggling voice in the back of my mind had almost convinced me this was some sort of prank. That any moment now a cheesy TV host would jump out from beneath the desk, shout 'Just kidding!' and slime me with green goo. I took a quick peek around the desk just in case, but all I could see were Filly's thick, hairy legs in khaki shorts.

'Josie, it's time to stop questioning every good thing that comes your way,' he continued. 'Be honest, be daring — and meet their deadline, yeah? Email the piece to me when you're done and I'll forward it on.'

'Thanks, Filly. I appreciate it.' I folded the brief in half and tucked it into my handbag. 'So, ah, have *Sash* magazine called lately?'

'Yep, Liani rang the other day and told me she's pleased with your work.'

'Great … She didn't mention anything else?' Such as my clumsy coffee-carrying skills, celebrity-kissing abilities or internet-troll magnetism.

Filly shrugged. 'Nope, that was it. Now, get out of here and put your writer's cap on.'

I was smiling as I left his office, as I got the bus home and as I walked to our front door. But when I got inside, there was no one to hear my big announcement.

The lounge room didn't provide any clues — it was still spotless from my clean-up after Mum's meltdown. I walked down the hallway. As usual, Kat's door was shut. Loud music blared from inside and I heard her singing along with the lyrics, drifting in and out of tune. When

I peeked in the master bedroom, Mum was asleep on the bed, fully clothed, apparently deaf to the bad karaoke pulsating through the house. I sighed, feeling guilty that I'd had such a good morning while things at home were still shaky.

I tiptoed into the kitchen and pulled out a chopping board, knife, some cheese and crackers. A food coma seemed a good idea right about now, even though I knew that overdoing it on cheese would end with me wailing 'Why?!' while clutching my stomach. Let Future Me deal with the tummy-ache, I thought as I unwrapped the cheese block. Now Me needed to blot out the twisted, all-consuming pangs of guilt about what was happening to my family.

'Step away from the camembert,' Kat said, appearing in front of me. 'I bet those fancy magazine girls don't OD on cheese. Go and have a celery stick or a glass of air.'

I rolled my eyes. 'Are you and Mum talking yet?' I asked, smearing a creamy chunk of cheese onto a biscuit.

Kat shrugged and reached for a cracker.

'So that's a no, then?' I said. 'Maybe you should chat to her when she wakes up.'

'Whatever. So what did your teacher want? Did you forget another assignment deadline?'

I told Kat about the *Weekly Mail* piece, leaving out the part about not getting paid. I knew she'd bag me for that. 'Hey,' I continued, 'look, I'm sorry I haven't been here and stuff's got ... hard, you know, with Mum and everything.'

My awkwardness was evident. We'd never been good at talking about serious things. We were great at arguing about TV and music, or teasing each other's haircuts and crushes, but when it came to saying what we really felt, we sucked.

Kat's jaw hardened. 'Ah, okay.'

'I'm serious. You've done an awesome job with everything and Mum's going to be fine. I think she's just exhausted and needs to sleep it off.'

I didn't know if that was true, or whether I was being naive, but it was what I'd chosen to believe.

'Thanks, Jose. Pretty cool about the article, by the way,' she added, changing the subject. 'Hey, are you okay after what happened at the cafe yesterday? Stacey's a real bitch.'

'Yeah, I'm fine.' If fine meant wanting to go all Jackie Chan on Pete Jordan's girlfriend.

'Good. I'm going to chill for a bit. Save some cheese for the rest of us, yeah?' Kat disappeared back down the hallway. It took me a few seconds to realise she'd taken the biscuits.

I was bursting to tell Mum that I was going to be a writer — a real writer published in a newspaper that people actually read — but I restrained myself from barging into the bedroom and waking her up to my news and a cup of Earl Grey. Her recent mood didn't give the impression she'd be ecstatic about ... well, anything much. So, instead, I settled for diving deep into my imagination, a technique that had helped me survive many of life's tragic, dull and frustrating moments. If Mum wasn't going to jump for joy in real life, then I would concoct a fantasy universe where she did. In my mind, she cheered, then pulled me into a hug — one of those bone-crunchers that left you simultaneously blissful and out of breath. She'd say, 'I'm so proud of you, love,' and I'd sink even deeper into her hug. She'd smell of coriander, Turkish delight and fabric softener. She'd smell like home.

Hours later, Kat was still tucked away in her room, Mum was awake, drinking tea and playing Solitaire on the dining table, and I was enjoying a moment's peace in my bedroom without: (a) someone publishing a photo of me that almost ruined my life; (b) my mum or sister throwing a hissy fit; or (c) having a nasty encounter with a sleazy guy from my past.

And then my phone rang. Steph's name flashed on the screen. I answered it.

'Hey lady, what's up?'

'It's happened,' Steph said breathlessly. 'This is not a drill. They've broken up. It's over.'

My mind raced. 'Who? Billy and Kara?'

'Even better,' said Steph without skipping a beat. 'James and Summer.'

My heart fluttered and anxious tremors shot through my body. Every fibre of my being wanted to organise a flash mob to celebrate this news, film it and put it on YouTube.

'Oh?' I said in my best whatever-like-I-care voice.

Steph saw straight through my attempt at nonchalance. '*Oh* indeed, Miss Playing It Cool. It's over. Did you hear what I said? James is single.'

'Righto, detective. What happened?'

'Oh, it was brutal.'

'Wait, how do you know? Did you bump into James in the city or something?'

'Um ... wait a second.'

I heard fumbling, followed by a guy clearing his throat.

'Hey, cuz. How are you?'

'Tim? Hey! What are you doing with Steph?'

'So, ah, Steph wants me to tell you something. She's too scared — right — well, she thinks it's better coming from me.' There was more fumbling and I heard Steph whispering in the background but couldn't make out what she was saying. Tim cleared his throat again. 'Cuz, so, ah, we're kinda together.'

'Who's together? You and ... you and Steph?'

'Well, we're not getting married or anything, but yeah, we're hanging.'

I experienced a slight WTF moment and forgot how to string a sentence together.

Tim murmured, 'Um … I'll just put Steph back on.'

'I'm back,' announced Steph, sounding sheepish. 'Oh J, you hate me, don't you?'

'No, of course not. I just …' I fumbled around for the right words. 'No, I definitely don't hate you. Or Tim. I'm taking it in … Um … so does this mean we're kind of related now?'

'Yeah, for sure.'

'Well, you better tell me *everything* when he's out of earshot. Well, not everything-everything, but you know what I mean.'

She laughed. 'I will. But how nuts is that about James and Summer? Tim told me and I had to call. Huge news, right?'

'I guess.'

Massive news, my mind shouted. The biggest news I'd heard in ages. I couldn't think of any other news that was bigger.

A horrible thought dawned on me. James was hot, smart and nice — the trifecta, and a total catch. He was classic boyfriend material, the type of guy any girl would love to take home to her folks — and I didn't want some gorgeous, leggy specimen swooping in to do just that. As far as I was concerned, if anyone was swooping, it was going to be me.

18.

My hair shone, eyes sparkled and I smelled incredible (perhaps a little *too* incredible, as I'd doused myself in perfume instead of spritzing as Sia had encouraged). Steph had shown me how to re-create the gorgeous, wavy hairstyle from my birthday night and she was right, it had been easy to do. I pinned the last strand of hair and secured the fishtail braid. Perfect. My dress was new: I'd braved the shops with Kat again and she'd helped me pick out a dusty blue cap-sleeved number that was on sale. A touch of cherry lip gloss finished my outfit. I'd never felt better — and it was only fifty per cent to do with making James fall desperately in love with me.

'Josie, are you here?' I heard him call out from the hallway.

'Yep, in the bathroom,' I said, before realising that sounded a little wrong. 'Like, I'm in the bathroom, but not *innnn* the bathroom, if you need to come in. I mean, I'm not on anything or using anything or doing anything, if you know what I mean?'

Of course he knew what I meant. The dead ants on the balcony knew what I meant. Moments like this certainly encouraged the idea of sewing my lips together.

When James popped his head in, I was coating on an extra layer of bronzer.

'Jose ...' he started, then, when he saw my face, 'Whoa! What's with the tandoori tan?'

'Oh, you know, just adding a healthy glow.' I paused. 'I look like a lobster, don't I?'

He grinned. 'Little bit. Just wipe some of it off and you'll look great.'

My cheeks flushed. Or maybe that was still the bronzer. 'Thanks.'

I searched his face for any sign of distress after the break-up, but there were no visible tear stains or puffed eyes.

'So, ah, Steph told me things have been pretty hectic for you at home and at *Sash*,' said James.

'Yeah.' Hectic was one way to put it. Jaw-droppingly nuts was another.

'I'm here if you need to, you know, talk about anything.'

I shrugged. 'Thanks, but there's nothing to tell, really.'

As much as I wanted to spend time with James, I didn't want my roller-coaster life to be the sole focus of our friendship. Instead, I would've rather talked about how much he wanted to rip my bra off, or something equally X-rated.

'Okay, if you're sure.' He smiled and sat down on the edge of the bathtub. 'So what else is happening? Keeping busy?'

'Does trying to stop Mum from tearing her hair out count?'

'You bet.' James tilted his head to one side. It was a seemingly innocent movement, but his eyes staring into mine pushed every logical thought from my brain.

'I, ah, I actually heard a little something about you,' I started.

The words hung in the air. There was no going back.

'Yeah? What's that? Oh, did Tim tell you I'm scoring the music for a mate's short film?'

'No! That's huge.'

'Thanks,' he said. 'After our chat I started thinking, so I put some feelers out and one thing led to another … Anyway! What's the thing you heard about me?'

'Um. Never mind,' I said, rubbing away some more bronzer to avoid eye contact. 'Awesome news for you. Very impressive and well-deserved —'

'Jose, what did you hear?'

I stopped, unsure how to continue. This was my chance, my moment — I just never pictured it would take place in a bathroom at eight in the morning. Somewhere in the back of my mind, a niggly voice reminded me that this probably wasn't the best idea. But then I remembered the hot, smart, nice girls lurking in my imagination, waiting to swoop.

'I heard you and Summer broke up,' I said. 'Steph told me.'

'Oh, that. Well —'

'James,' I butted in. The words were flooding out whether I wanted them to or not. 'You probably already know this, but I'm going to tell you anyway.'

'Okay ...'

'Well, you know how some people meet each other and it's like ... like peanut butter and honey? It just works.'

'I never really liked peanut butter,' said James, wrinkling his nose. 'It's so sludgy.'

'You don't like peanut butter? Okay, not the point. You know how some people fit together perfectly? Like Minnie and Mickey.'

James grinned. 'You mean the talking mice?'

'Bad example. Okay, okay ... like Batman and Robin? Those dudes can't stay away from each other.'

'What are you trying to say?'

'Argh! Forget the rodents, forget the superhero bromance! Think of two things that work together ... like noughts and crosses, or peas and corn —'

'You know, I'm more of a peas and carrots kinda guy.'

'Just ... shut up for a sec!'

'Excuse me?'

'I like you,' I blurted out. 'I've liked you for ages.'

My breathy sentiment rang out loud and clear, almost echoing off the tiles as I waited for James's response. You know those movie scenes where two people profess their undying love and it ends with them tearing each other's clothes off? Well, that didn't happen.

'Jose,' James said, 'the thing is —'

His phone rang, loud, shrill and dominating. He looked at the number.

'Look, I hate to do this right now, but I'd better take it. I'm so sorry. We'll talk soon, okay? I promise.' He patted me on the shoulder and left the bathroom. Even though he'd shut the door behind him, I heard him say, 'Hey, Summer'.

I glared in the mirror at my made-up face, now ruined by a stream of hot tears. Some were fuelled by embarrassment, others by the fact that the hottest, smartest, nicest guy I'd ever met was walking away to chat with another girl. The girl he was meant to have broken up with.

What had he been about to say before he was interrupted? I couldn't believe he'd walked out, leaving me to drive myself batty attempting to decode the rest of the sentence. Was it: (a) 'Jose, the thing is ... I'm about to start the physically and emotionally draining process of becoming a woman; (b) 'Jose, the thing is ... I'm in love with you. I want to get your name tattooed on my left bicep; or (c) 'Jose, the thing is ... Summer and I are back together. She's the one for me, we have amazing sex four times a day and I want to be the father of her children.'

Bingo. That was it. They were back together. *Of course*. It made sense. Moments after I'd confessed how I felt, Summer had called and he'd run away faster than an Olympic sprinter with a rocket strapped to his butt.

Annoyed for throwing myself at James (okay, so my glamorous look had been about eighty-nine per cent for him), I wiped off the extra bronzer, repinned my flashy hairstyle and slicked on an extra coat of lip gloss. If James wanted to waste time with Summer, that was his choice. I just didn't want to know anything about it (especially if my prediction of amazing sex was true). I grabbed my jacket and slipped out the door without saying goodbye. I was braced for another day at *Sash* and I wasn't going to let a guy — albeit a hot, smart, nice guy — cloud my judgement and ruin my chances of winning the internship prize ever again.

When I arrived at *Sash* HQ, Liani's office blinds were pulled across but not fully closed. I could see her chatting on the phone, her hand over the receiver. I couldn't make out much, only a faint 'Yes, I agree', 'You really think so?' and 'Sounds great', which could have meant anything from 'Yes, let's have butter chicken for dinner tonight' to 'I'd love to come to your music launch'.

Not wanting to interrupt her, I walked back to reception to wait on the couch. Rae's office door was closed and the blinds were drawn. The rest of the team were working in silence. It was so quiet I could hear the sharp clicking of the art department's fan and the tapping of manicured fingernails on computer keyboards. A quick glance into the features department showed Esmeralda and two others typing madly. Eloise had earphones in and was watching a TV episode. I couldn't believe she was paid to stay up-to-date with all things entertainment. A job where you could write and watch TV? Hello, dream career.

'Josie, how are you, sweetie?' a sweet, silky voice said.

I looked up to see the gorgeous Sia beaming down at me. Her hair was pulled back into a chunky side braid and her generous lips were sparkling with a bright coral lipstick.

'Nice braid, Sia.'

'You too,' she said, stepping in for a closer look at my new hairstyle. 'Someone's been hitting up Beauty DIY School. I'm impressed. Did you check out that website I showed you?'

I was about to tell her that Steph had taught me when Rae's blinds pelted open, her office door swung out wide and she strutted out into the main office. 'Everyone. Meeting!' she announced to the room. 'Yes, yes, I know it wasn't in the calendar. Can someone grab the fashion girls from their department? Oh, interns, feel free to sit and watch. This will be a good opportunity to see how things work behind the scenes. Has anyone seen my big purple planning book? Someone get Liani, now!'

The team assembled themselves in a circle, some trudging to their seats, other gliding with the gracefulness of ballerinas. I took a seat on the opposite side to Rae, between Sia and another girl with a friendly, freckly face who I hadn't met.

Steph plonked down across from me, wearing a leopard-print jersey dress. 'Oops, running late,' she mouthed. 'What's going on?'

I shrugged. 'Don't know.'

The queen of making an entrance, Ava stalked into the circle in her purple stilettos, then perched next to Rae, her slim frame upright as always. She linked her slender hands, then unlinked them, then linked them again. This drew attention to the three rings on her fingers today: a large green emerald stone, a thin gold band and a black rock-chick ring. Her diamond engagement ring must've still been getting cleaned.

Liani rushed out of her office to join the meeting, looking flushed after her phone call. Rae glared at her, as though it mattered she was five seconds later than everyone else. All thoughts of Ava's missing ring and James getting back with Summer disappeared as I waited for Rae to speak.

She began by telling everyone they needed to address *Sash*'s strengths and weaknesses and find room for improvement, then asked the team to brainstorm ideas on the spot. One girl's suggestion of a scratch 'n' sniff nude male poster was scoffed at, and Gen's pitch for a fashion shoot shot in Egypt was dismissed as a direct copy from *Marilyn* magazine. Esmeralda's idea for a competition to discover the country's hottest new blogger was a winner, as was Eloise's pitch for an 'Inside My Handbag' feature on five of the country's hottest stars. The meeting went on for almost two hours and Liani took notes throughout. By the end, her pad was filled with scrawled ideas and our stomachs were grumbling in sync.

'Finally, I want to bring some closure to the matter that's been haunting us in the media for the past few weeks,' Rae said. 'Billy's alleged affair.'

Steph rolled her eyes and fake-yawned. I wanted to hug her for that. Every other foundation-clad, designer-wearing magazine girl in the circle looked at me. How do they know, I wondered, as I avoided eye contact — even with Steph and Liani — and focused on a marketing poster to the right of Rae's head. As long as I focused on that poster I'd be okay.

'The main reason *Sash* has been dragged into it,' Rae continued, 'is because Billy recently spoke to our magazine and declared he was a changed man. Obviously, that turned out to be a lie, but we have to live with it.

Celebrities make mistakes like the rest of us, but it doesn't stop readers from wanting more. They just can't seem to get enough of this guy. In fact, on that note, I'd like to thank our hardworking intern Josie for the publicity.'

My jaw dropped and Sia squeezed my hand. Did Rae seriously out me to the entire *Sash* team as Billy's nightclub pash? I waited to hear more before I ran out the door shouting 'I slapped him away, I promise'.

'Thanks to Josie's exclusive interviews with Billy we've managed to maintain our circulation — just — in a very competitive market,' Rae said, giving me a short, sharp nod. I forced a smile, relieved that Rae hadn't revealed all. Although, based on the way everyone was staring at me, they seemed to know anyway.

'But Billy's light won't shine forever, so we need to put on our thinking caps to predict the next hottest person, trends and icons,' Rae went on. 'Yes, even more than we already have been. I want everyone moving onwards and upwards, and thinking outside the square. Enough of the copycat ideas or the been-there-done-thats. I want fresh ideas and so do our readers.'

Everyone was scribbling madly in their notebooks.

'Advertisers are playing hardball at the moment so we've got to create reasons to get them paying up,' she continued. 'A big month awaits us — a huge one — and I need everyone giving a hundred and ten per cent. That's it from me. Do you have anything to add, Liani?'

'Just keep working hard, everyone, we appreciate it,' Liani said. 'We're in a tough market, that's no secret, but, ah ... look, if we're stuck back late on deadline again, the dumplings are on me, okay? I'm thinking Shanghai-style ones — you know, with soup inside. Delicious.'

Everyone smiled. Typical Liani: she always knew how to brighten the mood with her down-to-earth sweetness.

'Well, that's it from us, guys,' she said. 'Thanks again, and we'll let your brains stew on all that for a while.'

The team drew a silent, collective sigh of relief. I could tell from the awkward shuffling in seats and mass stomach rumbling that, like me, they were counting down the seconds to run to the bathroom, stretch their legs and get a bite to eat.

'Okay, back to work, everyone,' announced Rae with a small flick of her wrist. The boss had spoken.

The team packed up their belongings and headed to their desks, leaving me, Steph and Ava sitting there, unsure where we were needed.

Rae stalked over. 'Josie, a quick word?'

'Of course,' I said, sounding like an overeager student keen to make amends. Which, in reality, I was.

I followed her into the office. The blinds stayed down and door remained ajar. Rae sat down in the chair behind her desk, so I walked toward the pouf.

'Don't bother — this will be quick,' she said.

'Okay …' Hopefully painless, too, I thought. I fiddled with my bracelet, swallowed and glanced toward the door. Ava was now standing outside Rae's office, flipping through a book.

Rae pursed her lips. 'Josie, I wanted to say, don't be alarmed if you see Billy around the building today.'

'He's here?' I stammered. 'Not that I care, I mean … I … great. That's great. Brilliant news for the mag.'

'Billy's manager has paid a lot of money to use our studios, creative direction and photographers for a photo shoot — and, despite everything, all the history, it's money we can't refuse at this point.'

'Oh, sure, that makes sense,' I rambled. No, it didn't. He was here? I wanted to scream. After everything he'd done!

'The shoot was meant to be yesterday when, ah, you weren't here, but his girlfriend's morning sickness kicked in and he wanted to look after her, so it was moved to today.'

'Oh.' I lowered my head.

'For reasons that you and I both know, I think it's best if you avoid Studio 8B and stay busy up here. The girls have plenty for you to do while I'm keeping an eye on things over there.'

'I can do that.'

'Wonderful,' Rae said. 'That will be all.'

'Okay, great.'

'Close the door behind you.'

'Thanks, Rae,' I said, walking out in a daze.

'Everything okay?' a voice piped up.

I turned to see Ava. Her dress was tiny, but it still hung off her loosely and her eye make-up was dark and eerie, giving her a ghoulish appearance.

'Ava, you scared me,' I stammered, my heart still pounding after my conversation with Rae.

'I didn't realise I was so frightening,' said Ava, her eyes widening. 'Rae really rattled you in there, huh?'

I swallowed. 'Sorry, I'm all good, it was … internship stuff, you know how it is.'

'Sure, internship stuff,' she replied, but judging by her tone she knew I was lying.

Yet again, life had found a new way to inject awkwardness into my world. Competitive interns, arrogant pop stars — what next? I didn't dare think of anything specific in case it came true.

Keen to avoid any more uncomfortable moments in the office, I offered to do the features writers' photocopying for them. It was a boring task and surely even I couldn't stuff it up.

19.

'That looks fun,' a sarcastic voice said behind me.

I looked around from the whirring, wheezing photocopier to see Ava towering next to me again, her long, lanky arms crossed over her skinny frame.

I shrugged. 'It's okay.'

'So, did you hear? Rae's asked me to escort Billy and his crew to the photo shoot. Meet them, show them around, be their personal assistant for the day. Like, *his* personal assistant.'

'Are you sure that's a good idea?' I blurted out.

'Jealous?' She raised an eyebrow.

'No, I just … No, of course not, why would I be?' I said, returning to the photocopying. 'Anyway … so … you're still not wearing your engagement ring. Is everything okay?'

Ava's jaw tightened. 'Everything's fine. I just left it at home.'

'Oh? I thought it was at the jewellers getting cleaned?'

'Yeah, it was,' she said, rubbing at her naked ring finger. 'It was *filthy*. You'd know what I mean if you ever bothered to get your hands dirty around here.'

'Excuse me?' My jaw dropped, thinking back to the number of times Steph and I had cleaned, sorted and dusted the fashion storeroom while Ava 'helped with a beauty shoot' or 'inspired Rae and the fashion department with her modelling portfolio'.

'Anyway, I'd better go to the shoot — Billy probably needs me.' She sighed. 'Oh, and one other thing. Billy's girlfriend, Kara — you know, the one he's having a baby with — is around the building, too. Just thought you should know.'

She strode off, flicking her voluminous red hair. I turned back to the photocopying and suddenly it didn't seem like such a boring task. My palms sweated, my brain was punctured with the same thoughts on repeat: What if Kara recognised me from the photos? Worse still: what if she recognised me before I recognised her and I didn't have a chance to hide? In the past few weeks I must have seen more than two hundred photos of her on the internet. She had long jet-black hair, blue eyes and flawless pale skin. I was sure of it.

I would have spent the rest of the day stressing about Kara but Eloise came to my rescue. More accurately, I came to hers. Eloise had done her best to hide a raging hangover, but since Rae, Liani, Ava and half the editorial team had gone to the studio, she couldn't hold it together any longer: she wanted junk food, and she wanted it now — she was just too seedy to venture outside.

Happy for the distraction, I walked the two blocks to the closest takeaway store and ordered two cheeseburgers, large chips, a chocolate sundae — and twelve nuggets. Eloise really stressed that part to me. It turned out magazine girls did eat more than carrot sticks and fresh vegetable juices after all.

The pimply-faced kid behind the counter gaped at my enormous paper bag for so long I couldn't tell whether he was repulsed or impressed.

Back at the office, Eloise groaned with excitement when I plonked the greasy food on her desk. 'I could hug you right now,' she said, yawning and rubbing her temples. 'Did you get something for yourself?'

'No, I wasn't hungry.'

That was a lie; I was always hungry. I didn't mind though: walking to the shops for hangover food was more fun than photocopying, sorting through the mail and tidying up the office combined. Plus, chatting with Eloise like this made me feel included in the *Sash* team, like I was one of the features girls.

'Don't be silly,' Eloise scoffed, emptying the chips onto a paper plate and pushing them toward me. 'Have a chip. Have ten chips.' She tore open the first burger wrapper and took a bite.

I heard a voice cry 'Ewww' and turned to see Steph walking over.

'Is that a plastic burger?' asked Steph, learning forward to take a closer look. 'Surely that's not real — it looks like a toy!'

'That's my plastic food, thank you very much.' Eloise grinned. Red sauce oozed out of the bun, coating her fingers. 'You'd think you'd never seen a burger before.'

'Do curried mushroom sliders in Thailand count?' said Steph, balancing between cheeky and downright pretentious. With her cute little face, fun energy and worldliness, she pulled it off.

Eloise wiped sauce from her lips. 'Okay, you two, this has been fun, but I'd love to enjoy the rest without judgement. And between you and me, before Rae gets back from the shoot. Maybe go and see what the art team are up to, yeah?'

'Okay,' we chimed at the same time.

'And Jose?' she went on. 'Take a sneaky cheeseburger with you. I think I've over-ordered.'

I couldn't help but agree. Steph sniggered as we loaded the plate with the untouched burger and soggy fries. We were walking toward the art department when I heard Ava's shrill voice again.

'Where have you been, Josie?' she said. 'I've been looking everywhere for you. Rae needs to see you immediately.'

'See me? Again?' My heart pounded. This was the final straw in a long line of straws. I knew it. 'Where? Her office?'

'No, the shoot. She said it'd only take a second. I offered to pass on a message but she specifically requested to see you.'

My palms dampened. 'No, she wanted me to stay away from the shoot.'

'That's weird.' Ava shrugged. 'Oh well, do what you like. Just don't blame me if you get in trouble again. I know how much you hate that.'

'Okay, I believe you. What level are the studios on again?' I asked. 'Four?'

'No, that's *Marilyn* mag,' said Ava. 'Try level eight.'

'I've heard the *Marilyn* girls have hair straighteners set up at their desks and check each other's clothing tags to make sure they're wearing designer gear. Do you think that's true?'

Ava shrugged. 'Makes sense to me. I'll meet you there.' She stalked away, flicking her hair (the girl seriously belonged in a shampoo commercial).

I threw the junk food I was carrying in the bin, hopped in the lift and, moments later, was up on level eight, where the fluorescent lighting was so harsh I wished I'd worn safety goggles. Several beauties walked past me, some holding notebooks, others nursing large bags of goodies, most likely from PR agencies.

I found a sign directing me to Studio 8B, and on my way there passed Jeremy the photographer.

He waved. 'Well, hello you. How have you been? Enjoying the internship?'

'It's great,' I replied. 'Hey, have you seen Rae?'

'She's through there.' He pointed toward a door. 'We're on a break. Want a coffee? I'm getting a double shot.'

'No, thanks.' I smiled, enjoying the warmth of chatting in the corridor for once. Many of the people in the building — guys and girls — were like plastic robots with the personalities of flat diet lemonade. Jeremy's phone rang so he said goodbye and walked off.

They were on a break. That was probably why Rae wanted to see me now. Billy and Kara were most likely tucked away in a VIP dressing room, feeding each other grapes and getting massages or something equally lavish. I took a deep breath and opened the door.

The studio looked like a zoo as usual. There was a king-size bed in the middle of the room, with luxurious-looking sheets and pillows, all glowing pristine white under the lighting. Two girls fluffed the pillows and messed up the sheets, creating a sexy just-slept-in look. A bright red motorbike was parked in a corner of the studio; across the room, a litter of puppies played in a large cardboard box, yapping and nuzzling each other. I nearly OD'd on cuteness.

Rae, Liani, Esmeralda and some of the crew had their backs to me as they chatted to a busty woman with a parrot tattoo down her arm. She was talking hoarsely about 'hair energy' and how 'we don't want him to look lifeless'. Rae appeared to be listening but her arms were folded over her chest; defensive and ready to strike as always. I couldn't see Billy — or anyone who looked like Kara — anywhere. Billy's manager was nowhere to be seen either. Phew.

I took a shaky step toward the group.

'Josie, Josie, Josie,' a slick voice drawled behind me.

I turned to see Billy, arms folded across his chest and smirking (of course). He wore a tight black T-shirt and dark denim jeans, and his usually floppy hair was slicked into a sharp twenties style.

'Billy,' I muttered, lowering my eyes. 'I should leave … I thought you'd be gone.'

'It's cool. Stay and chat. Did you see the puppies?'

'*Puppies?* What's the matter with you? Stop pretending that everything's cool,' I whispered, narrowing my eyes. 'I thought you were better than this. The lies you've been spreading about me —'

'Calm down. It's not like we spent the night together.'

'No, but you wanted to.'

'It was a kiss.' He rolled his eyes. 'One kiss. And stop acting like you didn't enjoy it.'

'What gave it away? The slap or the fact I vomited afterwards?' I snapped.

'It's you,' I heard a soft, feminine voice say. I turned to see a girl with jet-black hair, green eyes and tanned skin (not pale, as I'd thought) staring at me, her lip trembling. Her right hand cupped her swollen belly. 'You're the girl from the club who kissed Billy — I recognise you from the photos.'

'I … I …' My hand raced to my hair. Why did I choose today of all days to repeat Steph's style?

'You threw yourself at my boyfriend,' Kara said, her face hardening to reveal strong cheekbones and a prominent jaw.

'No, no, I promise,' I said, shaking my head. 'It's complicated. He was the one who —'

'Save it. I don't know what Billy was thinking when he let you kiss him,' Kara said, rolling each word off her tongue for added effect.

Anger bubbled inside me, winding its way from my toes, around my ankles, jetting up my thighs toward my mouth. 'Let *me* kiss *him*? I don't know what lies he's fed you, but you've got it all wrong. Billy asked me to go back to his hotel room.'

'How dare you!' Kara snapped, stepping forward, her left palm raised.

Suddenly, a hand grabbed hold of my arm and yanked me away, sending a painful jolt through my upper body.

'What are you doing here?' Rae hissed, towering over me. Her hand gripped my arm like a vice. Nearby, Billy was trying to console Kara, who was pushing him away. 'Josie, I told you to stay in the office. Now look what you've done.'

'I know, but then Ava told me to come and —'

'What on earth were you thinking?'

'It's just that it wasn't my —'

'Oh, it's never *you*, is it?' Rae snapped. 'It's never your fault. Never your problem.'

'There's been a misunderstanding —'

'No. You're the one misunderstanding. I've got more important things to deal with than this. I'm trying to run a goddamn magazine. I've had it, Josie. Your internship is over.'

'What? No, Rae. Please.' This wasn't happening. It couldn't be happening.

'Check the guidelines — you're dismissed. Now get the hell out of here.'

Lips trembling, I glanced around. Billy and Kara now stood next to each other, holding hands in silence. The busty red-haired woman was picking at her fingernails, bored. I didn't dare look at Liani or Esmeralda; the shame was too much.

'I really am sorry,' I spluttered. I spun on my heel and raced out of the studio.

20.

I felt like I'd been punched in the stomach. Maybe kicked too. I sat crying on the grass in the park near *Sash*, ignoring the strangers staring as they walked by. I realised this was one screw-up I couldn't bounce back from.

As much as I tried, I couldn't stop replaying everything in my mind: the blatant set-up from Ava, the heated argument with Kara, the public firing. It seemed so surreal, so shocking: me, fired? The same girl who geeked her way through high school? Who received nothing but praise, gold stars and straight As from teachers? Who wore her goodie-two-shoes badge with pride? I wiped my tears away with my hand; it came away smudged with mascara.

'Josie, here you are!' Steph cried out, appearing by my side in the park. 'The girls told me you ran out. I've been looking for you everywhere. Here's your handbag.' She plonked it down next to me.

'Thanks,' I said, rearranging my position beneath a grand old tree with thick leafy branches that blocked out the sun and cast a huge shadow across the grass. 'I'm sorry, I had to get out of there. It was too much. Rae fired me.'

'I know.' Steph sighed, sat down and put her arm around me. 'But you're stronger than this. Do you really want Rae to know you had a breakdown?'

I shrugged. 'It's not really a breakdown.'

'I'm just worried you're seconds away from going nuts and shaving your head.'

Only Steph could've got away with being cheeky at that moment.

'Everything's a mess,' I said, eyes welling up again. 'The internship's over and I really needed that money. And everyone at *Sash* knows about me and Billy. Ava framed me for no reason. Mum's all over the place, plus I'm meant to be writing an article for the *Weekly Mail* and I haven't even started thinking about it … And man, some of those comments about me on the websites. Wow. They were —'

'Awful. I know.'

'One person told me to throw myself off a building because I looked fat in that dress.'

'That anonymous *coward* is probably forty years old with raging BO and still living in his mum's granny flat.' Steph squeezed me tighter. 'Don't worry about those comments. They're lies, okay? As for the internship? This will work out, I promise. You're too talented and lovely and positive for it to go any other way.'

I smiled through my tears, touched by Steph's kindness.

'Plus,' she continued, 'you wanna talk about crazy parents? Did I tell you Mum's taken a second lover? Some guy she met at an organic farmers' market. Isn't that the lamest thing you've ever heard?'

'A second one? Yikes.' I couldn't even hang onto one, let alone two.

Steph shrugged. 'My family are skilled at making weird seem perfectly normal. I don't think Tim would be too keen if I tried to do the same, though!'

'I told James I liked him,' I confessed.

The words had been brewing all morning, but I'd been too embarrassed to tell her. Now, wiping away my tears in the park, I figured I'd already hit a low, so I might as well share the shameful secret.

'*And?*'

'He took a phone call.'

'Okay, but what did he say to you before that?'

'I said it, then he took a phone call. From her. I think they're back together.'

'Him and Summer?' Steph groaned.

'I want to go to sleep now,' I said, lying back on the grass and looking up into the leafy branches of the tree. They blocked out the sky; blocked out everything.

'Thanks for trying, Steph. You'd better head back before you get in trouble, too.'

'I was thinking we could have pizza at Tim's later on.'

'I don't know. James might be there.'

'With extra cheese?'

'Maybe.' I pushed myself up to my feet and pulled Steph into a hug. 'Thanks for the pep talk. And as for your mum: two lovers and a husband? She must be busy! Does she have a timetable to fit them all in or something?'

And then I had a horrible thought. 'Damn! I have to return my security pass to the front desk. I really don't want to go back ...'

Steph squeezed my hand. 'It's fine, Jose. I'll go with you.'

'You will? Thanks,' I sighed.

We walked back to the office together, weaving our way through the park, passing lazy suits sipping coffee in the sunshine, a group of schoolkids tucking into fish and chips, and a lone old woman huddled on a bench using a newspaper as a blanket.

We arrived at the *Sash* building and, trying not to cry again, I hugged Steph, who said goodbye then disappeared into the lifts. That was it. Our internship together was over.

I was waiting in line at the front desk when I saw Ava in the foyer, struggling to push a large metal rack holding an assortment of colourful outfits. She hummed and batted her eyelids as she passed me, acting as though she hadn't just lied to my face and got me kicked out of the internship program.

Ignore her, just ignore her, I told myself. Rise above it; accept that maybe you're just an ordinary girl with dreams that were too big to come true. Rae had made it clear my plans of becoming a successful writer were trashed and I had no one to blame but myself. It was my fault. Except, deep down, I knew it wasn't *entirely* my fault.

Sure, I'd let Billy mouth-maul me in the club, but I'd copped the flack and moved on. It was Ava who'd manipulated me into going to the photo shoot — she'd set a trap and I'd taken the bait.

As I stood there, her gaunt figure mere metres away, all I could think about was ripping her annoyingly pretty face off.

But there was a problem and a big one at that: I'd never been in a fight. Not a real fight anyway, where everyone crowded onto the school oval and screamed 'Fight, fight, fight!' The closest I'd come was slapping Billy at the club, or yelling 'No, *you* suck!' to the neighbours' kids a few years back.

And so, like everything else I'd been doing lately, I winged it. Fists clenched, lips pursed and hair flying out behind me like a psychotic witch, I charged toward Ava, who'd stopped to rehang a dress that had slipped off the rack.

'Ava, I need to talk to you,' I said.

I wondered when it would be appropriate for me to throw my first punch. Or jab. Or hook. Or was that fishing lingo? I had no idea. I just wanted Ava to hurt as much as I did.

Ava turned to face me, eyelashes fluttering, feigning innocence. 'Something the matter, Josie?'

'You set me up.'

'Excuse me?' she said, eyes widening.

'You heard me,' I continued, my heartbeat quickening. 'You lied to me and then, to top it off, you got me kicked out of *Sash*.'

'You give me too much credit,' she said, raising an eyebrow. 'I'm sure you stuffed it up in there all on your own.'

That was it. I couldn't stand another nanosecond of her cruel taunts.

'What have I ever done to you, Ava?' I snapped. 'I've complimented you, I've offered my help, I worried about you when you were sick, and you know what? You've been nothing but horrible.'

Ava glared at me. Her perfect nostrils flared but she said nothing.

'Well?' I pushed, searching her face for answers. 'Tell me. What's your problem?'

'You really want to know?' she said, lowering her voice so the people in the foyer wouldn't hear. 'You went to Liani about me.'

'I … I … Okay, you're right,' I stammered. 'But I was worried and —'

'You told her I had bulimia.'

'What? No, I didn't!'

'Don't lie to my face. The least you can do is tell the truth.'

'I swear I only told her about the bad pork and how I heard you getting sick and —'

'Keep your voice down,' she hissed, fake-smiling at a group of magazine glamours as they strutted past us. 'And that's rubbish. Josie, I have good genes, that's why I'm slim. Besides, you don't see me eat breakfast and dinner at home. And you were right — I ate some dodgy pork that made me sick. That's it. But thanks to you, I've got Rae and Liani breathing down my back, 'keeping an eye' on me. Do you know what that's like? Do you know how it makes me feel? Well, do you?'

Despite everything, I felt the anger fizzle out of me, leaving me tongue-tied. But Ava's rant wasn't over.

'You think you're so perfect! Better than everyone, and smarter and …' Her voice trailed off and her long, slim hand went to her head. 'Oh …'

'Ava? What's wrong?'

'I don't feel well,' she murmured, her skin drained of colour. 'Everything's gone all ... blurry.'

'Here, hold onto my arm,' I said, stepping forward.

But I was too late. She wobbled on her feet, then her knees gave out and she collapsed to the floor. Her head hit the marble with a dull thud that sent bile leaping into my throat. Her eyes flickered shut and her long legs and arms splayed lifelessly on the floor.

'Ava!' I threw myself to the ground to see if she was breathing. She was. After that, everything slowed down.

I remember crying out, 'Help, someone please help! My friend's fainted.' I remember Ava murmuring, 'Am I bleeding? My head hurts.' I remember someone trying — and failing — to peel me away from Ava's body. I remember Liani arriving and patting me on the back.

Security guards shooed everyone else away to make space for two burly ambulance officers to bring a stretcher into the foyer.

'Is she going to be okay?' I asked.

'It's just a precaution, Josie,' Liani told me before giving me a hug and hopping in the back of the ambulance with Ava. 'Go home, honey. Go home and rest.'

I nodded, too stunned to respond.

'Everything will be fine, I promise,' she said, rummaging in her bag and handing me a small rectangular piece of paper. 'Take this cab charge and go straight home. Use the taxi rank around the corner, and sign on the line when they drop you off. It won't cost you a thing.'

I nodded again.

The ambulance door slammed closed, cutting off our conversation. Liani gave me a small wave through the window and I watched her and Ava speed away, the ambulance sirens sounding like screams in my head.

While I threw my clothes, accessories and toiletries into my suitcase at Tim's place, I couldn't stop stressing about whether Ava was okay. Why had she fainted? I couldn't shake the sound of the ambulance sirens from my ears, or the thud of her head against the ground. I wanted to call the office to find out what was going on, but since I was no longer a *Sash* intern I figured that wouldn't go down well.

Packing took longer than I'd expected because somehow over the past few months of crashing with Tim and James each week, I'd made myself at home. My possessions were strewn everywhere, so before I could pack I had to endure a treasure hunt to find them all. My favourite silver pen was on top of the fridge, a hair comb was nestled in a pot plant and a pair of black undies (thankfully clean) were stuffed behind the couch in the lounge room. I pushed everything into my suitcase, squashing colours, materials and toiletries together. It took three attempts — and lots of swearing — to close it, but I managed. Once it was zipped and locked I realised

I'd forgotten to pack my towel, which was still damp and hanging in the bathroom. I decided the guys could keep it. They needed all the household items they could get.

I sat down on the couch, remembering all the nights it had served as my bed. My favourite memories were, without a doubt, my chill-out sessions with James. The fake talk-show interviews, the flirting, the cups of tea, the awkward dancing, the telling of secrets — they seemed so long ago now.

What the hell was the matter with me? I'd promised myself I'd stop dragging up the past, but it seemed impossible. James kept wriggling his way into my mind, and no matter how many times I swatted him away, there he was again.

Keen to distract myself, I scoured the train timetable. I could be on the train within an hour and home by nightfall.

After the afternoon's events, I was ready to go home. I needed familiarity, peace and quiet. The city, for all its expansive choices and fun, didn't offer any of those. My craving for my own soft warm bed to burrow into was too strong to ignore. Even if things weren't so great with my family right now, I knew home was where I needed to be.

I picked up my suitcase and wheeled it toward the front door, then looked back for one final breath at the apartment. I hated to admit it, but I was going to miss its mismatched charm — even Tim's smelly socks and week-old Thai takeaway containers. All of a sudden the door burst open and Tim and Steph crashed through and knocked me down. The three of us lay in a tangled mess on the floor, our legs, arms and bags intertwined into a human pretzel. Tim burst into a fit of laughter.

Steph slapped him lightly on the shoulder. 'This is supposed to be serious, remember? Give her the cupcakes.'

'Oh yeah, sorry.' He grinned and held up a container of squashed cakes. 'Sat on them, babe.'

I raised my eyebrow. Babe? I couldn't believe it: my lazy, laidback cousin was completely under Steph's thumb. Aunt Julie would be thrilled!

'So, ah …' I couldn't find the words. 'Did you hear …?'

'About Ava?' said Steph. 'Yeah, everyone's talking about it.' She unthreaded herself from our tangle. 'Half the *Sash* girls have gone to the hospital to wait with her; they didn't want her to be by herself. The rest of us were sent home.'

I was confused. 'Her fiancé couldn't make it? Is he working? You'd think your boss would give you time off if your fiancée was in hospital!'

'Yeah, it's just … Ava hasn't been completely honest about that,' said Steph.

'What do you mean?'

'Sia texted me from the hospital. Apparently he called off the wedding ages ago. He left her for someone else.'

'No! You're kidding?'

'She didn't tell anyone. Isn't it awful? Like, hide-in-your-bedroom-forever awful.'

'The engagement ring,' I muttered. 'She told me it was getting cleaned.'

'Apparently it was one of her friends he hooked up with, too.'

'Far out, is everyone cheating these days?'

'I'm not,' said Tim.

Steph elbowed him, but I saw a small smile escape. She was obviously falling for my cousin, too.

'So, what was wrong with Ava?' I asked. 'Does she have to stay the night?'

'Sia said they're running tests, but they don't think she's been eating properly for months, maybe even longer. Or when she does, she'll make herself sick.'

My stomach churned as I thought back to the day I'd heard Ava vomiting in the bathroom. I remembered her painful sobbing. Despite Ava's accusation, I hadn't told Liani any of that. I'd only offered my bad pork/upset tummy theory. Liani and Rae must have drawn their own conclusions before they'd pulled her in for a confidential chat. But that didn't soften my recollection of Ava hissing at me in the company foyer, or how angry and bloodshot her eyes had looked as she'd denied having an eating disorder.

'Do you think she'll be okay?' I asked, nervous about the answer.

'Yeah,' said Steph. She paused. 'If she gets the right help.'

We sat in silence for a moment, and I watched Tim play mindlessly with Steph's hair.

My mobile rang. I saw Kat's name pop up and I pressed 'ignore', then switched my phone on to silent; I'd talk to her later, once I got on the train.

'It's scary to think she thought she was fat, isn't it?' I said. 'I mean, she's the skinniest person I've ever seen in real life. It blows me away … I tried to help her, but …'

'Jose, some things can't be explained,' Steph said.

She and Tim glanced at each other. It was quick, but not quick enough that I didn't catch it.

'What?' I asked, self-conscious. 'Do I have something on my face? Or in my teeth? I do, don't I?' I covered my mouth just in case.

'Jose, how are *you* doing?' asked Tim, pulling my hand down.

I shrugged. 'I'm okay. I'm worried for Ava.'

'You're allowed to be angry at her, you know,' said Steph. 'Everyone with half a brain at *Sash* knows it was Ava who tripped you up. Rae will come around, for sure. You'll be pocketing that five thousand before you know it.'

'You're kidding, right? There's no way Rae would

reconsider me for the internship — you should have heard what she said. Plus, I'm not even angry any more.'

And I wasn't. Every last piece of hatred toward Ava had been snatched away when that wailing ambulance sped off.

'*Really?*' Steph narrowed her eyes at me.

'Really, guys,' I insisted. 'I'll get an internship somewhere else. It's fine.'

'Fine?' scoffed Tim. 'Isn't fine girl code for "This is the worst thing I could be feeling right now, I just don't know how to tell you"?'

Steph nodded. 'Pretty much. Get talking, Jose.'

'I can't, I'm leaving,' I said. 'I'm going home to Mum.'

'What?' they shouted in unison.

'Yeah, as in right now.' I gestured to the suitcase.

'Now? No!' said Steph. 'What about pizza?'

'I'm so sorry, I have a train to catch.'

Steph and Tim exchanged looks again, this time for even longer.

'So this is for real?' Steph asked. 'You're not coming back?'

'I guess not.'

Tim swore. 'Man, this blows.'

I wanted to squeeze their hands and tell them we'd still see each other loads. But I didn't. I couldn't imagine Steph with her too-cool shoes and edgy haircut chilling at the local pub over a chicken parmie with me and

Angel. Something told me her idea of living didn't include lapping up and down the main street, visiting the same cafe day in, day out, and trying to avoid old Mr Rickston whose onion breath was famous around town for scaring people away. As for Tim, he was so flaked out half the time that getting to a uni lecture was a huge effort, let alone catching the train to a town way outside his band-party-sleeping bubble.

I shouldn't have been surprised that My Dream Life Where I Was A Successful And Seemingly Normal Human Being And Mega Magazine Star didn't work out. I wasn't cut out for that world. Rae's world. The glamours' world. Sure, there'd been moments when I'd let myself believe that I'd changed into a new-and-improved Josie (now with added guy magnetism), but I'd only been kidding myself. I wasn't a babe, not like the other magazine girls. Never had been. I knew that at age twelve, when I had a face full of acne, a fear of mascara and an embarrassing stain on my physical culture leotard. But if I knew this (and I *did*), why did it still hurt so much to leave the city?

Steph's lip quivered and we threw our arms around each other. Tim leaned in, too, squeezing us both.

'It's been great having you here, cuz,' he said. 'Oh! I almost forgot. Did James already give you his laptop?'

'His laptop? No ...'

Tim raced around the apartment, looking in the

kitchen, on the bookshelf (which didn't contain a single book) and on the coffee table, before finally unearthing it from under a heap of papers on the dining table.

'Here,' he said, passing me the dusty laptop. 'He was going to give it to you next time he saw you.'

'No, I couldn't —'

'Jose, take it — he said you're the writer and you'll need it more than he does.'

'Are you sure?'

'Dude, the guy's already perving on a newer model that he can produce music on,' Tim said.

'Wow ... tell him thanks, okay? That's ... really nice of him.' I bit my lip to stop a flood of gushing remarks.

'Why don't you stay and tell him yourself?' said Steph. 'He'll probably be home soon.'

'Just tell him for me, okay? I better go,' I said, lowering my head. 'Thanks for everything, guys.'

I kissed Steph's cheek, waved at Tim, then wheeled my suitcase from the apartment. I had a train to catch.

21.

The train station hummed around me. I was so lost in my thoughts that I hardly noticed the pungent smell of urine wafting from the public toilets or the plodding, tapping and striding of hundreds of pairs of feet on the concrete. With no Harry-Potter-style invisibility cloak at my disposal, I'd settled for pulling my hoodie over my head and hunching over a table to hide away. As far as anyone could see I was just another nobody in the city. Another sucker trying to make a living then get home without being spat on or pestered for spare change.

I couldn't believe how my so-boring-I'd-almost-fall-asleep-thinking-about-it life had changed in the last couple of months. I'd had years of working hard to get good grades, attending dull family events and spending Saturday nights watching Mum unpack the dishwasher. Then ... *bam!* I'd written two features for a national magazine's website, accidentally hooked up with a celebrity, been harassed by online bullies, been rejected by a gorgeous guy, been booted out of *Sash* by its infamous editor-in-chief, and seen someone's life fall apart in front of me. I didn't know what to think about anything any more.

How could I have been so wrong about Ava? I felt awful for her. Dumped, depressed, not eating, making herself sick ... and I'd thought she was the confidence queen. She should have been. Not only was she beautiful, but she was smart and talented — I'd seen her as a triple threat for the internship prize. But beneath all those layers of expensive make-up and designer clothes, she was as scared, alone and anxious about her place in the world as the rest of us. Maybe even more so. If seemingly have-it-all girls like Ava felt like insignificant ants scuttling around trying not to get stamped on, then what chance did we, the non-glamazons, have?

And then, like a glorious sign from above, the idea for my *Weekly Mail* opinion piece came to me. It didn't tap me on the shoulder or whisper in my ear. No, it whacked me over the head with an almighty wallop. 'Write me,' it pleaded. 'Write me now.' I could feel the words rattling around inside me, forming sentences and wanting to spill onto the page. They didn't care that I'd got the flick from Rae and from James, or give a rat's that I was kilometres away from the comforts of home. They were ready to be written and I wasn't going to argue with them, lest they explode into specks of dust, never to be found again. I was a writer. Okay, a wannabe writer, but I needed words on my team.

A booming voice plagued with static came across the loudspeaker, shouting that my train wasn't far away — but I couldn't wait any longer. I needed to get the words out now before I lost them.

I raced toward the ticket counter and bustled my way to the front of the line, past two gum-chewing kids, three guys in faux-leather jackets and a dazed-looking businessman. I pleaded with the attendant to swap my ticket for a later train, bribing him with a half-eaten packet of lollies and a chocolate bar. *Finally* he handed me a new ticket for the next train, which gave me a good two and a half hours to write in the station's cafe — hello wi-fi and food.

Stomach clenched, I sat down at a table, turned on James's laptop and waited for it to load. I hoped his desktop background wasn't a photo of him and Summer kissing. The Polaroids had been bad enough. Luckily, the computer's welcome page only revealed a black and white photo of Jimi Hendrix carving it up on his guitar. Phew.

Tracing my fingers over the keyboard, I felt connected to James; he was probably the last person to have touched these keys. But my tough-love side didn't let me sink into that thought for long; it's a laptop, Josie, not a diamond ring, I told myself. Summer was still James's girlfriend. I was just the dorky writer chick who inherited the old computer and I had to be okay with that.

I opened up a new Word document and forced myself to focus on the Big Idea. My mind brimmed over with Ava's body-image struggles, the awful attacks on my appearance by the online trolls, feeling inadequate alongside picture-perfect magazine babes and something as simple — and crushing — as being dumped and left broken-hearted. Oh yeah, that emotion was universal. When you're single, it can seem like everyone else comes in pairs. Steph had Tim, Kara had Billy, Summer had James. Me? Well, I had a deadline.

It was time to get writing.

When I was done, I saved and closed the piece, then started on a longwinded email to Filly. I told him about the failed internship at *Sash*, the lessons I'd learned and the ones I hadn't, the embarrassment of being sacked and my secret fears for my future. Despite how nonchalant I'd been to Steph and Tim, I'd convinced myself that the only career option left for me was shovelling animal poo at the local zoo. But most of all, I told him about the importance of what I'd attached to the email. I'd met my deadline for the *Weekly Mail* and wanted him to read every word.

The next step was getting it accepted by the paper. I didn't care about the glory, or the by-line or my portfolio. Sure, I wanted to see my words in print, but my name or face didn't need to be in golden lights next to them.

I'd seen enough of myself in the media to last a lifetime. The story was the important part. After all, I wasn't just speaking for me — I'd written this piece for every mother, daughter, friend or sister who'd ever beaten herself up for the way she looked or felt about her body.

I hovered over the 'send' button. Unsure, I reopened the article for a final look. I skim-read it, soaking up every word until I felt ready. Well, ready enough. The words were unlike any I'd poured onto a page before; they were deeply personal. I knew Kat would tease me for being 'soft' or for 'wearing my heart on my sleeve'. It felt like reading over an old diary, only this piece was going to be published in black and white next to ads for second-hand lawnmowers and escort services.

Almost satisfied, I added one final sentence to the email: *I hate to ask, but based on the magazine internship incident, does this mean I have failed the subject?* I signed off. Then, without letting myself question anything else, I pressed 'send'.

I shut the laptop down and bundled it into its bag. I wasn't ready to hear Filly's response yet. But as I wheeled my suitcase to the platform, a little part of my brain wondered what I would do if his answer was 'Yes, you have failed the subject'.

I glanced at my watch again. Only a few minutes had passed since I'd last checked. The train ride dragged on, as though the universe had conspired to make me suffer one final time. The punishment? Torture by boredom — and it was working. All I could hear was a man snoring across the aisle, while the two young girls with him squabbled over a grubby ragdoll. There was nothing to do and no one interesting to make polite chitchat with to pass the time. The darkness of night was creeping in, so there weren't even paddocks to stare at while I gazed out the window and dreamed of home. Desperate for something — *anything* — to do, I turned on my phone. My jaw dropped. Twenty-one missed calls. All from Kat.

I called her number, but it rang out. I tried again; this time it went straight to voicemail.

'Crap,' I muttered.

I tried once more. Still no answer. Next, I tried Mum. No answer from her either. My eyes welled up as worst-case scenarios planted themselves deep into my brain, growing darker by the second. I tried Mum again, redialling once, twice, three times, until I lost count.

Just when I was about to cry onto the shoulder of the man sitting near me, my phone burst to life and Kat's name appeared on the screen.

'Josie, where are you?' she said. 'I've been trying to call you for hours.'

'I'm so sorry,' I said. 'My phone was on silent. What's going on? Are you okay? Kat?' My questions fired so fast that she didn't have time to answer.

Instead, she sighed. 'Jose, Mum's in hospital. There was an accident.'

'What? What happened?'

'I don't want to talk about it on the phone.'

'Freaking hell. Is she okay?'

'Yeah, I think so. She had a fall … and there's some other stuff. Just come home, Jose. Please.'

I told her I'd be home as soon as I could. At least, I thought that's what I said, because by then it felt as though I'd floated out of my body and was watching this happen to someone else. I let the shock sweep me up and push me through the train ride, spilling me out onto the familiar platform of home. Except even that looked different now.

All I could hear in Mum's hospital room was the soft hum of electronic medical equipment and my own fast nervous breaths. Mum was asleep. Earlier, a nurse had pulled her hair into a low bun and I could see every wrinkle and freckle on her face. It was unsettling at first — Mum's face was usually surrounded by her wild hair — but gradually I could see her beauty. Mum looked at peace while she slept, maybe lost in a dream of a time when everything was okay.

'Well, that took about an hour,' Kat said, walking into the room holding two teas. 'They can save people's lives but they can't get the kettle to work. Want one?'

I didn't, but I took it anyway. 'Thanks.'

She crashed onto the seat next to me. 'So ... Mum's right arm's broken in five places. It'll be in a cast for a while.'

'Far out. I can't believe she was up that ladder. She's lucky she didn't break her neck! What was she doing?'

'Getting Dad's golf gear from the attic, apparently, so she could try to sell it. Her mood's been pretty weird lately.'

'Weird?'

'Yeah. Laughing. Crying. Snapping. Apologising. She broke her phone this morning and I'd never seen her so upset. It was though she'd been told her left ear had to be cut off or something.'

'Geez.'

Mum's odd behaviour the other day with the rest of Dad's stuff and her reaction to the cutlery on the floor came to mind. 'Do you think she'll be alright?'

'Eventually.'

Kat and I sat in silence, watching her rest. I knew Mum had been struggling since Dad left — we both knew — but I had no idea it would ever come to this. An accident. An ambulance. A trip to Emergency. In a way, it was a relief that there were nurses and doctors to fuss, and take her temperature, and tell us what to do. But mainly it felt awful, like I hadn't done enough to help. Like I should have prevented this somehow. Like I'd been so caught up in my own drama that I'd failed her as a daughter.

I also felt terrible for Kat. When I'd arrived at the hospital, I'd found her teary and wringing her hands in the waiting room, so it was good to see she'd calmed down.

To think I'd been so stressed about a stupid internship and an off-the-market cute guy while my little sister tried to cope with a sick, worn-out mum with broken bones.

'I'm so sorry I wasn't here, Kat.'

'Don't be. You're here now.'

I glanced at Mum, but there was no difference. Part of me had hoped our voices would have woken her up and had her springing out of bed to shower us with kisses and hugs.

But she didn't move.

For the first time in a while, I wished Dad was here. I wanted to scream at him, hit him; I wanted to yell, 'Mum's falling apart and it's all because you had a midlife crisis and ran away.' I knew where my anger was coming from. It was guilt for not being there when Mum needed someone. It wasn't up to Kat to watch over her. I was the older sister, it was my job, my responsibility.

A little moan escaped Mum's lips. Kat and I sat up straight, waiting for more. We needed more. And then, as though she could read our minds, she gave a small cough.

She opened her eyes, saw us and smiled. 'My darling girls, you're here,' she murmured.

Her eyes closed again. I squeezed her hand, and Kat and I went back to watching her in silence.

22.

The next morning, Mum barely spoke as we fawned over her at the hospital, collecting her bag and tying up loose ends with the nursing staff. She didn't say anything when I drove us home in her car, even though seeing me behind the wheel usually terrified her. Or when we took over her chores at home, putting on loads of washing, mopping the tiles, stacking the dishwasher and vacuuming the carpet. While we rushed around proving our uselessness by calling out things like 'Where do we keep the duster?' and 'How do you turn the dishwasher on?', Mum sat quietly in her usual spot at the head of the dining table, established many years ago for its easy access to the kitchen.

Finally, with most of the bigger chores done, Kat and I plonked down across from each other at the table, in the same seats we'd had since childhood.

'How's your arm?' I asked Mum, nodding at her cast, which was already covered with her name, hearts and flowers drawn by Kat. 'I guess you won't be able to write for a while.'

'Or work,' she sighed, linking the fingers of her left hand through mine. 'I need two hands to make cakes and garden. But we'll get by … we always do.'

I shook my head, furious with myself for losing the chance to win five thousand dollars. But if I couldn't earn that kind of money myself, then I was going to do my best to come up with a solution.

'What about the library?' I suggested. 'Surely they'll be happy to keep you around?'

'With this thing?' Mum asked, pointing at her cast. 'I don't know, love, I'm only casual. But I'll have a yarn to them, okay?'

'Don't you get sick pay?' asked Kat. 'Brenna Jadenson's dad fell over at work and scored an awesome payout. Maybe you could do that? He gets to bludge around all the time now.'

'This is a bit different,' Mum said. 'And we're not bludgers.'

'There is another option,' I began, tongue-tied by Mum's and Kat's eager expressions. 'Um … well … we could try to track him down.'

'Who?' asked Kat.

'Dad,' I forced out.

I'd barely said his name out loud since he'd left and, judging by Mum's face, I should have kept it that way.

'That man has done enough,' she said, lip quivering.

'It's just … I'm worried,' I said. 'We have to pay the bills somehow.'

'Yeah, let's make him suffer for what he's done,' added Kat, eyes blazing.

'Not a chance,' said Mum.

My mind raced. 'Well, I'll get a job — two new jobs — and help out,' I said. 'And Kat's old enough to work, too. We'll both pitch in and sort this out —'

'Girls!' Mum interrupted, her voice raised and face flushed. 'I'm the parent around here and I'll pay the bills, you hear me? I want Kat focused on school and you focused on your degree. It's my house, my responsibility, my choice. Now, I don't want to hear another word about money, or jobs, or *him*. We're done here.'

'But, Mum —' tried Kat.

'End of discussion,' she said. 'Now, I'm going to have a lie-down before lunch. Are you two okay to pull something together for us?'

'Yes,' we said at the same time, then swapped unsure glances as she shuffled to the couch in the next room. We were going to have to be okay, whether we felt ready or not.

Our first challenge: we had lunch to prepare.

Capsicums, carrots, cucumber, tomatoes, Spanish onion — I mentally ticked off the ingredients for a salad. Ah, rocket! I rummaged around in the fridge until I unearthed a packet of spicy green leaves and tossed them through the bowl, admiring the rainbow of colours.

'I know Mum's trying to play it cool on the whole money issue, but I heard her freaking out on the phone to Aunt Julie,' whispered Kat, frying sausages in a pan next to me.

'Again?'

'Yeah, at the hospital. She was rambling about bills and medical fees and being out of work and ... This is serious, Jose. I feel kinda helpless.'

I did too, although I couldn't let my little sister know.

On top of the broken arm, the doctor had told us she had a mild case of situational depression, most likely brought on from the stresses of the past year. He said she needed to eat healthily and exercise. Kat had promised to drag Mum out for an hour's walk most days and I'd planned to dust off the exercise bike in the garage. But none of it seemed like enough.

I crunched on a piece of cucumber as I struggled to think of a worthy idea.

'Maybe I should call Aunt Julie?' I said, immediately wishing I hadn't suggested it. Aunt Julie was a clean freak and, worst of all, she smelled of disinfectant. I cringed at the thought of her showing up on our doorstop with a list of chores and a suitcase spilling with stinky soaps and cleaning products.

Luckily, Kat thought the same. 'Argh, no way,' she groaned. 'She's such a freak. You know she irons her underpants? Who does that?'

I let out a sigh. 'Okay, well … what can we do? There's got to be something.'

Kat cocked her head, thinking. 'You're going to be home for a while, right? Now the internship's done?'

I nodded. We'd briefly talked about the failed internship at the hospital but I couldn't bear the thought of reliving it again.

'Let's wait and see,' shrugged Kat. 'We'll give it a few days and if we need help, then we'll call Aunt Julie.'

'But only if we're really desperate.'

'Agreed.'

'It's a total Plan B.'

'Sausages are done,' said Kat. 'I've nailed this cooking thing. How's your salad?'

'Yeah, it's ready,' I replied, naively hoping my salad was tasty enough to distract us all from Mum's health problems, our growing expenses and my firing from *Sash*.

Something told me it wasn't, though.

I'd eaten half the cucumber.

No new email messages. *Again*. I slammed my laptop shut and wondered what was taking Filly so long to get back to me about my article for the *Weekly Mail*, the internship and my chances of failing the course.

I hadn't heard a word from him, not a peep. I'd called the uni and one of the tutors had told me Filly had extended his latest fishing trip into a 'working holiday', whatever that meant. The longer I didn't receive a reply, the more I panicked. My mindset had switched from 'It's fine, Filly will help me get through this' to 'I'm going to get kicked out of university because I annoyed a magazine editor and there's nothing anyone can do about it'.

I refreshed my inbox for the zillionth time. You know, just in case. And there it was, again: *no new emails*.

Surely it wasn't that hard to reply? I mean, you type a few words, throw in some spaces and full stops here and there, then press 'send'. Easy, right? Apparently not for Filly.

And, like a really annoying song that gets stuck in your head, I wondered what James was doing and whether he'd thought about me lately.

No, I convinced myself. He'd be too busy having sex-capades with Summer.

Sighing, I trudged into the lounge room and collapsed on the couch. Mum was out in the backyard, watching two sparrows dart and prance on the lawn.

She'd seemed happier over the last couple of days. Calmer. The hospital had put her in touch with a counsellor and he had her using phrases like 'True confidence comes from within' and 'Every day, I am grateful to be alive'. She'd repeat them to herself while she was doing her make-up or brushing her teeth. It all sounded a bit lame to me, but I couldn't complain: it seemed to be working. We had our mum back, and nothing was more important than that. Kat and I had helped her clear out the rest of Dad's belongings — old faded shirts, workboots, stuff like that — and she'd been humming, admiring the rosebushes, even showing us how to bake banana muffins, ever since.

The ladies at the library had been good to Mum, too: they'd organised a bake sale to help cover her medical costs and even created a new casual role just for her so she didn't have to worry about carrying heavy piles of books. Her main duty? Reading to kids at after-school care. I think she'd always dreamed of being a film actress or musical-theatre star, so she was delighted to start the following week (and wear a green wig to make even the toughest kids giggle). Money was still tight but Mum had been true to her promise: she'd handled it her way. Kat and I were thrilled to see her doing so well and secretly relieved that we didn't have to fall back on Plan B.

I was wrenched from my thoughts by someone trying to knock down the front door.

'Can you get that, love?' Mum hollered from outside.

'Yeah, yeah,' I mumbled, and rushed to the door before whoever was bashing on it put their fist through the wood.

I heard Kat call out, 'Sorry, forgot my keys. Can someone let me in, please?'

Just as I put my hand to the lock, the door burst open, nearly whacking me in the face.

'Found them,' Kat grinned, waving her keys in a manicured hand.

I rolled my eyes and walked back to the couch.

'Hey, Lady Grump-a-Lot, where are you going? You'll want to see this,' Kat said, waving a newspaper at me. 'Josie, did you hear me? This'll wake you up.'

I turned back to face her. 'It's not another story about Billy cheating, is it? I'm not in the mood.'

She laughed. 'Billy's probably pashed a dozen girls since you. In fact, Shirley Piper's hairdresser's roommate in the city said he asked for her phone number in some club last week.'

I sighed. Clearly Billy hadn't changed at all. 'Well, what is it?' I dawdled over to the dining table where Kat had spread out the newspaper. She pointed to a medium-sized story in the upper corner of a right-hand page. Half asleep, I started reading. It only took one and half sentences for it to click.

It was my story.

My article for the *Weekly Mail* that Filly had never emailed me back about.

'Oh my god!' I shrieked. 'This is mine! Why didn't you say so?'

Kat dragged her long hair into a plait. 'So, am I an awesome sister or what?'

'The best.' I stopped reading and looked up. 'Thank you! How'd you know it was in the paper? I had no idea.'

'The ugly guy in the newsagent — you know the one with the foul earrings — was reading it,' said Kat, screwing up her nose. 'Hey, it's pretty good — your story, I mean.'

'Yeah?' I lapped up the moment; compliments from my little sister were a rare, wonderful thing.

'So those online freaks were pretty brutal to you, huh?'

'I suppose you could say they taught me a thing or two,' I said. 'Hey, did the *Mail* editors keep the bit about where to find help for eating disorders like bulimia, anorexia, distorted body image ...' I checked, running my eyes over the words so fast I almost couldn't take them in. 'They did. This is amazing. They published it all.'

'Have you seen what's at the end yet?' Kat said. 'That's the *really* cool bit.'

I glanced at the bottom of the piece and there it was: a little dash with my name after it in bold type. I swallowed. This was real. I had an article published in the paper, an article that actually meant something to me, an article with a real message.

Kat cleared her throat. 'So, like, not meaning to change the subject, but did you hear?'

'Hear what?'

'Stacey dumped Pete Jordan.'

'Serious?'

'Yeah. And now everyone knows he has a tiny you-know-what.' Kat wiggled her little finger. 'Apparently he sent a selfie of it to her phone, but her dad saw it, then accidentally messaged it to all her contacts.'

'No way!'

'They *all* got to see Pete in his … well, lack of glory.'

Speechless, all I could do was shake my head and grin. My luck had changed and it felt wonderful. I wanted to knock on wood, throw salt over my shoulder and avoid black cats to stop it from ever changing back again.

Happy with her good deed for the day, Kat hummed as she retreated to her bedroom for some loud music and texting. The tune was catchy and its cheeky bubble-gum pop sounded familiar. It didn't take me long to realise she was humming Greed's new song — I'd heard it on the radio earlier. Despite myself, I hadn't been able to help tapping along to the beat.

Energy fizzed through my body. I wanted to scream with happiness over my first official newspaper by-line. But mostly, I wanted to thank Filly for the opportunity to write something real and get it published. I had to talk to him.

The phone rang out twice before I gave up; it didn't go to voicemail either. When my phone burst to life a few moments later, I answered it without checking who it was.

'Hello, I just had a missed call from this number?' a gruff voice said.

'Filly? It's Josie!'

'Josie, how are you?'

'I'm great. I, er, wanted to tell you some news.'

I felt a bit desperate and sad. Actually, I felt really desperate and sad. I'd been waiting days for a response from Filly, and nothing, not even a crummy voicemail message. And here I was, calling him over and over like an annoying salesman.

'Sorry, are you on holidays?' I added.

He cleared his throat. 'Let me guess — you've seen today's paper?'

'Oh, um, yes. I just saw it.'

'And?'

'I'm giddy.'

'Hey, *you* wrote it and they *loved* it,' he said. 'And so did I. The part about standing up against body-image bullies was brilliant. My daughter loved it, too. She said she's going to show all her friends at school tomorrow. Great work, Josie. Easily your best so far.'

'Thanks,' I said, my face hurting from smiling so hard. 'When I didn't hear from you, I thought you hated it.'

'Sorry, I've been spending long days fishing … er … writing reports, and by the time I resurfaced I figured you deserved a nice surprise.'

I smiled, but then remembered the other thing. 'Did you, um, read the bit in my email about me losing the internship?'

Filly paused. 'I did, it's a tricky one. I may need you to come in to chat about it some more.'

'Will I fail the subject —'

'Sorry, Josie, can you hang on a minute? I have another call coming through — actually, can I call you back? This is the third time this number has called today, it must be urgent.'

'Oh, okay,' I stammered, but Filly had hung up before I'd finished.

I lay back on the couch and traced my eyes over the by-line: *By Josephine Browning*. I'd done it. Sure, I hadn't won five thousand dollars for Mum or a monthly column in a national magazine, but things were moving in the right direction. Who knew, maybe I wouldn't end up scrubbing tiles or unclogging toilets after all.

I was halfway through reading the feature again when my phone rang. 'Hey Filly, so I wanted to —' I began.

'Josie, it's Liani.'

'Oh, hey!'

My heart swelled as I heard her voice. I hadn't spoken to her since ... well, since ... you know. I'd been too embarrassed.

'I know this is out of the blue ... really, really out of the blue,' she said, 'but is there any chance you can come into the city? I'd love to chat with you about something important.'

I sat up. 'Oh? When are you thinking?'

'As soon as you can get here. Is that possible?'

'I, ah, sure. I'll get the next train.'

I didn't ask why or what was going on. Liani had summoned me and that was all that mattered.

When I hung up the phone, I went to ask Mum if she'd be okay on her own. She was concerned about me returning to *Sash* after what had happened — I couldn't blame her; I was trembling on the inside myself — but I assured her I'd be fine. I just hoped that was true.

Forty-one minutes later, I was packed, preened and on a train back to the city, unsure what was waiting for me. Was I making a huge mistake? Or was Steph right? Were they reconsidering me for the internship? Would this mean I wouldn't fail uni after all?

My mind wouldn't stop racing so I rang Steph to debrief. The chugging of the train was so noisy I had to shout my news down the line. Two kids reading on the seat across from me glowered. One raised his finger to his lips, the international sign for 'Shut up'.

'Liani rang me too!' Steph said. 'She didn't mention anything about calling you, though.'

'What do you think's going on?' I whispered, glancing at the guys who now had earphones plugged in. They didn't look up, so I figured I was in the clear.

'I have no idea … Maybe they're going to announce who won the internship prize?'

I leaned against the window. 'That can't be it. I'm out, remember? Well, unless they want to rub my nose in it.'

'What else … Oh! Maybe Rae wants to apologise to you, like in barbershop-quartet style with bells, whistles and matching red-and-white striped dresses?'

'That would be sweet,' I said. 'Let me know if you find out any more goss, okay? Hey Steph, am I crazy for going back there?'

'You'd be crazy not to. What have you got to lose?' Steph was right: I'd already lost my dignity.

We both promised to call if we heard anything more, then hung up. Alone with my thoughts, my brain got to wondering — a dangerous pastime. If Steph and I had been summoned to the *Sash* office, did that mean Ava would be there, too?

I was so preoccupied with the excitement and mystery of Liani's call that I didn't even notice Filly hadn't rung back.

23.

The suffocating smell of perfume was the same, and the receptionist greeted me with a smile as always, but something was up at *Sash* HQ. There was an air of franticness, stress in every voice, worried frowns creasing the glamours' perfectly made-up faces. I glanced around for Steph; no sign of her yet. Ava wasn't perched on the reception couch either.

I took a deep breath and walked into the office. Five men in white overalls were taking down posters, frames and books and placing them into black garbage bags. Shocked, I watched them work. The girls typed in silence amid the upheaval, exchanging sneaky glances but mainly glaring at their computers. A quick look at their screens revealed most of them were in the middle of writing lengthy emails that probably weren't work-related. There's only so much you can write in an email about calling in oil-free foundations for a beauty shoot.

As requested, I headed for Liani's office. My palms were sweating and every muscle in my body was tensed.

I kept my head down and focused on making it without bumping into Rae. But I couldn't avoid her dominating presence: she was everywhere — in clippings from newspapers and photos of her chatting with celebrities on red carpets. I'd forgotten that her face was plastered all around the office. Two minutes at *Sash* and I felt like I was in the enemy's camp. And it was my fault: I'd walked in voluntarily, like a sacrificial lamb.

'Hey Liani,' I said, poking my head through her office door.

She turned and her face opened into a grin. For once, her cheeks weren't flushed and I could see the pale, luminescent softness of her skin — like a baby's. Unlike everyone else in the office, Liani had a peaceful aura, despite the four boxes heaving with folders on the floor and the empty shelf above her desk.

'Josie — you came!' She walked over and pulled me into a hug. She was spongy and warm; a human-sized hot water bottle that squished in all the right places.

She gestured for me to take a seat. 'I apologise for all the secrecy. I suppose you're wondering why you're here?'

'Just a little bit.' I smiled, crossing my legs. 'But before you say anything, I never got a chance to explain about my last day, or to apologise. It was such a mess and —'

'I know, honey, it's okay,' interrupted Liani. 'Ava told me everything at the hospital.'

'Everything?'

A lump formed in my throat. I could only imagine what lies Ava had been spreading.

'Everything,' Liani repeated. 'She's out of hospital and resting at home, but she feels awful about what happened between you two.'

'It's just that ... Wait, *she* feels awful?'

'I know it's a lot to take in,' Liani said, then glanced at her watch.

'So you know that I didn't ... I mean, you know? But no one rang. I'm so confused —'

'Josie, I'm sorry. Things around here have been a little ... Well, you'll soon find out. We'll talk later about everything, every little detail, I promise — but first I need you to come with me. The meeting's about to start.'

'Oh, okay, great.' I stood up and smoothed down my dress. 'Hang on, what meeting? Does Rae know I'm here?'

I didn't know if I could handle another verbal assault from Rae's poisonous tongue.

'Yes, she knows.' Liani must have noticed that my face had frozen because she patted me on my shoulder. I couldn't respond; I was too busy trying not to crumple at the prospect of sitting through a meeting with Rae at the helm. 'In fact, she encouraged me to invite you along. You ready?'

Not one iota. But I followed Liani out of the office door toward the semicircle of designer clothes, spray tans, glossy hairstyles and patterned notebooks. Rae stood at the front, avoiding any direct eye contact. Instead, she stared at her clipboard and admired her perfectly polished nails. She hadn't so much as glanced in my direction, so I told myself to quit over-thinking and focus on getting through the meeting.

I noticed that, while Rae wrote notes in long, loopy handwriting, every other *Sash* girl had her own focus point in the room: a book on the shelf, a framed print by the window, anything other than Rae or another staff member. For me, it was a black stain on the wall to the right of Rae's head. Oddly, it reminded me of an elephant sitting on a bike, which calmed my nerves (and almost set me off in a fit of nervous laughter).

Rae placed her notebook on her lap and the meeting began. The first red flag was Rae sprinkling her sentences with corporate buzz words like 'economic climate' and 'moving forward'. It was business jargon and I had no idea what it meant. Judging by the others' faces, I wasn't alone.

'It will come as no surprise, to some of you at least, that things are changing around here,' Rae said, crossing and recrossing her legs.

At the mention of change, some of the girls sat upright in their seats, while others shrank down low.

'I may as well just say it, because if I don't, you're going to hear it from someone or somewhere else.' Rae shot an apprehensive look at Liani, who lowered her head. 'Girls, we gave it everything … and I know this will seem sudden, but we've been fighting for our place for a long time …' She paused — a long, painful pause — and I realised I'd never seen her lost for words like this. 'Liani and I have been told to tell you the magazine is folding.'

'What?' blurted out Eloise, Gen and Carla in unison. The others covered their mouths or hung their heads.

Shania, a production coordinator with bad acne and greasy hair, piped up. 'Wait, what does that mean?'

Needless to say, she wasn't the sharpest pencil in the pencil case. But for once Rae didn't shoot back a scathing reply. Instead, she spoke calmly and slowly.

'We're closing, Shania.' She turned to the group again. 'I'm so sorry, everyone. This market is rough, really rough, and there's not enough space for both *Marilyn* and us in the company any more. With ad pages not selling and our dropping circulation, we just can't compete, even though our editorial — your hard work — is first class.'

Everyone stared at Rae; some eyes were already red and teary. No one uttered a word so she continued.

'We're not the first to close, and we won't be the last, so please don't take this personally. I know — management knows — you have all given this magazine everything and I thank you for that.'

'What's … what's going to happen to us?' Eloise asked, her voice shaking.

'Bella from HR will come and talk to you all about options,' Rae said. 'And there are options for everyone, so don't be afraid to ask.'

It looked as though Rae was about to say something else, but a chorus of chattering and chirping overpowered her. Teary girls whispered to each other, already making plans and promising to 'stick together'. Others sat in silence, their heads lowered, too shocked, angry or upset to react.

Janice, an older woman who helped out the subeditors part-time, called out over the babble. 'Rae, what does this mean for the current issue? We'll finish it, right?'

'Yeah,' chimed in Sia. 'We will, won't we? I've called in some gorgeous products that I've been saving for this issue.'

Rae clasped her hands together. 'I'm sorry to say that we won't. In fact, we've been ordered to delete what we've done so far — delete it all. They don't want to risk it leaking to our competitors.'

'But all our work …' muttered Carla, shaking her head.

'We will get through this,' Liani said, the familiar red flush back on her cheeks and spreading quickly.

'We all will. *You* will,' added Rae defiantly, to no one in particular. I was sure everyone in the room hoped she meant them.

As the group broke into another frenzied buzz of speculation, I gave Steph an awkward little wave across the room. She mouthed 'Whoa' back to me and gestured for me to come over. I weaved my way through the frazzled group, tripping on handbag straps and stomping on toes. When I eventually made it to Steph, we fell onto each other in a big hug.

'Did you know?' I asked.

'No way! Seriously, I'm sitting here thinking why are we here?' she whispered. 'I had no idea about any of this. Dad didn't breathe a word, and Rae seemed fine last night. Well, uptight and snooty, but she's always like that.'

'It's so weird,' I said, looking around the room. The men in overalls were still tossing keyboards, magazines, posters, even pot plants into bags. 'It's the end of an era. I feel like we're intruders or something, watching this.'

It felt inappropriate to approach the *Sash* girls so we huddled together and continued whispering.

'So did you two girls hear?' interrupted Gen, snapping us to attention. 'Apparently Rae's been made editor-in-chief of *Marilyn* magazine — one of the other girls just told me. We lose our jobs and she gets a promotion. I love how she left that part out of her speech.'

'Are you serious?' I asked. 'She's going to *Marilyn*? The competition?'

'Yeah,' said Gen. 'They've ditched the old ed — you know, that loud chain-smoking woman with the hooked nose — and brought Rae in. Rumour has it she got a pay rise when she threatened to work for another company.'

'Unbelievable,' said Steph. 'She's ruthless.'

'Oh yeah, and that's not all,' fired off Gen, the filter between her brain and mouth clearly on strike. 'Esmeralda's pregnant.'

'What?' My head whipped over to where Esmeralda was standing with one hand on her hip and the other resting on her stomach.

'Yep, she's going freelance. I overheard her telling one of the others. Get out while you can, guys — this industry chews people up and spits them out left, right and centre.' And she rushed off to join Eloise and the editorial girls who were crying in the foyer.

'Well, that's motivating,' said Steph grimly.

'I wonder what everyone else will do?' I said. 'Liani must be devastated.'

Steph pulled a face. 'I know. With her mortgage and the baby ...'

'Eloise will be okay, right?' I asked, watching Eloise wipe away tears. 'I mean, she's awesome.'

'I'm sure someone will snap her up,' said Steph. 'And Sia — that girl's so charismatic she's probably got people calling her for interviews already.' Steph and I knew we had no idea what we were prattling about; we just wanted the best for the women who'd been so good to us.

Rae coughed, dragging everyone's attention back to herself. 'I know that news was hard to hear, but I wanted to say thank you,' she told us. 'Together we have been through good times, tough times and, let's be honest, shitty times. But one day, your time at *Sash* will be a blip on your career, a tiny pink dot nestled among other successes and failures and delights and dislikes and, hopefully, you'll look back on it fondly.'

She glanced over at Liani, who nodded.

'As I said, HR will talk to you, but in the meantime I have written you all excellent references and, who knows, maybe we'll work together one day in the future. As some of you may have heard, I'm moving on to edit another title — not too far, I'll still be in the building — and I'd love to stay in touch. This is all a lot to take in, so I've sent for a few bottles of bubbly and some cheese and crackers. A little brie should help us all with the office pack-up that lies ahead. Thank you.'

Her speech complete, Rae excused herself and walked back into her office. She closed the door behind her and left the blinds down.

'She thinks cheese is going to fix this? Fool. Half of us don't eat dairy!' I heard Gen hiss behind me. Two girls chimed agreement, swearing loudly to make their point.

I wondered if Rae was crying her in office, nursing herself through the pain of having to shatter the worlds of her staff. But another part of me imagined her cackling and raking her long fingernails together, excited about her next queen-of-the-empire role at *Marilyn*. I settled on a blurring of both options, because that was Rae: hot and cold, happy and serious, friendly and chilly, all at the same time.

Sure, I didn't love every minute I'd spent with her — in fact, they'd go down as some of the most nail-biting minutes of my life — but the woman was a genius at what she did and I respected that (despite the fact she was an A-grade tyrant who'd scare the designer dresses off her new team at *Marilyn*). The internship may have been over, the five thousand dollars and chance of a by-line had evaporated, but my time at *Sash* was worth it anyway. I had interned for one of Australia's fiercest, most respected editors. Rae's passion for her work and nonstop energy was astounding. But most of all, she deserved a gold-plated trophy for wearing six-inch heels every day without snapping an ankle.

'Hey Josie, are you free for our chat now?' Liani asked with a smile. Chaos was in full swing around her but her signature red flush was gone. 'We'll pick up where we left off.'

'Sure,' I replied, and followed her into her office.

This is it, I thought, I'm going to find out what's going on. Any attempt to play it cool was left in the main office; every part of me, down to the pores of my skin, waited in anticipation for Liani's news. Was I goosebumping from the adrenaline? Abso-freaking-lutely.

Liani's posters were rolled up in a corner and notepads and stationery were in neat piles on her desk. Things were never going to be the same again.

'Wow, so big news, huh?' I said, taking a seat opposite Liani. 'I mean, who'd have thought that was about to happen? Well, I mean, I'm guessing you knew, and Rae obviously, oh, and maybe Es, but anyway, big news for everyone else.'

Liani nodded. 'Yes, it's been a tough day.'

'I mean, it's like one hit of news after the other, isn't it? No internship for you, Josie! *Bam!* Wait, no internship for anyone! *Bam!* And no magazine for everyone! *Bam, bam, bam!*' My arms flailed in the air like a demented Mexican wave.

'It's huge. Huge news.'

'I know everyone will be fine, though, especially you. I bet you'll have job offers lining up at your door soon and you won't know which one to pick. Or maybe you'll want some time at home with your bub. Or a holiday. Or a —'

'Josie, can I talk now?' asked Liani, without the slightest hint of frustration in her voice.

'Oh, right. Of course. Sorry. You know I do that thing where I'm nervous and I ramble and I … yeah. You know.'

'I suppose you're wondering what you're doing here?'

That shut me up. I nodded.

'I've been in touch with your uni lecturer —'

'Filly? He didn't tell you about that stupid essay I handed in late, did he? Because it was by accident!' I paused, realising what I'd done. 'Sorry, did that whole interrupting thing again.'

'No,' she said. 'But he did send me a copy of the piece you had published in the *Weekly Mail*.'

'Oh.' Wow, Filly. I'd have to pay him a publicist's fee.

'Josie, it was wonderful and moving and ... powerful.' Liani said. 'And the topic — body image and bullying in the media. Breathtaking. Your piece was so current and, more than anything, *needed*. It got me thinking ... people need to know more about this! They need to read your words.'

'Really?' I blurted out.

I couldn't tell whether this was one of my vivid daydreams or not. I needed to pinch the top of my arm to find out. And so I did. And it hurt. A lot. This was happening.

'Over the years I've read hundreds of articles on body image, but to see one that covered it so delicately and from a softer, younger perspective — well, it hooked me. I wanted to read more about it, more from you. And there were some heavy issues in there, too — bulimia, bullying, feeling out of place. They're issues that need to be discussed, over and over again, until something changes in the world.'

'I agree,' I forced out.

'And to think your story's been syndicated to the national papers and you'll get to invoice for it. That's just —'

'National what?' I interrupted. 'Invoice?'

'Professor Fillsmore didn't tell you? You'll be getting paid for it — it's been picked up by the bigger papers.'

'I ... I ...'

'They loved it.'

My tear ducts ached. I pinched my arm again to distract myself, but it only made my eyes well up faster.

Liani leaned forward. 'Josie, the piece was heart-wrenching, real and one hundred and fifty per cent you. It was the perfect style for your voice.'

'My voice?'

'Your writer's voice.'

'This is ... I can't believe it,' I said. 'I think this is the best moment of my life.'

Liani's smile broadened into a full-blown, light-up-the-night beam. 'Josie, I want to offer you a fulltime job as my junior writer.'

I wanted to scream, 'Yes, yes, a thousand times yes!' but I was shocked into silence. My mouth moved but nothing came out. I felt like scarfing down waffles — it was as though my brain had overloaded and all I could handle was the thought of a big bowl of comfort food. With extra caramel topping.

'I ... I ... I ...' I stammered.

'I'm the new editor of *indi*, Josie, an online magazine. The owners want to take it in a new direction — aim it at real girls and real women. It's going to be fabulous, heartfelt and hard work. I know how much you love writing, and I'm sorry that everything's crashed here, but if you come and work for me you'll have your very own column every week.'

The letters Y, E and S danced on my tongue and shimmied between my teeth. *Yes, yes, yes,* I yelled in my head.

'It's a start-up company so the office won't be this fancy,' Liani continued. 'But I can promise you a stable salary, a lolly jar that never runs out and flexible working hours. What do you think?'

'Yes,' I spluttered, bearhugging my boss-to-be. 'Thank you so much.'

'Something tells me you'll like this, too — Sia will be our online features and beauty director.'

'That's amazing,' I said, already imagining the onslaught of free cupcakes and chocolates she'd share around the new office.

'It sure will be,' said Liani. 'In a few days we'll have a producer and then we'll be set.'

'It sounds perfect.' And then it hit me. Hard. 'Oh no, uni! I've still got lectures and classes back home.'

I should've known it was too good to be true. The thing I needed to get a job was going to be the thing that stopped me from getting a job. Would I have to drop out? Or transfer? Or turn down this incredible writing position? My mind raced with possibilities.

'Now, now, one step at a time,' said Liani, rearranging herself in the chair. 'If you're keen, Professor Fillsmore has agreed to you studying long distance, as long as you keep up your marks and pop down to see him at least once a semester.'

'So, let me get this straight,' I said. 'I'll be living, working, breathing in the city? And I don't have to quit uni? And I'll be a fulltime website writer? On *indi*? Seriously?'

She grinned. 'Almost — a fulltime *junior* website writer. Well? Is that still a yes?'

'Yes!' I laughed.

'Wonderful. You start Monday. Now get out of here and celebrate.'

I grinned. 'Thanks, this is incredible … boss.'

24.

Thrilled to bits, I walked out into the main office, which was still abuzz with a range of emotions. Most of the girls were in groups, whispering furiously, their manicured hands flailing. My good mood instantly disappeared and my stomach backflipped for them, especially Eloise, who'd always been so sweet.

I went over and tapped her on the shoulder. She turned around, red-eyed, and gave me a hug.

'The last time I felt this rubbish I was hungover, remember? Maybe we should do another cheeseburger run?' Eloise attempted to joke, but her heart wasn't in it.

'You'll get snatched up for a great job, I know you will,' I said.

'I hope so,' she muttered. 'If not, there's always PR. I've heard it pays more anyway.'

Gen, Carla and Sia rushed over. 'Eloise, we're going to the pub right now — you in?'

'I'm technically unemployed, right?' Eloise said. 'Probably shouldn't.'

Sia waved an envelope. 'The beauty sale money will cover everything. And forget about cleaning up — Rae's given us the okay to leave it.'

'It's the least this company can do for us,' spat Gen, still fired up.

'Josie, you in?' asked Carla.

'Ah, thanks, but I'd better get going,' I said. 'Thanks for everything, guys.' I hugged them all, squeezing Eloise and Sia extra tight.

'I'll see you soon, colleague,' whispered Sia, keeping her exciting new job a secret for the sake of the others.

I watched them walk away, knowing I'd never see them all together in the *Sash* office again.

Steph was standing alone in the corner. I walked over to tell her my news, but as I drew closer I realised her face was white. 'What? What is it, Steph?'

'Rae wants to see me in her office. Right now, apparently. Maybe she knows I stole Dad's car the other night and drove up the coast.'

'You stole your dad's car?'

That made her giggle. 'Shhhhh.'

The receptionist called over to us. 'Steph, Rae's ready to see you now.'

'Okay,' Steph replied. She turned back to me. 'Will I catch you later? You're staying at Tim's, right?'

'I'm meant to be,' I said, 'but I was thinking of killing time in the city. I don't want to walk in on James and Summer hooking up on the couch.'

Steph wrinkled her nose. 'Firstly, gross. Secondly, he's working.'

'Really?'

'Yeah, take this key and let yourself in. I'll be back later on and we can debrief.'

'Sounds perfect,' I replied. 'Good luck in there. Hope you're not done for grand theft auto.'

'Me too.' She rolled her eyes.

Goodbyes done, I left the office, soaking it all in one last time. On the street, I punched Kat's number into my phone — I had to tell her my news. Then I wondered if she'd throw a hissy fit over the death of her favourite magazine, so I decided I'd only tell her about moving to the city for now, and the fact she'd get my bedroom with the larger wardrobe. The RIP *Sash* news could wait for a face-to-face chat.

'What?' she said when she answered.

'Hey, how you doing?'

'Pretty busy.'

'Oh, okay … So how's Mum?'

'Same old. Reading books, napping in the garden, eating cake …'

'Cool. And how are you? Coping?'

'Yeah, why wouldn't I be?' The old Kat was back, and this time around she had extra bite.

'Fair enough … So, I kinda have some big news. Is Mum there? Put me on speaker phone.'

Kat burst into laughter. 'Oh, that's hilarious.'

'It is?'

'Sorry, what did you say?' She giggled. 'Koby just sent me the funniest video. There's, like, this dog who falls into a box of biscuits. Okay, it sounds lame but it's awesome.'

I shook my head, confused. 'Koby?'

'Yeah. My boyfriend. Duh.'

Of course. I mean, I'd never heard of the guy, but *of course*.

'I might call you back at a better time,' I said.

'Righto,' she said and hung up before I could add anything else.

In the past, Kat blowing me off for a canine YouTube clip would have annoyed me — a lot. But after everything we'd been through, it just made me laugh. Some things never changed, and in the case of my feisty, larger-than-life sister that wasn't such a bad thing. My news could wait.

At Tim's, I lay full-length on the couch and daydreamed. Everything was falling into place. *Finally*. Uni was back on track, I had an amazing job lined up, my family life was on the mend and I had a group of awesome friends. Sure, there were still some murky areas — the whole James situation, for one — but generally life was kicking butt. And for once, not mine.

It dawned on me that I needed to tell Angel the news and I had no idea how she was going to react.

'Hang on, I'm flossing,' she said when she answered my call, her voice muffled.

After she'd finished, I rambled on about the magazine closing down, the amazing writing job at *indi* with Liani, and how she and Rae knew that Ava had set me up after all.

When I'd finished, rather than scream, shout or squeal like I'd been expecting, Angel's voice softened. 'Wow, Jose, it's happening,' she said. 'The job in the city — you're really doing it.'

I swallowed. 'Yeah, it's kinda scary, huh?'

Angel went quiet. 'I'm going to miss you.'

'Oh, shut up before you make me cry, I'm not going that far,' I said, but it was too late. Warm, salty tears rolled down my cheeks and I wondered whether our friendship would ever be the same again. Together Angel and I had survived braces, bullying, parties (usually not being invited to them), crushes, broken hearts, exams, assignments and family dramas. But for some reason I couldn't shake the strange feeling that things were about to change, big time.

'So, actually, I've been dying to tell you something ...' Angel said.

I thought I had all her tones down, but this one was unreadable — it lingered somewhere between her I-just-made-out-with-a-boy voice and her I-just-heard-the-craziest-gossip-about-that-bully-we-hate voice.

'Tell me,' I said.

'I'm dropping out of uni.'

Shocked, I sat upright on the sofa. '*What?* Does your dad know?'

'Yeah, he's not happy about it, but he knows,' Angel said. 'Uni wasn't for me. I mean, *arts*. What was I thinking? Everyone knows an arts degree is just an excuse to wear a tea-cosy as a beanie and make out with your tutor.'

'It is?'

Angel's voice became more serious. 'Look, you've done so well being away from this place, and if I don't get out of here now, I'm never going to. I'll end up stacking shelves at night like Tahnee's aunt. I'm eighteen! I want what you've got.'

'So what's the plan?' I asked.

'I'm going to Europe,' she squealed. I couldn't remember the last time I'd heard her sound so happy. 'Staying in hostels, overdosing on pasta, working in bars ...'

'Are you serious?'

'Want me to save space in my backpack for you?'

I avoided her question. 'When are you leaving?'

Angel paused. 'Next week.'

'Next week? No, you can't. That's so soon!' Too soon. I couldn't believe it. My hands were drenched in sweat.

'You could come, too, Jose. Picture it: you and me taking on Europe. It'd be rad. We could get matching neck pillows for the plane.'

I bit my lip. Angel was my best friend, and it would be amazing to travel with her. But I wanted to write. I wanted to tell stories. I wanted to dig up facts and report them. I wanted to be a journalist, and Liani was giving me the opportunity to do exactly that before I'd even finished my degree. As awesome as it would be to have a picnic underneath the Eiffel Tower with Angel, that wasn't going to make my dream come true.

'I can't come,' I said, 'I just can't. But you'd better send me a buttload of postcards.'

'Postcards! Haven't you heard of Skype, grandma?' Angel laughed, and I knew it was going to be okay.

'Well, we can always Face-stalk each other. And you'd better learn how to read a map before you go.'

'You were always the navigation queen,' she said. 'I'd just get us lost in the dodgy part of town.'

'Remember that time you took us down the wrong street and we saw that drug deal happen next to the butcher's? We thought they were going to come after us and kill us.'

Angel let out a small snort of laughter, which set us both off.

'Now it'll just be me, all alone in big, bad Europe,' she said when she could talk again. 'Reckon they do map-reading courses for dummies over there? And what if I can't understand any of the languages? Maybe I'll hire a hot tutor or something. The only word I know in French is "hello" — "adios", right?'

I almost didn't have the heart to tell her 'adios' meant goodbye in Spanish, but then imagined her offending a sexy French waiter while ordering a chocolate-filled croissant, so I filled her in — and taught her a few French words. As Angel freaked out, it hit me like a sharp slap in the face: she wasn't the only one who needed to brush up on her solo skills.

In a matter of days, I was going to know how it felt to be alone, really alone, without my beautiful, brave best friend to call on. Was I scared of losing her? Terrified. But I didn't want to bring her down, so I gulped and forced a laugh as she ranted about her flight's carry-on rules; and pushed aside the thought that my life was changing again and there was absolutely nothing I could do about it.

25.

When Angel had hung up, I lay down on the sofa, contemplating whether I could be bothered undressing, filling the bathtub with water and bubbles and chilling out properly. Easy answer: no.

The lounge room door opened and James poked his head in with a smile that ... oh, you get the idea. The guy looked so cute I may have blushed just from breathing the same air as him. His dimples were dimpling, his shaggy hair was shagging and his jacket made him look like an indie rock star. 'Hey, James,' I said, struggling to concoct anything intelligible to say to the guy who'd turned me into a pining angst-ridden mess.

'Hey, stranger,' he said, walking into the room. 'I thought I heard talking coming from in here. Having a party for one?'

'How are you?' I asked. 'I thought you'd be at work.'

'Yeah, I was.' He shrugged. 'Answered a few calls, wrote a few emails, served a few customers ... got fired.'

'No way! What happened?'

'I called my boss a jackass,' he said, leaning against the wall. 'Oops.' He bit his lip. 'It's for the best, though.'

'Yeah?'

'There's a pretty cool music production course down the road. I won't have money to eat, but who needs food when you're a rock star, right?' He grinned, showing off those dimples again.

'Your dad will be so proud,' I teased. 'Seriously, though, it sounds really great ... Oh, and thanks for the laptop, by the way. I love it.'

'All good.'

James took a seat on the arm of the couch. Now that he was closer, I could smell his cologne — a light but masculine fragrance that made me think of an ocean breeze. With him perched so close and me lying down, it almost felt like we were breaking the rules. But we weren't. Everything was innocent and above board and focused on safe topics like 'work' and 'parents'.

Until I spoke again.

'So, ah, Summer must be worried about you losing your job,' I said, pulling my knees up to my chest. 'I mean, not worried about the money, just, you know, worried about you. Like all girlfriends would be, or so I imagine ...'

Shut up, Josie, I thought to myself.

James lowered his eyes. 'I don't know about that.'

'Oh?' I cocked my head to one side. 'Why? I thought you guys were stronger than ever.'

'Are you kidding?' he said. 'Jose, she convinced herself I'd been cheating on her for months and lost it.'

'What?'

'Constant phone calls at home, at work — she even hassled my mates about it.'

'Oh,' I said.

'Then she hooked up with my boss.'

'Oh! I can see why you called him a jackass.'

'And two of my boss's mates.'

'That's awful.' The words sounded empty, fake, but I didn't know what else to say. 'I'm sorry, I had no idea,' I rambled on. 'Tim didn't say anything.'

'Tim? He wouldn't know if his boxers were on backwards.'

I nodded. 'True.'

I couldn't believe James had been single and getting his heart run over by Summer The Bulldozer all this time.

'The craziest part is, I wasn't even cheating!' he said 'Not at all. Although ...'

Uh-oh, I thought, my entire faith in guys was about to be shot here. If James turned out to be a cheater like Billy, I'd sign up to the nunnery that afternoon.

'Well, the thing is, a while back Summer caught me ... um ...'

'Caught you ...?' I almost didn't want to know. But at the same time I had to know. I wanted — needed — to know everything.

'I was sleeptalking, Jose, and, I, ah, may have said your name. Something about you being hot and wanting to kiss you. Allegedly.'

'Oh.' I gulped. 'Allegedly, hey?'

'Well, it got Summer all fired up and, yeah ... didn't go down too well.'

In shock over James's confession, I swallowed, blushed and sighed all at once, which caused a spluttering coughing attack. One hand flew to my mouth, while the other clung onto the side of the sofa for support. I felt like a wheezy old man coughing over the carrots and broccoli in the supermarket.

'Are you okay?' James kneeled on the floor and stroked my back while I coughed.

I nodded. 'Um, yeah, I'm good. You were saying ...'

'Summer and I were meant to be right for each other, you know? Everyone said so. I didn't question it. And then I met you. You were so ... so ... annoying!'

'Excuse me?' I knew I was annoying, but I didn't want Super Hot Guy Of My Dreams to think that, too.

'But in a cute way,' he went on. 'Without even realising or trying, you got me.'

'I did?'

'I tried to ignore it. You were seventeen and —'

'Eighteen now.'

'Ahhh, would you let me talk?'

'Sorry.' I tried not to smile. I failed.

'And then Summer and I broke up, and you told me that you — well, that you … you know what you said.'

'Right.' I sighed. 'I know. I ruined it. But you've got to understand — I'm a battler. A dork. Seriously, I deserve some kind of award for making it through today without getting my hand caught in a door.'

James grinned. 'But the thing is —'

'This sounds familiar,' I interrupted.

'Would you just … I'm crazy about you.'

I gulped. 'Can you say that again? I think I imagined you telling me you like me.'

James climbed onto the sofa so we were facing each other. His long legs were crossed and squeezed up toward his chin, like a praying mantis. 'No, I didn't. I said I'm *crazy* about you.'

'But I'm so —'

'It doesn't matter.'

'And what about my —'

'I don't care.'

'But I like eating Nutella straight from the jar while watching musicals.'

He laughed. 'Yeah, we can work on that. But when you're not busting my balls for breaking in to my own apartment, or eating all my Hawaiian pizza, I can't stop thinking about you.'

I stared at him in stunned silence as our entire history flashed before my eyes. (If my life were a movie I'd have cued eighties music for a montage scene at that moment.)

'Well?' he said. 'Don't leave me hanging out here.'

What was I meant to say to the guy I'd liked for months? I love you! Marry me! Have my babies! Maybe not. I settled for the truth.

'James, I've never done this before —'

And then he leaned forward and kissed me. Our lips grazed softly and his hand cupped my face.

I pulled away. 'This is really happening, right? If this turns out to be a dream ...'

James laughed and pulled me closer so I was sitting in his lap. We kissed again, hesitantly at first, but the kisses quickly grew faster and more heated. Tingles surged through my body.

Suddenly, the front door burst open, causing me to squeal.

'Josssssie!' hollered Tim.

'Oh, god, they're kissing!' yelled Steph.

We all looked at each other, swapping smirks and awkward smiles. Then we collapsed into laughter. As I cackled along with everyone else, I noticed James's arm was still wrapped around me.

'You guys!' cooed Steph.

'Oi, mate, am I meant to give you some kind of pep talk about hooking up with my little cousin?' Tim asked.

James laughed. 'If you want.'

With the awkwardness over — well, as much as it could be — I noticed the familiar scent of ham, cheese, pineapple and tomato wafting up my nostrils. 'Is that …?'

'Come with me, child,' said Steph. 'Dinner is served.'

I snuck a look at James, who grinned and helped me up. The passionate moment was over but I wanted to repeat it thirty times a day for as long as my lips could handle it.

The moon glinted through the lounge room window, casting its dull light over our group. Steph and Tim were curled on the couch, Tim rubbing his belly after taking on our challenge to devour twelve slices of pizza. James and I sat on the floor. Only our pinkie fingers were laced together, but it was enough to send shudders of electricity through my hand. I wondered if he felt it, too. The television hummed in the background.

'Quick, turn it off,' Steph hissed to Tim, pointing at the remote next to him.

He fumbled for it, but didn't pick it up fast enough (his reflexes slowed down by all that cheese, no doubt) and I saw what Steph was desperate to hide from me. Billy and Kara were being interviewed on *Your Night*, a trashy tabloid news program. The caption 'Billy: I can't wait to be a dad' flashed up on the bottom of the screen below footage of Billy rubbing Kara's engorged belly.

Steph, Tim and James all looked at me, wincing, but I shrugged. 'Here he goes again.'

'He's consistent, I'll give him that,' sighed Steph. 'Man, what a douche-canoe. You've definitely upgraded to a better model.' She winked at James.

'Hey, I forgot to ask, what happened with Rae?' I said. 'Was it about the stolen car?'

'Stolen car, babe?' asked Tim.

Steph brushed him off. 'Ah, I'll tell you later. No, well … actually Rae offered me a job with her at the new mag.'

'At *Marilyn*? That's fantastic!' I said. 'And you reckon I have *my* life together! What's the job?'

'Design assistant, or features assistant, or editorial something — I wasn't really listening.'

I stared at her. 'You took it, right?'

Steph glanced at Tim. 'Well, the thing is …' Those words again.

'Turns out we're going to India for a few months,' Tim said. 'Surprise.'

James slapped him on the back. 'Mate, that's unbelievable.'

'Are you joking?' I asked, stunned that travel's magnetic pull had claimed two more friends in a matter of hours. 'Where did that come from?'

'Jose, you know me, I've been going mad trying to be a normal person with a normal office gig,' said Steph.

'It feels so wrong. Well, me and Tim got to talking and we're going to do some volunteer work over there, learn yoga, eat curries … make it up as we go.'

'Wow, I … I …' For the billionth time that day, I lost the power of speech.

Steph hopped off the couch and wrapped her arms around me. 'You'll be fine, kiddo. Hey, who knows, we may get to the end of the first week and realise we hate it. If that happens, we'll be on the first plane back.'

'When do you leave? In a few days?' I had to ask. I couldn't lose three friends in one week. I just couldn't.

'No way, we're not that organised,' laughed Steph.

'So what did Rae say when you turned her down?'

'You know what? I think she got it. It was Dad who was pushing her to find something for me — as always.' She gave me another squeeze and a crumpled piece of paper fell from her pocket onto the floor.

'What's that?' I asked.

Steph looked down. 'Oh man! I almost forgot. Liani was meant to give it to you back at the office.' She thrust the paper into my hand. 'I've read it already, sorry.'

I smoothed it out. There were a few words written in swirly old-style script in the middle of the page. *'Josie, I'm so sorry for how I treated you,'* I read aloud. *'Please forgive me. Liani passed on your article. I don't know what to say other than thank you for being there, even when I didn't deserve it. Ava.'*

'Whoa,' said Tim.

I folded up the note and tucked it in my pocket.

'Aren't you going to say anything?' asked Steph. 'Jose, aren't you still angry?'

'Nope.' And I wasn't.

'That girl ruined everything!' Steph said, her voice rising. 'She got you thrown out of the internship.'

'There is no internship, remember?' I said, shrugging. 'No life-changing five thousand dollars. No magical by-line. No column. None of that.'

'You're right,' said Steph. 'So why aren't you having a fit, then? The Josie I know would be in spiral of crazy right now.'

I looked around at their concerned and curious faces, and I laughed as I saw Steph tap Tim's hand away as he reached for another slice of pizza.

'Well?' asked James, his eyes lighting up. 'What's going on?'

'Yeah,' said Tim. 'Tell us.'

And so I told them about my new job in the city.

I waited for the thunderous applause and cheers. For balloons to fall from the ceiling and everyone to high-five me, then hoist me onto their shoulders to run a lap of the neighbourhood. But nothing. Not even a burp from Tim after his fifth glass of Coke.

'Did you hear me?' I said. 'I got a job. I'm going to be a junior writer here in the city. Guys?'

Without warning, they roared with excitement and enveloped me into a group hug that almost knocked me flat on the floor. There were arms and legs everywhere; James's elbow nearly poked me in the eye and Steph's hair got caught in my mouth, but I didn't care — although Tim's garlic breath took the wind out of me when he smacked a kiss on my cheek.

Eventually Steph and Tim wriggled out of the clinch, leaving me and James in our own embrace. Our eyes locked and, for a moment, we were the only ones in the room. James tucked a curl behind my ear and smiled. Heart pounding, I leaned forward so our lips could meet again.

'Let's give them some space,' I heard Steph whisper to Tim, and I sensed them slip away.

James and I were finally alone. All I could feel were his fingers stroking my cheek, our tongues brushing together, his warm skin when I pressed my lips against his neck — and it was all I wanted to feel. But, ever the over-thinker, I kept waiting for something to ruin it. A freak fire in the building. A call from Mum reminding me it was my turn to do the laundry. A hairy spider scuttling up the nearest wall. But nothing bad happened, and I wasn't going to waste time wondering why life had spared me for once. So, with Hawaiian pizza in my belly, a gorgeous guy in my arms and a writing job in my future, I relaxed into James's kisses — no interruptions, chaos or drama allowed.

Except for Steph and Tim. Less than a minute later, they charged in with a ginormous tub of chocolate ice-cream and four spoons.

James and I pulled apart, half-breathless and half-laughing at being interrupted again.

'Dude!' said James, hitting Tim on the leg.

'I know, I know, but giving you space to hook up or whatever got boring,' said Tim, planting himself on the sofa and shovelling his spoon into the tub.

'Sorry,' said Steph. 'I tried to hold him back.'

James caught my eye, his cheeky dimples making me wish we were still alone. Then, clearly not wanting to be outdone by Tim, he jammed a chocolatey scoop the size of a tennis ball into his mouth. The two guys exploded with laughter, moaning about their competing ice-cream headaches. It wasn't obvious in the dimmed room, but I could see that Steph's eyes had misted over. She didn't say a word, though, just squeezed my hand.

I smiled and reached for a spoon.

ACKNOWLEDGMENTS

Taking *The Intern* from my imagination to publication was like riding a roller-coaster — there was plenty of laughter, shrieking and nausea. With much love and my deepest thanks to those of you who lined up with me and buckled in for the ride:

The wonderful Helen Littleton, who saw something in me that I was yet to see in myself. You nudged me in the right direction and for that I am eternally grateful.

To the publisher of my dreams, Lisa Berryman: without you, none of this would have been possible. Thank you for taking a chance, trusting in me and cheering every step of the way. I can't wait to do it all again soon.

The brilliant and kind Nicola O'Shea, who edited, wrangled and coaxed *The Intern* into the best shape of its life. It's been an absolute privilege to work with you.

For their guidance, support and hard work, I wish to thank the rest of HarperCollins, especially Rachel Dennis, Gemma Fahy, Amanda Diaz, Tim Miller, Libby Volke and Hazel Lam.

To Sam Faull, Amanda Ryan and Simone McClenaughan, your friendship, feedback on the first draft and pep talks throughout the process were invaluable.

Thanks to the teachers, editors, authors and writers who have nurtured my creativity and inspired me to follow this path (some intentionally, some from afar): Cathy Edwards, Marg Ryan, Peter Cox, Felicity Packard, Simone 'Boss Lady' Amelia, Fiona Wright, Gemma Crisp, Jacqueline Mooney, Zoë Foster Blake, Andrew Humphries, Gretel Killeen, Martine Allars, Kylie Ladd, Kerri Sackville, Margaret Clark and John Marsden.

A special note for Sarah Ayoub, who bravely rode this roller-coaster first, and squeezed my hand through the scariest twists and turns. And to Georgia Kemmis, another creative pea in my pod, it's been a pleasure collaborating in the lead-up to *The Intern*'s release.

My darling friends — you know who you are — you inspire me to aim for the stars (and thanks for understanding when I was too busy working on the book to catch up).

To the McMillans and the Tozers, I love you all. For introducing me to the joys of reading, I want to thank the best parents a girl could hope for, Allan and Annette. All those MS Readathons and books for Christmas paid off! Much love and gratitude to my little sister, Jacqui, who styled my outfit for my first job interview in the big smoke (yes, that part in *The Intern* may have been semi-true ...).

And finally to my beloved husband and first reader, Jason — for your patience, for your creativity, for your logic, for your enthusiasm and, most of all, for loving me at my best *and* worst (even those times when I was eating peanut butter from the jar when the finish line seemed so far away). We did it.

Now, let's ride the roller-coaster again.

Gabrielle Tozer is an author, journalist and copywriter from Wagga Wagga, New South Wales. Since moving to Sydney almost a decade ago, she has worked as a managing editor, deputy editor, chief subeditor, senior features writer and freelancer for publications including *DOLLY*, *Girlfriend*, *Cosmopolitan*, *Bride to Be*, *DisneyGiRL*, *Disney Adventures*, *The Canberra Times* and *Mamamia*. Gabrielle's writing has also appeared in the creative anthologies *Take It As Red* and *GOfish* and she is a previous winner of the ABC's Heywire competition. When she is not churning out her next novel (yes, that's why she hasn't brushed her hair for a while), she loves tweeting, eating chocolate and watching too much television.

Say hello:
gabrielletozer.com
facebook.com/hellogabrielletozer
twitter and instagram: @gabrielletozer